"You think I'm [barcode: D0446896]

"Aren't you?"

AJ opened her mouth to deny it, but the words caught in her throat. "I…I don't know…. It seems as though, if I am married, I should feel something, some sense of urgency to get back. And I don't."

"So you're running from something," Ryan said. "Maybe it's not a good marriage. Are you afraid to go back?"

"No. It's not that. It's more like…"

"Like what?"

"Sadness. Like I've lost something and I'll never find it again."

Ryan knew that sadness too well. He could no more ignore the pain in AJ's voice than he could stop the tide from rising.

He wanted to pull her into his arms, to apologize for the pain his conversation had brought. The need to protect her kept growing.

All he would allow himself was a touch. Only one touch. He tucked her hair behind her ear and traced the line of her jaw with the tip of his finger. The velvet softness of her skin sent a bolt of desire crashing headlong into his best intention to keep his distance…

Dear Harlequin Intrigue Reader,

We have a superb lineup of outstanding romantic suspense this month starting with another round of QUANTUM MEN from Amanda Stevens. A *Silent Storm* is brewing in Texas and it's about to break....

More great series continue with Harper Allen's MEN OF THE DOUBLE B RANCH trilogy. *A Desperado Lawman* has his hands full with a spitfire who is every bit his match. As well, B.J. Daniels adds the second installment to her CASCADES CONCEALED miniseries with *Day of Reckoning*.

In *Secret Witness* by Jessica Andersen, a woman finds herself caught between a rock—a killer threatening her child—and a hard place—the detective in charge of the case. What will happen when she has to make the most inconceivable choice any woman can make?

Launching this month is a new promotion we are calling COWBOY COPS. Need I say more? Look for *Behind the Shield* by veteran Harlequin Intrigue author Sheryl Lynn. And newcomer, Rosemary Heim, contributes to DEAD BOLT with *Memory Reload*.

Enjoy!

Sincerely,

Denise O'Sullivan
Senior Editor
Harlequin Intrigue

MEMORY RELOAD

ROSEMARY HEIM

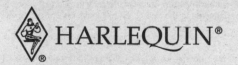

HARLEQUIN®

TORONTO • NEW YORK • LONDON
AMSTERDAM • PARIS • SYDNEY • HAMBURG
STOCKHOLM • ATHENS • TOKYO • MILAN • MADRID
PRAGUE • WARSAW • BUDAPEST • AUCKLAND

ISBN 0-373-22764-7

MEMORY RELOAD

Copyright © 2004 by Rosemary Heim

This edition published by arrangement with Harlequin Books S.A.

® and TM are trademarks of the publisher. Trademarks indicated with ® are registered in the United States Patent and Trademark Office, the Canadian Trade Marks Office and in other countries.

Visit us at www.eHarlequin.com

Printed in U.S.A.

ABOUT THE AUTHOR

Rosemary Heim grew up on a dairy farm, attended a one-room schoolhouse, lived in an English castle and settled in Minneapolis. She shares a charming (needs work) old house with her husband and four cats. Rosemary would love to hear from readers. You can visit her Web site at www.rosemaryheim.com or mail her c/o Midwest Fiction Writers, P.O. Box 24107, Minneapolis, MN 55424.

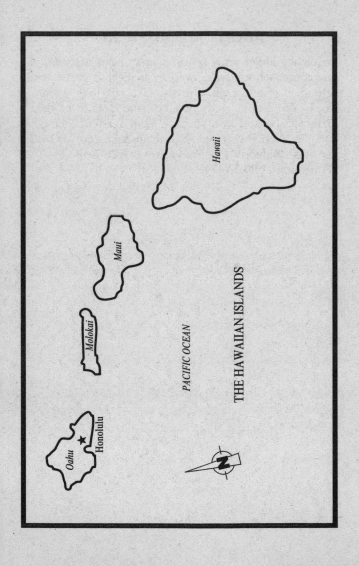

THE HAWAIIAN ISLANDS

PACIFIC OCEAN

Hawaii

Maui

Molokai

Oahu

Honolulu

CAST OF CHARACTERS

AJ—woke with a camera, a loaded gun and no memory. All she wants is to find her home.

Ryan Williams—FBI Special Agent. Between assignments, he's returned to this island hideaway for a little R and R.

Jacquelyn Kingston—FBI Special Agent in Charge. She watches over her team members from a distance.

Justin Angelini—He started an investigation and ended up dead.

David Angelini—He picked up the investigation after his brother's death. Now he's disappeared.

Jamison McRobbie—Mysterious and gifted, he offers shelter to his friends.

Kimo Kealoha—Photo lab owner and friend to AJ. He seems to have information everyone wants.

Tim Pela—FBI Special Agent. He has a few secrets of his own.

Frank Sullivan—A man pulling the strings behind the scenes.

John Danse, Carly and Matt Adams—FBI Special Agents. Will their help cost Ryan and AJ their chance for a future?

First, last, always,
To Will

ACKNOWLEDGMENTS

As with many books, especially first books,
there is a plethora of people to thank.

First off, thank you to Susan Litman,
for opening the door and providing gentle
(and patient) guidance on this new journey.

On the technical side, thank you to Maureen Lease
and David Kitchen for answering my questions about the
FBI. Any errors or inaccuracies are due to my
flights of fancy, not their information.

Thank you to Jackye Plummer, Penelope Neri and
Andi Sisco Pike for answering my Hawaii questions
and to Sandy Morris for the medical info.

Kat Baldwin and Karen Sanders, there aren't words
enough to express my appreciation of your patience
while I learned all those pesky writing skills.

Jade Taylor, thank you for the wonderful title.
Stacy Verdick Case, your "drainstorming"
led to a satisfying A.F. and so much more.
Yea to the power of three!

Thanks to my friends and family who believed
in the dream and encouraged me, to the wonderful
members of MFW, and Rex, the best German shepherd
I never knew.

Chapter One

Ryan Williams ran as if the devil was dogging his tail. Too bad some devils couldn't be outrun. Like memories of betrayal.

He slowed from his flat-out run. Wave-packed sand gave a little with each step, cushioning his bare feet as he raced along the shoreline. Bloodred fingers of light streaked the sparse clouds as the sun breached the horizon.

Blood red.

The thought raised goose bumps along his arms in spite of the tropical warmth.

Day two of his leave and he hadn't shaken the images from the last mission yet. Dealing with a traitor was never easy. It became doubly hard when innocent people were hurt. Thank God everyone was going to be okay.

And thank God for well-to-do friends who issued standing invitations. Once again, Jamie's ''guest cottage'' offered Ryan refuge, a safe place far away from the Bureau and all its intrigues. The north shore of Oahu was about as far away from Quantico as he could get. He needed every inch of that distance.

His breathing approached normal as he continued slowing down, cooling off from his customary five-mile run. He rounded the small bend in the shore, passing the tall palm trees that marked the final leg of the course he'd laid out four years earlier on his first visit.

He headed away from the ocean, winding through the small grove of coconut palms. He loved the quiet of the beach at sunrise, the solitude, the freedom. It provided exactly the break he needed.

He cleared the tree line high on the beach, skidded to a stop and quickly stepped back behind the nearest trunk. Up ahead, a figure crouched in the sand.

Who the devil was that? Ryan wasn't particularly pleased with the idea that someone had managed to invade this private stretch of heaven.

A quick scan of the surrounding area came up empty. No other intruders staked out on the beach. No boats in the water. No movement among the trees. No vehicles within eyesight. Not much could have gotten past the estate's security defenses, even this early in the morning. So how had this intruder gotten so close?

Regretting the absence of his gun, he left the tree cover and crossed down the beach to confront the intruder. The shushing waves masked what little sound his footsteps made.

From behind, he couldn't tell much about the person except that it was female. Long black hair lifted on the gentle breeze, seeming to defy gravity. He had a brief view of a slender back, narrow waist and softly rounded hips before the breeze died. The hair settled back into a solid curtain.

Oh yes. Definitely female. Interest of another sort stirred.

He adjusted the angle of his approach so he could get a better look at her. It didn't do much good. An expensive-looking 35mm camera obscured the woman's face. A large black camera bag rested in the sand next to her. She kneeled, facing the water, motionless except for her fingers on the camera lens and shutter release.

He glanced out over the horizon, searching for what held her attention. Just empty water met the morning sky. The few clouds stretched and shredded colors as the sun rose higher.

Was that what held her attention? That play of color?

When was the last time he'd been so engrossed by something as simple, as innocent as a sunrise?

Probably never.

He stopped a few feet from her and waited for her to notice him.

A minute passed. Then several more. The sun rose higher, breaking free from the ocean. Still the woman kept taking pictures, not stopping until she ran out of film. She never looked away from the rising sun as she quickly rewound the film, opened the camera back and removed the film cassette.

Ryan's eyes narrowed as he watched her quick movements. It took her less than a minute to reload the camera and begin shooting again.

She must be nuts. All alone on a deserted beach and she was oblivious to everything but the horizon. That was a good way to get hurt. Or worse.

Unless she wasn't alone. He performed another recon of the beach and nearby tree line. Still empty. All appeared as it should.

He stepped closer. When that failed to draw her attention, he cleared his throat. Still no response. Finally he spoke. "Excuse me, miss. This is a private beach."

She hesitated long enough to glance in his direction. He caught a glimpse of one pale gray eye edged with thick black lashes as she gave him a thorough up and down. She turned back to her camera and the sun without a comment.

Such a dismissal might have irritated Ryan if he hadn't

noticed other details. She wasn't as unconcerned as she tried to appear. He could see her chewing on her lower lip and her throat worked around a swallow.

Good. She should be nervous. He stepped closer.

"Thirty-eight seconds. That's all I need."

He stopped short as her soft voice floated to him on the morning sea breeze. He checked his watch, noted the sweep of the second hand, marked the time. The old habit, left over from days of split-second, life-and-death missions, hadn't faded with the passage of time. He made another quick scan of their surroundings. The last thing he wanted was to be the sitting duck caught by this pretty decoy.

She finally lowered her camera, clipped the lens cap in place and returned her equipment to her camera bag. Ryan glanced at his watch. Thirty-eight seconds, exactly.

"As I was saying, this is private property. How'd you get here?"

The woman glanced around. A small frown creased her wide forehead. "I...walked."

"That's a fair piece of walking. It's a few miles from the nearest road. Unless you crossed the estate grounds." He stepped closer.

She closed the quick-release catches on her bag and stood with a fluid movement. He got his first good look at her and a tiny alarm went off.

Her T-shirt and leggings were black and snug fitting, like something worn to hide in nighttime shadows. The pale skin of her bare feet blended into the sand. Her left hand clutched the wide black nylon strap of the bag over her right shoulder, her right hugged the bag close to her hip. "Then I'd better be on my way."

A haunted look passed over her finely molded features as she looked around the beach. She didn't move.

Something was definitely off here. She looked like a

deer caught in the headlights of an oncoming semi. Ryan didn't need Jamie's psychic powers to feel the waves of panic rolling through her. The need to protect, a need rooted deep in his childhood, rose up, stronger than his government training of self-preservation. He held out one hand and stepped toward her. "I'm staying with a friend. His place is just up the beach. I could give you a lift back to your car if you'd like."

"No!" She backed up a step. Her right hand slipped into the wide front pocket of the camera bag.

"What's wrong? I maybe could be of some assistance to you." He kept his voice soft, calming, letting his southern-gentleman drawl come on thick. That sometimes did the trick when he needed to get around personal defenses.

"No. I...I didn't mean any harm. I didn't see anything.... Just...let me go."

"I'd like to oblige, miss, but my mama raised me to be a gentleman. She'd tear a strip offa me a mile wide if I left a woman on a deserted beach to fend for herself." He smiled, hoping to reassure her.

It didn't work.

Her right hand swung up and pointed a pistol in the general vicinity of his chest. "Please, just let me go. Forget you ever saw me."

Ryan held both hands up, palms out. The gun was a matte black, 9mm Glock. Standard issue for the FBI and many other law enforcement groups. Not only didn't she have the first clue how to use it, she was terrified of it. Both hands, knuckles white, clutched the grip. The gun dipped and wavered as she held it as far away from her body as she could.

He kept steady eye contact with her, not bothering to watch the gun. "Are you sure you want to do this?"

Her shoulders hunched tighter and her eyes narrowed.

"Uh, miss? That gun isn't going to do you much good, unless you're fixin' to throw it at me."

A frown drew her dark eyebrows together. "You don't think I'll shoot?"

"Well, you can certainly try, but the ammo magazine is loose, the safety's on and your finger's nowhere near the trigger." He couldn't really tell about the mag from where he stood but the last bit, at least, was true. As long as she kept her finger off the trigger. He closed the gap between them with a single stride, wrapped one hand around her wrist and eased the gun from her trembling fingers. "Now, maybe you better tell me what this is all about."

"Are you a cop?"

"Not exactly."

"What do you mean, 'not exactly'? Who are you?" She tugged slightly at the hand still holding her, but she didn't struggle.

Her skin felt like silk, smooth, and warm. The pulse in her slender wrist raced against his fingertips. He stood too close but couldn't bring himself to step away and break the physical contact with her.

"You know, for a trespasser, you sure do ask a lot of questions."

"Wouldn't you? Alone on a beach, accosted by a stranger…"

"One you just pulled a gun on." He sighed and the tantalizing fragrance of something soft and tropical blended with the aroma of the sea and sand around them. The delicate scent teased his senses. The wrong kind of curiosity stirred again. He released her wrist and put a little distance between them. "Look, maybe we should start over."

He tucked the confiscated gun into the back waistband of his ragged cutoff fatigues, dusted his hands clean of sand and perspiration and held out his right hand. "My name's Ryan Williams."

She gave his hand a quick shake, releasing it as though she'd been shocked. He sure had been. The quick voluntary contact had sent a tingle racing straight from the palm of his hand to his belly.

"How do I know you're really who you say you are?"

Ryan grinned and shook his head. She was an intriguing mix of wariness and innocence. His fingers tapped a drumroll against his hips as he thought for a moment. His grin widened and he snapped his fingers. "I've got it. How'd a picture ID do?"

He reached into his hip pocket and pulled out a thin leather case. Flipping it open, he handed it to her. He watched her reactions as she looked at his Bureau identity cards. Her shoulders loosened a little.

"Okay." She handed the wallet back. "Unless of course it's a fake."

"No, ma'am." He crossed his heart and held up his hand in the old Boy Scout salute. "I swear it's genuine, certified real."

She nibbled on her generous lower lip as she looked around. Ryan wondered what her lip tasted like. Sunshine and sea? Awareness zinged across his nerves, warming him at the thought. The silence lengthened as he waited for her to reveal her name.

When it became clear she wasn't about to trust him with that bit of information, he pulled her gun from his waistband. She took a quick step away from him.

"Whoa, whoa. Take it easy." He released the ammo mag, emptied the bullets into his palm and dropped them into his pocket. Reinserting the mag, he emptied the remaining round from the firing chamber before holding the gun out to her on the palm of his hand. "Here, why don't you hang on to this. You really can't shoot me now, but it might come in handy if you feel the need to hit me with something.''

A hint of a smile rewarded his small jest.

''Do you need a ride someplace? Or is there someone you want to call?''

She shook her head as she slipped the gun back into the camera case. He was caught for a moment, watching the sun dance off the silky ripples of her hair. Her soft sigh brought his attention back to her mouth. Dang, she was biting her lip again.

''You said you live near here?'' Her words brought him back.

''My friend does. I'm staying in his guest cottage. Why don't we go back there, have a glass of lemonade and, if you want, you can tell me what's going on?''

Her pale gray eyes looked him over. Silence stretched between them as her study extended to their surroundings.

Ryan waited, tamping down his impatience. Some instinct told him it was important for her to make the decision without pressure.

''All right. I'll come with you, but only long enough to call a taxi.''

''Fair enough.'' Instead of pumping his fist in victory as he wanted, Ryan swept his arm in front of himself. ''Right this way.''

They headed down the beach in silence. She kept up with him, walking with an easy grace in spite of the soft sand dragging at their feet. He was acutely aware of her slender form beside him, just out of reach, but near enough to keep his senses on red alert.

She was the perfect height, tall enough to tuck under his chin, but not so short he'd get a kink in his neck bending down to kiss her. *Hold your horses, boyo. This is not an appropriate direction to be thinking.*

The small bungalow, hidden among another bunch of

palms, came into view none too soon. He held the back door open for her and she stepped past him. She stopped just inside the tidy little kitchen, inspecting her surroundings.

Ryan made a production of brushing the sand from his feet before stepping onto the clean terra-cotta tile floor, giving her as much time as he could to look around. The more comfortable she was with her surroundings, the more likely she would be to confide in him.

The door clicked shut behind him. If he hadn't been watching her so closely, he would have missed her slight flinch.

He stepped around her and moved to the other side of the room. Maybe she'd relax some if he kept his distance a bit better than he had been. "I imagine you might want to freshen up a bit." He pointed down the hall. "Why don't you go on through to the bathroom while I get that lemonade?"

She hesitated, her hand clenching and releasing on the camera bag's shoulder strap.

Ryan cleared his laptop and paperwork from the small round kitchen table, turned away and began opening cupboards, setting out glasses and a plate. He waited until he heard the bathroom door close before turning around. A swift survey of the room confirmed his suspicion. She wasn't letting that bag out of her sight.

When she returned he was sitting in one of the ladder-back chairs, leafing through a recent *Smithsonian* magazine. A plate of gingersnaps, a frosty pitcher of lemonade and two tall glasses filled with ice covered the bright yellow tabletop. The second chair at the table turned out, an open invitation for her to sit down.

Ryan sat up straight and tossed the magazine onto the counter behind him. He squelched the urge to stand and hold the chair for her as she joined him.

She slid onto the chair without changing its position. The camera bag settled on her lap, her hands curled into white-knuckled fists around the bag's handle. She flexed her hands a couple of times, then lowered the case to the floor, looping the shoulder strap over her knee. Her back never touched the chair's ladder-back. An air of quiet panic swirled around her.

The clinking of ice filled the room as Ryan poured them each a glass. He took a cookie for himself, then pushed the plate closer to her. "Not exactly the breakfast of champions, I know, but I figure it's got the same basic ingredients—grain, eggs, sugar."

A fleeting smile answered his attempt at humor.

She took a tiny sip of the lemonade and set the glass back on the table. "Thank you." She cleared her throat. "For suggesting I come back here."

Ryan shrugged. "My mama raised me to be a gentleman."

Another smile flickered across those full lips of hers. He couldn't help noticing how they shone with moisture from the lemonade. He shifted, trying to get comfortable, damning himself for noticing every little detail of her appearance.

"She did a fine job. Are you from…" She cleared her throat again. "I can't quite place your accent."

"Don't guess I sound much like any one place. I moved around quite a bit when I was growing up, mostly in the South."

She nodded and the silence crept back in. Ryan wanted to ask her some questions of his own, but decided to bide his time. Maybe if she asked a few more questions, got to know a bit more about him, felt a little more comfortable, she'd begin to open up herself.

"You don't live here?" She looked around the retro-chic kitchen.

"No, just visiting. Jamie lets me stay here whenever I have the time."

"Nice friend."

"Yeah." Ryan took another swallow of lemonade to keep from asking her anything.

"Where do you call home?"

"Nowhere in particular." He shrugged. "I'm kind of a nomad. My job takes me away for extended periods of time, so I've never really set up a permanent base."

"How sad," she murmured. Her face reddened. "I'm sorry. I didn't mean…"

Ryan shook his head and waved away her concern. "No offense taken. I just never saw any reason to settle down. Homebody is not in my nature."

"What do you do?"

"At the moment, nothing. I'm…between assignments."

"But a government job?" She busied herself wiping the condensation from the sides of her glass.

Ryan nodded and waited for the next question. He had a pretty good idea what it might be.

"So, what, are you a secret agent, or something like that?"

"Something like that."

"Oh." She laughed, a bit nervously he thought. "I guess you probably can't tell me much more."

"Not much more to tell. I'm posted to the Office of Professional Responsibility. It's my job to smoke out bad agents and see that they pay for their treason."

She straightened in her chair, looking at him with a slight tilt to her head.

"I could give you a number to call. A couple numbers, actually. My boss and a buddy. They'll vouch that I'm on the up-and-up."

"I can call them directly? Any time?" The idea seemed to reassure her. She eased back into her chair.

"Any time. It's not a problem." He leaned back in his chair, balancing on the back legs. It wasn't much of a stretch for him to reach the little message pad and pen hanging on a hook by the cordless wall phone. The chair settled back on all four legs. He wrote the numbers, explaining as he went. "The first number is for Jacquelyn Kingston. She's my supervisor at the Bureau. John Danse is a fellow agent I just worked with. He's not exactly a buddy, but he'll vouch for me. The last number is for this house."

He pushed the paper across the table. She studied it for a moment, then carefully folded it and tucked it into her T-shirt pocket.

Ryan's mouth went dry. The sharp edges of the paper stood outlined between the softness of the cotton material and the fullness of her breast. He lifted his glass and downed most of its contents. The icy liquid had little cooling effect.

"You work for a woman?" Her voice pulled him back to the issue at hand.

"Yeah. She runs a tight ship. That's not easy with the bunch of retired military personnel she's got in her organization. We all tend to be pretty independent. Except when we're working as a team."

"You don't look old enough to be retired."

"I reckon thirty-two is old enough for pretty near anything." His smile widened as a soft blush colored her cheeks. "Did you want to make that call now?"

"Call? Oh." She refused to meet his steady look. Her glance darted about the room, resting momentarily on the phone behind him. "Well, actually…that may be a bit more difficult to do than I thought."

"Do you need the phone book?" He stood this time and opened a drawer, pulling out the phone book. He set it and the cordless phone's bright red handset on the table in front of her.

She stared at them as if they might change into snakes and bite her. She tentatively picked up the phone. Her long, slender fingers stroked the keypad. Ryan shifted again and pushed away the image of those same fingers running over his chest and belly.

This was crazy. He didn't care how long it'd been since he'd been with a woman. Reactions this strong and immediate were not normal.

The thin pages rustled in the silence as she flipped through the phone book with one hand. Her other hand clutched the phone.

The soft overhead light played on the various rings she wore. Each finger hosted a different style—silver, gold, tiny gemstones trapped in the finest of wire, an openwork band. Only the ring finger on her left hand was bare. There, a wide patch of pale skin revealed a story all its own.

Great. Just what I need, a married woman. She's probably a runaway wife and having second thoughts but doesn't want to ask her husband to come fetch her.

The thought startled him. Why should he feel such disappointment that this woman might be tied to some other man? And none of that explained why she was carrying a gun she didn't know the first thing about using.

"I can leave you alone to make the call if you'd like," he offered, even though his mind shouted a denial. He wanted to know who she planned on calling.

"Thank you, but that's not necessary." She rubbed her forehead, hiding her eyes behind her hand. Her long black hair fell forward as her head bowed, curtaining her face from his view. "I'm not sure where I'd go."

Her quiet words stilled the noise of his inner voice. Without thinking, he reached across the table and touched her hand. "Are you in some kind of trouble?"

"I think I must be."

"Can you tell me?" He leaned close, straining to catch her soft words.

She shook her head.

"I might be able to help."

Finally, she lifted her head and met his look. Tears trailed over her cheeks. More pooled in her eyes. "Can you tell me who I am? Because I haven't a clue."

Chapter Two

Her words hung in the air.

Okay, so she's a runaway wife having an identity crisis. Tread lightly, boyo.

He ignored his mental warning and shifted out of his chair to kneel on the floor in front of her. He touched her hand, the hand once again clutching the shoulder strap draped over her knee, intending to lend some comfort and encouragement. The chill clinging to her long fingers startled him. Gathering both of her hands into his, he began chafing them, trying to ease the cold. He met her tear-filled eyes with a steady gaze. "It'll be okay."

She blinked her eyes closed and shook her head. "How can you know that?"

Ryan couldn't stop the grin pulling up one side of his mouth. He shrugged. "Because things always work out. You couldn't know this, but I live a charmed life. When I found you on the beach, you became part of it. So, I just naturally know everything will be all right."

"You really believe that?"

"Nothing's ever happened to show me different." He brushed away the tear trailing over her cheek. It began as an innocent touch, but the contact sent a vibration through him, relaying an unexpected intimacy.

"Then I'd say you've been very lucky."

"Like I said, sugar, a charmed life. So, why don't you tell me what's going on?" He gave her hands an encouraging squeeze before releasing them. Pulling his chair around the table, he sat down, scooting closer to her until their knees nearly touched.

She shifted on the cushioned chair seat, crossing then uncrossing her legs. With each movement, their knees brushed together, her dark leggings against his bare skin. Each brush sent heat curling up his leg. Ryan spread his legs, giving her a little more room. Giving himself a break from the unexpected torture of that oh-so-brief touch.

He took a sip of lemonade to ease the sudden dryness of his mouth. "Let's start at the beginning. Will you tell me your name?"

Confusion flickered across her face, she blinked, her gaze darted around the room. "I…I can't," she choked out.

"I promise you, if it's a matter of safety, no one else will know."

A fine tremble shook her fingers as she tucked her hair behind her ears. "It's not that. At least, I don't think so." Her voice was barely louder than a whisper.

"Then, what is it?" He kept his voice low and calm, then waited through the silence.

She sat up straighter, pulled her shoulders back and finally met his gaze head-on. "You want to start at the beginning?"

He nodded.

"That would be on the beach, when I woke up thirty-four minutes before you found me."

"You slept on the beach? All night?" He leaned forward, resting his elbows on his legs and cupping her knees in his hands. The scent of the beach—sunshine, sand and salt—clung to her clothes. Another fragrance, subtler, more feminine, teased his senses. He thought of pulling back, putting some distance, some breathing space between them, but the fear on her face drew him closer. The need to protect and comfort her ignited a slow-burning fire deep within him.

He searched her eyes, trying to find the answers hidden in the stormy depths. "What is it? What aren't you telling me?"

She shook her head.

"Sugar, I can't help you if you don't give me anything to work with."

"Ryan, I can't tell you my name, because I don't remember it." Her words came out in a rush, tumbling one over the next in her urgency to say them. "I don't remember why I was on the beach or how or when I got there. I don't recognize my own voice. I couldn't describe myself until I looked in the mirror. My mind is a huge void."

Ryan sat back, staring at her for a moment before releasing a soft whistle. "Well now, that is a fix, ain't it?"

Truth echoed in her words. Of course, she could just be a good actress. It wouldn't be the first time a beautiful woman had fooled a man with tears and a woeful smile.

He studied her, searched her face for clues to what was really going on. Her gray eyes never wavered from his. He saw honesty and a silent plea asking him to believe.

Her body language reinforced the image. She sat with her arms wrapped around her waist, as though trying to hold the fear in before it overpowered her. She still held on to the camera-bag strap as though it was her only anchor of certainty in an unknown world.

His instincts said this wasn't an act; she told the truth.

Another set of instincts, the undercover-survival instincts, kicked in. He leaned forward, reaching toward her.

She flinched at his first touch, but didn't pull away, just sat motionless as he burrowed his fingers through her hair. The dark mass slid over his hands in a soft caress. The sensation called up the image of her hair falling in a curtain around him. He tamped down his reaction. Now was not the time.

Starting at her temples, he conducted a thorough exam of her skull. ''Do you have any bruises, bumps, sore spots, anything to indicate some kind of injury?''

''No.'' Her whispered answer brushed over his inner arm, raising gooseflesh.

He smoothed the silken mass of her hair back over her shoulder and probed her neck and shoulders. None of his prodding elicited a flinch of pain. He broke the physical contact with her and leaned back in his chair. A silent sigh of relief escaped his lips. ''What about a headache?''

''Only when I strain to remember.''

''What about your ID? You must have something on you with a name.''

Early-morning sunlight slanted through the kitchen window, gleaming in her midnight hair as she shook her head. ''No. There's nothing. No pockets except this one.''

He followed her gesture toward her breast. The outline of the slip of paper he'd given her looked harsh against the roundness of her breast. His mouth went dry as cotton.

This was getting out of hand. He had to get his reactions to her under control before his libido completely took over. If he didn't, he'd be useless to both of them. He swallowed and forced his attention back to her face.

''What about the camera bag?'' He downed the rest of his lemonade and refilled the glass.

''I looked. There's nothing.''

''Everything looked normal?''

She nodded.

Ryan tugged at his earlobe. There had to be something, some clue to her identity. Maybe she hadn't noticed it because it looked normal. People sometimes missed the obvious because they were so intent on finding the obscure. Hide in plain sight.

Or maybe it was all there in the bag and she didn't want her little game to end just yet.

"Do you mind if I look?" He held out his right hand, testing her, wondering if she'd let him search the bag.

She leaned over, lifted the bag by the handle and set it in her lap. Her long fingers rubbed the bag, her fingertips pressing into the nylon as they slid over the surface. It was an odd gesture. Almost that of a child reluctant to give up a cherished security blanket. She hesitated, gnawing on her lower lip for a moment before handing the bag to him.

The weight of it caught him off guard. She'd been handling the bag with such ease there'd been no indication of its heft.

He pushed his chair back and stood. After clearing the small table, he set the camera case on the sunny yellow Formica top. He slanted a glance at her. "What've you got in here?"

"Cameras, lenses, film. Pretty much what you'd expect."

"I guess that depends on what you expect." He lifted it and let it drop back on the table with a soft thunk. "It seems mighty heavy."

"No more than usual." She shrugged.

Ryan hesitated. Had she just slipped? Or was this a spontaneous memory breaking through the amnesia? When she didn't say any more, he shifted back to the camera bag. He began his search with the outside pockets, snapping open each quick-release catch and pulling out the contents. He checked each item before laying it on the table. Packets of lens tissues, a shutter-release cable, several cases holding filters, a small cloth coin-purse. He spilled its contents onto the table, revealing a few coins and several small bills.

Once the pockets were emptied, he ran his hands over the interiors, double-checking for any items that may have escaped his initial notice.

He shifted a little, positioning himself so he could watch her reactions as he opened the body of the case. The zipper slipped over its teeth with surprising silence. The ticking of the kitchen clock sounded louder in the quiet room. As he folded back the cover he forgot about watching her, doing a classic double take when he saw the contents.

This was not a tourist's camera bag.

He'd seen one camera when he came across her on the beach. It was inside the case, along with a second camera body, each nestled in a cushioned compartment. Several lenses and a shrink-wrapped block of film boxes filled other sections. Individual film canisters were held in place across the inside top of the bag with elastic loops. One by one, he transferred the items from the camera bag to the table.

Underneath the block of film he found a small black beanbag. He held it up and raised a questioning eyebrow.

"It comes in handy as a cushion when I need to prop the camera against an uneven surface," she answered without hesitating.

He nodded, then pulled out the next items. Two disposable cameras. Again, he looked at her.

A smile lifted the corners of her full lips. "They're great for scouting. You'd be amazed at how good some of the shots are. There should be a notebook in there, too."

"Here it is." He pulled the small spiral-bound pad out from between two of the cushioned dividers and flipped through the pages before setting it aside. "No flash attachment or motor drive?"

"Not necessary and too noisy, in that order."

He nodded, his gaze steady on hers.

A frown creased her forehead. "Why are you looking at me like that?"

"I think we can safely say we know one thing about you."

"What? What do you know?"

Her answers had been automatic, not rehearsed. The difference was subtle but discernible if you knew what to listen for. And Ryan knew. "You're a professional photographer."

She rubbed her temples. "A lot of people carry camera bags. That doesn't make them photographers."

"True, but this is high-end equipment. Pretty pricey. Except for the disposables, it's not exactly standard vacation supplies. I've only met one other person who carries this kind of stuff with her and she's a pro."

"Maybe I'm just rich and waste a lot of money on a hobby." She picked up one of the cameras and fiddled with the settings.

Ryan shook his head. "Maybe so, but I don't really think that's it. You hold that camera with…authority. When I found you on the beach, you were completely absorbed with what you were shooting. You knew what you were doing, exactly how long it'd take you. Then, of course, there's your answers."

"My answers."

"Uh-huh. They come instinctively. You know what you're talking about."

"Oh." Her lips shaped the word more than said it. "Then why can't I tell you my name? Shouldn't that be instinctive?"

"Well now, ya got me there. Can't claim to know much about amnesia, but if you're running from some kind of danger…" He lifted his shoulders. "Guess your name might be one of the things your mind would want to keep hidden. First thing we do is see if we can get you in to see a doctor.''

"Is that really necessary? There's nothing wrong with me, physically. What can a doctor do?''

"Won't know 'til we ask. Is there any reason you don't want to see a doctor?'' He watched as she thought for a moment. Finally she shook her head.

"I'll give Jamie a call when it's a more civilized hour and see if he can recommend someone.'' He turned back to the camera bag. "These dividers look movable. Mind if I pull them out?''

"Go ahead. They're only Velcroed in place.''

He pulled each cushioned section out, checked them for hidden contents, then laid them on the table. The bottom cushion didn't budge when he tugged on it. Stitching held it tight at all four corners, making for a solid bottom. When the bag stood empty, he surveyed the items covering the tabletop then turned to her. "Does anything strike you as not being right?''

"You mean other than the gun?'' She shook her head, all the while massaging her temple with one hand. Her other hand cradled the camera to her chest.

Ryan tilted the bag, trying to get a better view of the interior. The dark fabric soaked up light like a sponge. The overhead light didn't help much in the way of illumination. He opened the drawer beneath the phone and pulled out a flashlight.

The intense beam of light played over the interior of the bag. Nothing looked out of the ordinary. None of the seams showed evidence of having been opened and re-sewn. Light bounced off something in the bottom. He tilted the bag more with a little shake.

The bottom cushion wasn't so solid after all. A dull silver bead chain fell into view, the short length slithering out from beneath that cushion. He tugged it free and probed beneath the cushion for any other hidden treasures. All he encountered was the nylon-covered base.

He settled into his chair and held his last find up to the light. Two items dangled from the chain looped over his finger, jingling softly in the still kitchen.

A rectangular matte silver medallion, about one inch in length, gleamed in the dull kitchen light. The tag wasn't new but hadn't come standard issue with the bag, either. From the weight, it could be real silver.

The second item held even more interest. Three gold bands intertwined to form a single ring.

His thumb brushed the lettering engraved across the surface of the medallion. He flipped it over. More engraving. Something in his chest shifted, tightened as he made out the words.

"What is it?" Her question pulled his attention from the tag.

"Do the letters *AJD* mean anything?"

She squinted, as if trying to focus on a distant image, then sighed. "I don't think so. Why?" –

"They're etched into this tag. They don't trigger anything for you?" He watched her, waiting for some sign, a flicker in her eyes, a tightening around her mouth, something that would reveal the truth of her coming answer.

"No." She sank against the chair's ladder-back. "Is there anything else?"

He nodded. His thumb rubbed the engraving again. He imagined he could feel the rest of the phrase, the words, each individual letter burning against his skin. His eyes narrowed and he waited for her reaction. "Together, always."

The blood drained from her face, leaving her pale beneath her slight tan. The kitchen's fluorescent light heightened the effect, making her look even more ashen, sickly.

It was the first automatic response from her with any

real emotional strength. The first crack in the defensive wall her mind seemed to have built. If he pushed her a little more, maybe he could widen the crack, and they would discover what she didn't want to remember.

The idea of using her pain left a sour taste in his mouth. His need to protect her battled their need to discover what lay hidden in her mind. He hated himself for it, but he had to take advantage of her reaction before her defense mechanism kicked in again. "There's more on the flip side. 'Remember' and some numbers. They could be a date. 'Three slash fifteen.'"

Her eyelids fluttered shut and she seemed to struggle to breathe for a moment. She set the camera back on the table with great precision. He didn't try to stop her when she stood. She wrapped her arms around her waist, holding herself tight.

Why did her reaction feel like a knife stabbing his chest? How had this woman managed to get so far under his skin?

She crossed the kitchen to stand by the wall of windows overlooking the beach. He followed her, coming to a stop beside her.

He wanted to comfort her, to put his arms around her and hold her close. All he would allow himself was to brush her hair back over her shoulder so he could see her face. He dangled the chain in front of her.

After a moment, she took it from him. Her fingers worried the clasp open, slipped the ring off the chain and onto her left ring finger. The trio of gold bands rolled over her knuckle and settled into place, neatly covering the lighter colored skin banding her finger. A perfect match.

She refastened the clasp and examined the silver medallion. A soft ting-ting-ting punctuated the silence. Ryan watched as she repeatedly rolled the triple bands over her knuckle, around her finger and back into place. All of her attention was focused on the medallion. Playing with the ring was an unconscious action, one born of an old habit.

''What does it mean?'' His words sounded harsh in his own ears and he couldn't say for sure if he was asking about the medallion or the ring. Either way, his hands itched to reach out to her. Instead, he jammed his fists onto his hips.

''It's…he…no, they…'' She struggled to find the words, her chin trembling with the effort. ''I don't remember.''

She impaled him with a haunted look before squeezing her eyes shut and turning away from him.

The pain in her eyes undid Ryan. Anger he could stand. Tears he could deal with. But this silent agony was too familiar, reminded him too much of another woman a lifetime ago. He'd been helpless then, just a little boy, powerless to ease a suffering he couldn't begin to comprehend. Not until it was too late and he never had a chance for atonement.

Maybe this was his chance. Years too late, it wouldn't erase the old memory. Nothing could do that. Nor would he want to lose that image. It was too much a part of him, too ingrained in his psyche. He wouldn't be who he was, where he was, what he was without it.

But maybe here, now, with this woman, he could do what he hadn't been able to do when he was six.

He drew her into his arms, resting his chin on her head. A soft tremor shook her body as she dragged in a breath.

''Why can't I remember?'' Her warm breath washed over his arm in a soft moan. ''It's so close. But it's all jumbled together….''

''It'll be okay. Shhh.'' He rubbed her back and shoulders, crooning in soothing tones. ''We'll sort it all out. Don't worry, sugar. If there's someone out there, he's probably looking for you. We'll…'' He stopped short of promising they would find him. *Don't make a promise you might not be able to keep, boyo.*

She pushed away from him and paced across the room. For a moment, he thought she might bolt out the door, but she turned and continued walking the perimeter of the kitchen.

"Why can't I remember?" Her voice trembled between tears and frustration. "It doesn't appear that I hit my head. There's no reason I shouldn't remember. I should know who I am." She spun to look at him. "I should know who gave me these things and why I feel nothing but empty when I think of him."

Ryan's stomach rolled into a giant knot. Whoever the guy was, the connection to her was strong. He couldn't keep his gaze from that blasted ring she still played with. Could this shadow be anyone other than her husband?

Damn, first woman to get my interest—

Whoa. Where'd that come from? Just because he was on R and R didn't make this any different from one of his undercover assignments. No personal involvement. She was a woman in need of help. That's all it was. That's all it could be.

He crossed the room to her. Resting his hands on her shoulders, he looked into the pale gray depths of her eyes. "We will solve this. I promise you that." He slid one hand down to her elbow and tugged. "Come'n sit down. Let's look through everything. Maybe something will jog loose."

She followed him back to the table like a tired puppy. He settled her in her chair and watched as her head sank into her hands. "Do you have a headache? Do you want some aspirin?"

"Yes. No." She glanced at him and he saw a glimmer of a weak smile. "Yes, I have a headache. No, I don't want any aspirin. The lemonade will do."

He refilled their glasses and sat next to her again. "Why don't you look through the notebook, see if you recognize anything."

The kitchen clock ticked the next few minutes off while she leafed through the small spiral-bound notebook, studying each page. He busied himself with the film canisters. They held nothing but film, a mix of color and black-and-white, most of it used, judging by the lack of any film leaders.

She flipped the last page of the notebook, closed it and pushed it aside. Slumping back in her chair, she combed her hair away from her face. "Nothing other than exposure settings and a few locations."

"Well, don't fret on it. We can check out the locations later, see if that shakes anything loose. We'll get this film developed, too. Maybe whatever you shot will tell us something. Come on, AJ." A shiver danced across his insides. Right or wrong, he'd just given her a name. "Let's get you tidied up some. Sleeping on the beach probably left you a mite gritty."

He stood and held a hand out to her. "The guest bedroom is right down the hall."

She glanced from his eyes to his hand and back again. "Why did you call me that?" she whispered.

"It…kinda slipped out." His hand dropped to his side. "'Hey' is too general and Jane Doe is too…well, it just doesn't seem to fit you. Those engraved letters look like a monogram and it seems pretty likely it's yours. AJ's the closest we've come to finding a name…." He tugged at his earlobe. "I'm sorry. If it bothers you, we can come up with something else until we find out your real name."

"It startled me is all. I rather like how it sounded just now." A soft blush darkened her cheeks. "Somehow, not being able to remember doesn't seem quite so hopeless, as long as I have an identity of some sort."

"Then AJ it is, until we find out otherwise." He pulled her to her feet and led her down the hallway. "You know, this could be the opportunity of a lifetime."

She looked at him, disbelief clear in her expression.

"No, really. Think about it." He pulled a towel from the hall linen closet and handed it to her, along with a facecloth, a new toothbrush and an array of small bottles of toiletries from various hotels. "Not everyone gets to start over with a clean slate. You're free to decide who you are, what you want to be."

"Well, I suppose you could look at it that way. I just wish the slate wasn't quite so clean. All I have is this sense of urgency, of something I need to do. But I have no idea what." Her eyes widened and she clutched his arm. "Omigod. What if I have a child? Or children. What if they're somewhere waiting for me? What if they're in danger because I've abandoned them?"

A chill raced through him. Her words hit him harder than she'd ever realize. The picture of a small child with AJ's eyes and thick black hair popped into his head. The little boy stared back at him with sadness and accusation. He shook his head, banishing the image. That particular shadow belonged to him, not AJ. At least, he hoped that was the case.

He covered her hand with his. "Take it easy, sugar. We've got enough on our plates without borrowing more trouble. While you're in there—" he nodded toward the bathroom "—why don't you see if there's any, um, evidence that you've had a child."

She frowned, confused.

"Like stretch marks or, well, um, I don't really know." His words trickled to an awkward halt. A dull heat crept up his neck. When had he ever turned red-faced in front of a woman?

Understanding dawned and a blush darkened her face as

well. She clutched the pile in her arms to her chest and backed into the bathroom. The door closed between them without either of them saying another word.

Ryan thumped his head on the doorframe. *Dumb, dumb, dumb.* He cleared his throat. "I'll, uh, leave some clean clothes for you on the bed. In the guest room."

A muffled "thanks" came from behind the door.

He didn't tarry over finding clothes for her. Grabbing the first clean items that came to hand, he dropped them on the bed in the guest room and beat a hasty escape back to the kitchen.

AJ's equipment still occupied the tabletop. He surveyed everything and shook his head. "Women and cameras," he muttered. "Bound to bring nothin' but trouble."

Only, he had the distinct feeling this woman didn't need a camera to bring him trouble. Just being near her had him thinking all kinds of crazy thoughts. What was it about her that had him wanting to be the knight in shining armor? That was the last role he wanted to be cast in.

Everything worked much better when he kept behind the scenes and did his thing. In and out like a shadow, then on to the next assignment. Alone. No entanglements. Responsible for no one but himself.

Not that it had been like that in Montana. That was the first and last time he ever wanted to go so deep undercover.

He leaned against the kitchen counter and washed away the memories with a gulp of lemonade. The past could stay in the then and gone. He needed to concentrate on the here and now.

AJ's equipment was as good a place to start as any. The fact that she'd left the room without the bag could be considered something of a breakthrough. Maybe she'd decided to trust him.

Or maybe she'd clung to it as the only connection to

her identity. Now, with a name, at least she had another piece of the puzzle.

Or maybe she thought whatever might be hidden there was safe.

He picked up the camera bag. While considerably lighter than when it had been packed, it still seemed heavy for a nylon bag this size. He sat down with the bag in his lap.

Maybe one of Jamie's focusing exercises would help. Taking a couple deep breaths, Ryan cleared his mind of conscious expectations and blocked out his surroundings. The only sounds he kept tuned to were those of AJ's movements in the bathroom. He closed his eyes and let his fingers drift over the surfaces of the bag, not seeking with expectations of finding anything in particular. Just feeling for whatever existed.

When nothing presented itself, he turned the bag over and repeated the process. The base seemed to be a solid piece set into the bottom of the bag. Four small pads punctuated each corner. He fiddled with each one, humming with surprised satisfaction when they loosened.

Down the hall, everything was quiet. His eyes snapped open. He held his breath, waiting. When the shower turned on, he blew out a sigh of relief. *Let's hope she likes long showers.*

The pads unscrewed easily. The solid base lifted off revealing a false bottom. There was only about an inch of space, but it was ample room for the small black book he found.

He lifted the thin volume from its hiding place and set it on the table. Using the very tips of his fingers, he opened the black vinyl cover. Letters and numbers filled the first page. He flipped through several more pages. Something had been written on all of them.

This didn't look like AJ's record book of locations and

settings. He flipped open her spiral-bound notebook. Her notes, easily decipherable, were written in a back-slanted looping hand.

A neat, angular handwriting filled the pages of the mystery book with nonsensical combinations of letters and numbers. About halfway through, the cursive writing changed to printed block letters. Neither sample matched AJ's penmanship.

He tugged on his earlobe. Whoever the author was, the contents had been sensitive enough to prompt the use of a code. He could think of a few reasons something like that would be hidden, none of them good.

AJ, sugar, whatever it is, you are in it deep. And it's not gonna get better anytime soon.

Whatever the information might be, it had been recorded in a code too complex for him to decipher at first viewing. He'd need some time to do a proper job of it.

The water shut off in the bathroom. He cursed. His window of opportunity had just slammed shut. The little black book would have to wait.

He pulled a sandwich bag from one of the counter drawers and slid the book inside, zipped the seal and slid the package into his pocket. He screwed the bottom panel back into place and set about repacking the camera equipment.

Moving quietly around the kitchen, Ryan tidied up, then settled back at the table with his laptop. He logged on to the Internet and began surfing a few of the medical information sites. Outside, he could hear waves brushing onto the shore. Down the hall, the bathroom door opened.

Chapter Three

Her shower left the bathroom steamy. Too steamy to stay hiding in there any longer. It had taken forever to get rid of all the grit and sand. As for the pain—no matter how long she'd stood under the pounding spray, the pain refused to leave.

When she opened the door and peeked out, cool air rushed into the room. A chill shivered over her skin and she pulled the huge bath sheet tighter around herself. Down the hall, she could only see Ryan's shoulder and arm as he sat at the kitchen table with his back to her. She padded across the hall to the guest bedroom, slipped inside and closed the door.

Whoever had decorated the room had had nice taste. The pale blond wood furnishings blended with the palette of soft colors used on the walls and bedding to give the room an airy, cool feel. A bowl of potpourri sat atop the dresser, scenting the room with a tangy citrus fragrance. Small handcrafted treasures nestled among the books on the shelves of a bookcase. A small bowl filled with an array of colorful semiprecious stones sat next to an elegant stained-glass lamp on the bedside table.

The overall effect was soothing, offering a sense of peace, of sanctuary. Everything looked so…homey. As though someone actually lived there, rather than a professional decorator had laid out a magazine spread.

She trailed her fingers over the quilted bedspread. Even that had the look of having been lovingly handmade from favorite bits of fabric.

Another shiver danced over her naked shoulders when she encountered the neatly folded pile of clothes. Were they Ryan's? Or did the owner—Jamie—keep a supply of extra clothing tucked away for his guests along with the extra toothbrushes?

She turned from the bed and came face-to-face with a stranger.

No, not exactly a stranger. She faced a large wood-framed mirror hanging on the closet door. That was the only reason she recognized the woman watching her with guarded eyes. No sense of familiarity stirred. No flood of memories rushed forth to fill in the blanks.

The woman just stared back. She concentrated on the reflection but recognition still eluded her.

Why can't I remember? She stepped closer, leaning in to search for some clue, some detail that would trigger her memory. *AJ?* A vague sense of recognition stirred as she tried connecting the name Ryan had dubbed her with the reflection in the mirror. She traced the outline of her face on the cool glass. Unfamiliar gray eyes stared back. She leaned closer, looked deeper into the eyes.

Nothing. Nothing except emptiness that went deep, all the way to her heart. She backed away from the stranger in the mirror and sank down on the edge of the bed.

Tears threatened but she forced them back. She'd cried enough already. In the shower where the running water washed away the tears and the sounds of her quiet sobs. And earlier.

She had awakened on the beach to the sound of her own sobs. Her dreams were a jumbled confusion of images, none of them making sense, all of them fading as she became aware of her surroundings. Then she'd realized the dreams weren't the only things fading from memory. She had no memory of anything. A void existed where her identity should have been. She had no idea why she had been sleeping on a beach, or even where that beach was.

"AJ, are you okay?"

She jumped at Ryan's voice coming from the other side of the bedroom door. "Yes, I'm fine. I'll only be a few more minutes."

"No rush, sugar. We can head into town to drop off that film whenever you're ready. If you feel up to it."

"Sure. Fine. That's…fine." She lied. She wasn't fine. How could she be with her mind so empty?

No. Not empty, not exactly. It was more like a drawn curtain, transparent enough to let shadowy images through but too opaque to allow any real detail to show.

She sensed rather than heard Ryan's quiet steps as he retreated, leaving her alone in the strange room, staring at her reflection, which should have been familiar, but wasn't.

She wanted to trust him. Her instincts told her she could, but why? All indications were that they'd never met, yet she'd followed him here, to a strange house, with barely a moment's hesitation. Who was he?

Her heart sped up at the memory of his touch. When they shook hands, it had been magnetic. The jolt hadn't startled her so much as the strange sense of familiarity had. She didn't know him, but there had been a sense of recognition on a deeper, more elemental level, as though they were kindred spirits. She hadn't experienced anything like that since…since…when? Who? Someone else, someone important to her. The knowledge slipped further behind that blasted curtain.

She rubbed her temples, working at the tightness that wrapped around her head like a huge rubber band. Every time she tried to remember, her head ached. She closed her eyes and took several deep breaths, relaxing with each slow exhalation, willing the pain to leave.

Standing, she rolled her shoulders, raised her arms over her head and stretched. Slowly her knotted muscles relaxed. She paced around the room as she worked the snarls from her long hair and braided it. This task at least seemed familiar, routine. The normalcy served to calm her a little more. She could almost pretend everything was normal. Until she picked up the T-shirt.

It was a man's V-neck T-shirt, the kind that comes three to a package. Nothing out of the ordinary. Except she knew it had to belong to Ryan. The soft, pale green cotton matched the material of the one he wore right now.

Another shiver, totally unrelated to a chill, swept over her, dragging with it an awareness of the man who'd found her on the beach and brought her into his home. Not an awareness of him as a kind person doing a good deed. But an awareness of him as a very masculine, very attractive man.

This wouldn't do. Not at all. She hadn't missed Ryan's attention to her rings, especially the one he'd found hidden in her camera bag. The one that looked like a wedding ring.

Her thumb rubbed over the twined bands, rolling them back and forth over her knuckle. The motion was familiar, comforting even. The three intertwined circles of gold rolled together easily as she slid them over her knuckle and off her finger. Sadness flowed over her. Her finger felt naked without the ring. She felt lost without that symbol of being connected to someone.

The bands were nicked and burnished, their shine muted with the patina of constant wear. Lettering etched on the inside surface of one of the bands caught her eye.

She switched on the stained-glass lamp and held the ring

close to the light. Tilting it back and forth, she found additional markings. Each band had been inscribed. She swallowed hard, fighting back the rush of grief threatening to swamp her tenuous composure.

The words were familiar. On some level, she'd even expected to find them. Still the emptiness swirled around her. *AJD, Together Always, Remember 3/15*. The same inscription Ryan had found on the silver tag.

She slipped the ring back on and hugged her hand close to her heart. Pacing the room did nothing to ease the knot in her chest. It wasn't fair. How could grief this strong exist without memory of the person?

The room began to close in on her. The welcoming coziness became smothering. The light scent of the potpourri turned cloying. She pulled on the loaned clothes, ignoring the rippling awareness of whom the items belonged to, intent on one thing—getting out of the room before she started crying again.

Once out of the bedroom, she regained some small measure of calm. She made her way down the short hall, aware of the soft murmur of Ryan's voice. As she neared the door to the kitchen, he stopped talking. She held her breath, wondering who was in the kitchen with him. She wasn't ready to face anyone else yet.

He started talking again and she let out a slow sigh. Whoever it was, they were on the other end of the phone line, not in the kitchen. Her calm façade slipped a notch as his quiet words sank into her awareness.

"I don't know. It could be a setup, but I don't think so. You're the only one who knows I'm here."

Setup? What was he talking about?

"Yeah, I know. You're the one with the super, weird-vibe detector, but my gut says she's okay. She comes off as…real, I guess."

He was talking about her. Her rubber-soled sandals

squeaked on the linoleum floor as she stumbled to a halt in the doorway.

Ryan turned to look at her, his steady gaze never wavering as he listened to whoever 'was on the other end of the line. He'd been leaning back against the counter by the door and now he shifted so his entire body faced her. He stood mere inches from her, relaxed, seemingly unbothered by her sudden appearance.

The clean scent of sea air mingled with the tang of the perspiration he'd worked up on his morning run. She was close, too close, too aware of him. Instinct warned her the situation was dangerous, she'd been foolish to trust him so easily.

Before she could step away, his warm fingers wound around her wrist. The pale green of his eyes darkened as he watched her. He swept her with an appreciative gaze, a smile quirking up one corner of his mouth.

"That sounds good," he said into the phone. "Right, see y'all later." He returned the phone to its cradle and turned the full strength of his attention to her. "Those clothes never looked better. How 'bout you? Are you feeling better?"

She nodded. "Who were you talking to?"

"The esteemed Jamison McRobbie. Better known as our host, Jamie. I thought he might be able to help us out. He works with the police sometimes—"

"No! No police." She pulled her arm free from his loose grip and took a quick step away from him.

"AJ?" His soft tone stopped her backward movement.

"No, please, we can't go to the police." She fought down the panic threatening to shatter what remained of her hard-gained peace.

"Okay, we won't." He reached for her, gently running his hand down her arm. "Can you tell me why we can't go to the police?"

She closed her eyes and swallowed. A shudder ran across her shoulders, down her back. "I...I don't know. I just get this huge wave of 'danger' at the thought."

"All right, sugar. Don't worry about it. We proved your instincts are still pretty sharp, and if they're telling you to stay away from the police, we will. For now." He lifted her chin on the edge of his hand.

She opened her eyes. For a moment she lost herself in the pale depths of his steady gaze. How could she not trust him? From the moment they'd met on the beach, his one concern seemed to be helping her. What could he possibly gain from her?

Time stood still as she searched for an answer in his face. "Am I foolish to trust you?" she whispered.

Ryan's focus shifted from her eyes to her lips. "Probably." His breath caressed her cheek. "But not for the reason you think."

His attention to her mouth lasted for a fraction of a second, but it was long enough for her to realize how close they were standing to each other, how easy it would be to close that small space. How much she wanted to do exactly that.

Awareness coursed through her, setting her nerve endings on fire. There was more than trust at issue here. She'd just been on the verge of tears over an inscription in a wedding ring, *her* wedding ring. Whoever her husband was, whatever the status of their relationship, he held a great deal of importance to her. She couldn't—shouldn't—be so attracted to Ryan so easily.

But she was. *What kind of person am I?*

He released her arm and stepped back, putting a little distance between them. Had he been as aware of her as she was of him?

"Now then." He cleared his throat. "We have something really serious to discuss. Breakfast."

The sudden change of topic granted her a momentary reprieve from her troubling thoughts.

"'Course, I need to clean up before we leave," he continued. "But that won't take long. There's this great little place about ten minutes away. They do a mean *loco moco*."

She realized she was nearly hungry enough to tackle the local dish of rice and hamburger patty topped with gravy.

"Or how does fresh fruit and waffles sound?" Ryan offered the alternative.

"Wonderful." Her stomach rumbled in agreement. How long had it been since she'd eaten?

"Great. I'll be ready in two shakes. Why don't you put your feet up in the living room, while I go get gorgeous?" His quick smile revealed teeth so white they would have seemed fake if not for a slight misalignment of the eyeteeth. He led her into a spacious room filled with wicker furniture.

She sank onto the bright floral cushions of the couch and watched Ryan disappear down the hall.

Her camera bag sat on the coffee table. She crossed her legs tailor style and settled the bag in her lap. Its weight was comforting in an odd way. When she opened the cover, she discovered the contents had been neatly stowed back in their proper compartments. Ryan had done an excellent job of returning the equipment to its original order. It all looked and felt…right.

She ran her fingers over her equipment and pulled out her camera. Everything else in her life might be a blank, but this at least held a familiar certainty. It was the same security she'd experienced earlier, when she'd awakened on the beach and reached out for the only solid object near her.

For a few brief moments she'd been able to forget that she had forgotten. The familiar weight of her trusty Nikon had comforted her. When the sunrise had begun, she'd been able to lose herself in capturing the beauty of it through her viewfinder and saving it on film.

She slipped the camera back into its compartment and pulled the notebook out. She leafed through the pages, looking for something, anything that might trigger her memory. Precise notations of locations, times of the day and camera settings filled the pages. The handwriting held a vague sense of familiarity. She dug a pen from one of the pockets, turned to a blank page and began writing. At first it was nothing more than random words, enough to know it really was her handwriting in the book. Then she refocused, became intentional about what she wrote.

My name is…

She couldn't finish the sentence. She tried again and again, each time starting on a new line, each time getting no further. She closed her eyes and tried again.

Failed again.

She tore the pages from the book, crumpled them into a tight ball and jammed it into a compartment in the bag. The pen and notebook went back into their pockets and she closed the bag with a snap.

People don't just go around forgetting who they are for no reason. Something terrible must have occurred to wipe out every bit of her conscious memory.

Relax. That's what she needed to do, just relax. Little things came when she didn't try so hard. She leaned her head back against the cushions. Her eyes drifted shut as she rubbed her hands over the bag. Each texture, each contour, felt familiar and reassuring beneath her fingers.

The silver pull on the zip hung cool and solid from its chain. Opening her eyes, she examined it, reading the inscription for herself. *Remember.* Remember what?

A tear traced a hot path down her cheek.

"AJ?"

She jumped at Ryan's voice, her hand flying to her chest to catch her wildly beating heart. "Jeez, you scared me! Don't you ever make any noise when you walk?"

"Sorry. Old habit. You seemed to be pretty deep in thought."

She wiped the tear away with the heel of her hand before turning to look at him.

His short, light brown hair was damp and standing on end, looking like the latest style in a trendy men's magazine. He wore khaki shorts and a brightly colored Hawaiian shirt that he'd left unbuttoned and untucked. The white T-shirt he'd changed into hugged the contours of his well-muscled torso and set off his tan. A small gold ring hung on a chain around his neck. With these clothes, he looked as if he'd fit right in with the tourist crowd. Provided the tourists were a bunch of Olympic competitors.

And she was still far too aware of him and his athletic body for her comfort.

"I've only been sitting here eight-and-a-half minutes. Did you get a real shower taken?" She shut out the brief image of him in the shower before it could fully develop.

"Yes, ma'am. Even washed behind my ears. Mind if I ask a question?" He waited for her consenting nod before continuing. "How do you know it's been eight minutes? There aren't any clocks in here and you aren't wearing a watch."

"Eight-and-a-half minutes." She corrected him. "I always know exactly how much time has elapsed. It comes in handy when timing exposures or developing film."

"Are you always right?"

"Always," she replied with absolute certainty. "My turn. How did you manage to shower and get dressed in such a short time?"

"Military training. Heck, anything over five minutes is

considered downright leisurely.'' He held out one hand to her. ''Now, how about that breakfast?''

He led her out the front door and handed her into the passenger seat of a cherry-red Corvette convertible.

''Nice little car.'' She watched as he buckled his seat belt and turned the ignition key. The engine came to life with a powerful rumble.

''Jamie's.''

''Ah, all part of the vacation package?''

Ryan nodded, slipped on a pair of RayBan Wayfarer sunglasses and nudged the stick shift into first gear. As they pulled onto the road, he launched into the story of his first stay on the island.

He kept her entertained all the way to the little restaurant and all through the meal.

For a brief period, she was able to pretend everything was normal.

Chapter Four

Ryan had run through the better part of his repertoire, regaling AJ with carefully sanitized stories of his childhood. It seemed to work. She had actually eaten some fresh fruit and even looked a bit relaxed until they got back into the car.

Now silence fell as they headed for Honolulu. He flipped on the radio, filling the quiet with KNUI's Hawaiian music. An ad for a photo finisher came on between songs.

AJ cleared her throat. "You mentioned getting the exposed film developed. Do you have a lab in mind?"

"None in particular. With all the tourist trade there's bound to be a slew of those one-hour places. We can drop the stuff off at one of them." He glanced at her in time to catch her grimace of distaste. "What?"

Her hands tightened on the camera bag. "Nothing. I'm sure that would be..."

"Like flossing with razor wire." He reached over and covered her white-knuckled hands. "Scratch the one-hour place. We can stop and check the phone book for professional labs. Maybe one of them will sound familiar."

"That's assuming I ever used one or, if I did, that I'll remember which one it was."

"Don't fret yourself. It's possible you might remember.

I did a little Web surfing while you were in the shower, found some information about amnesia. From what I found, the kind of amnesia you have is called psychogenic amnesia.''

''And that means what?''

''It means, sugar, that the memories aren't really lost, just sort of hidden for the time being.''

''Like a drawn curtain.'' She leaned forward a little, hope lighting her face. ''So, I'll remember everything? My name, where I live, all that?''

''Maybe.'' He didn't want to get her hopes up too high. While the research said the amnesia might only last a few hours, it could also last years. ''One of the articles said hypnosis or free association might help trigger memories. That's why looking through the yellow pages isn't such a crazy idea. You might see a name that's familiar.''

She nodded and leaned back into the seat, nibbling on her lip in thought.

''Once we get your film taken care of proper like, then we can do a little shopping. Cute as you look in my clothes, I don't imagine they're particularly comfortable.'' The discomfort was probably mostly his. Every time he thought of the way his shirt draped—he squashed the image before it fully formed. To distract himself, he launched into another story about one of his early visits to the island.

AJ visibly relaxed, watching the scenery flow by as they sped toward Honolulu. As they neared the city, she opened her camera bag, checked her equipment and began sorting through the canisters of exposed film.

Ryan eased up on the accelerator as the city traffic began building around them. AJ glanced up. ''Take the next exit. At the stoplight, take a right.''

He opened his mouth then closed it again. She was busy digging through her bag, and he decided not to interrupt her. This might be the beginning of the breakthrough they needed. He wasn't about to jinx it by asking her a pile of questions.

He made the turn, scooting through the intersection as the light changed from yellow to red. She directed him through a few more turns before telling him to pull over.

"Park in the next block. It's up ahead a little ways."

He parked the 'Vette, turned off the ignition and waited, watching her, wondering how she'd react to their surroundings.

She rearranged a few loose items in the camera bag then snapped it shut. When she finally looked at him, Ryan raised one eyebrow.

"What?" Confusion clouded her expression.

"What's up ahead?"

"The lab."

"What lab?"

"The film lab that does all…my…." Her voice trailed off on a breathy *oh*. She twisted in her seat, checking out the surrounding area.

Her directions had taken them away from the busy downtown area to the Kaimuki area. Here, a mix of neighborhood shops lined the street. Out of the tourist path, the merchandise displayed in these store windows catered to everyday life and the needs of the nearby residents. He'd be hard-pressed to find a puka bead necklace or picture postcard anywhere in the vicinity.

He held silent and waited. It took her a bit, but she did continue.

"This is where I get my film developed. They do custom printing for me, too. There's a little shop in front where they sell supplies, but their main business is processing and printing." Her voice faded to a whisper. She rubbed her forehead and tucked a stray wisp of hair behind her ear. "How'd I remember that when I can't remember my own name?"

"Don't fight it. The research said you'd remember basic functions. Getting film processed would be pretty basic for a photographer. Let's take anything that slips through and run with it. Are there any names attached to this place?"

"Uncle Kimo?" She lifted her hands in a questioning gesture.

"Good. Let's go see if Uncle Kimo can give us some information."

AJ laid her hand over his as he reached for the keys. Something tightened deep inside. Something he wanted to ignore but couldn't. Not as long as she touched him. He pulled the keys from the ignition and broke the contact with her hand.

"Ryan, I can't waltz in there and say 'Hi, guys, what's my name?' That's a sure bet for getting me hauled off to the loony bin. Or worse, what if I'm wrong and whatever I'm hiding from is linked to this shop?"

"You got a point there." Ryan tugged at his earlobe. "Do you think you can help me pull off a little undercover investigation?"

She frowned. "What do you mean?"

"You go in first. Just act normal, take your cue from their reactions. I'll come in a minute later. If there's any hostility, get out. Otherwise, you do your business and when you leave, I'll see what they'll tell me."

"Do you think it'll work?"

"Hey, I do this for a living." He was none too sure himself, but no sense telling her that.

"What if it doesn't work? What if they don't tell you anything?"

"Now don't go borrowin' trouble. If they don't give me any information, we'll come back when your film's ready and see what that tells us." He gave her an encouraging smile and nodded toward the car door. "Go on. I'll be right behind you."

"One minute?"

"That's all. You can time me." He winked and she rewarded him with a half smile before she got out of the car. He glanced at his watch and scanned the surrounding area. Pedestrian traffic was light. A few import sedans, minivans and a Jeep or two were parked at random intervals up and down the street. Everything looked mostly normal.

When AJ entered the shop, he strolled after her. He stopped to check out the large display window. Gold lettering arched across the glass, proclaiming Kimo Kealoha—Photography Services. The words formed a perfect frame for the reflection of the coffee shop across the street and the nondescript, dark blue sedan parked in front of it. A child's stuffed toys littered the car's dashboard. Ryan's mental radar blipped. Something wasn't quite right.

He tried to shrug off the sensation. Ever since he'd talked to Jamie he'd been running on yellow alert. If he wasn't careful, he'd be seeing spooks behind every bush.

A bell jangled overhead as a teenage girl exited the photo shop. Ryan slipped through the door before it swung closed. He wandered in, nodded to the man behind the counter and began browsing. Tucking his sunglasses in the neck of his T-shirt, he kept an eye on the street while keeping an ear on the conversation between the shop clerk and AJ.

"I've only got a few rolls of film, but I'm anxious to see how they turn out." The quaver in AJ's voice was barely noticeable.

The man behind the counter laughed. "When aren't you in a hurry?" His grizzled gray hair and rounded shape made him look like an overgrown elf. His voice matched the image. "And don't we always rush your stuff?"

"And don't I always appreciate your rushing my stuff?" Laughter eased a little of the tension from her voice. Ryan glanced her way just in time to see the dimple in her left cheek, near the corner of her mouth. He hadn't seen it before. He'd like to see it again.

The man shook his head as he began sorting the film canisters and writing out work-order tickets. "Some *haole* was in here looking for you earlier. Funny looking man, all dressed up in a dark suit and a very ugly tie."

"Really?" AJ's voice squeaked and Kimo paused in his scribbling to look at her. Ryan turned away to peruse a film display, doing everything he could to look disinterested in their topic of conversation as he worked his way around the store to have a better view of them.

Kimo continued after a short hesitation. "He was tall, skinny. Bad skin, eyes so pale, I'm not sure they had any real color. Seemed to think you'd be in sometime today. Guess he was right. Do you know him?"

AJ shook her head. "I don't think so. He asked for me by name?"

"Yes, but that doesn't mean much, now that you're starting to make a name for yourself—" He stopped in midsentence, holding up two canisters and shaking them at her. "You just picked this high-speed film up yesterday." He pointed at another canister. "That infrared, too. Don't tell me you stayed out all night shooting your experiment just so you could include it in the opening?"

AJ's eyes widened and she shrugged.

"Ya gotta slow down, girl. You're so busy shooting the island's beauty, you never see it. When you get done with that show, promise Uncle Kimo you'll take some time to look around you, without a camera in the way."

"Okay, Uncle Kimo. I promise."

"Maybe I could believe you if I didn't know you so well. But I do." Kimo shook his head and returned to writing the work orders. "I'd talk to David if I thought it'd do any good, but it wouldn't. You and he are too alike to be together so much.''

The color drained from AJ's face. Her eyes closed and she bit her lip. Kimo never looked up from his task so he missed her reaction.

"It was different when Justin was still alive.'' Regret colored Kimo's words. "He balanced you two. But now all either one of you do is work, work, work. That's no kind of life.''

It didn't take a genius to see how much the mention of the two men's names had shaken her. Ryan took a step toward AJ but stopped at the tiny shake of her head.

"How soon can I see these?'' Her voice cracked and Kimo pinned her with a stern look.

"Tomorrow. You go rest, before you collapse.''

AJ opened her mouth, but closed it again without voicing a protest.

Ryan decided it was time to move in. He walked over beside AJ, smiling at her as he leaned sideways against the counter, facing her. "Hi.''

"Hello.'' She gave him a once-over. The slight pause seemed to give her enough time to regroup. She turned her attention back to Kimo. "It's still early. Are you sure I can't see that film today?''

"Tomorrow.''

"Fine. I'll see you tomorrow morning. At nine.''

"Ten and not a minute before. Go home.'' Kimo glanced at Ryan. "And watch out for strangers.''

She shook her head at Kimo, looked Ryan up and down one more time.

He straightened away from the counter and watched, fascinated as a blush tinted her high cheekbones. He winked at her and her blush darkened before she turned on her heel and left the store. The bell jangled as the door closed behind her.

"Can I help you?" Kimo was all business. The laughter he'd shared with AJ clearly didn't extend to a stranger.

Ryan dragged his attention from AJ's retreating figure and turned back to the counter. "Nice lady. Are you really her uncle?"

Kimo waved a hand in the air. "I watch out for her. It's a responsibility I take very seriously." His midnight-dark eyes stared at Ryan, taking his measure and warning him all in one look. "You're a bit off the tourist track. Where can I give you directions to?"

"Nowhere, really. I'm staying with a friend up on the north shore and thought I'd explore some of the neighborhoods." Ryan smiled his easy, not-to-worry smile. "Do you have any of those disposable cameras? I hear they work pretty good."

Kimo pulled one from the shelf behind him and thumped it onto the counter. "That'll be $15.85. Anything else?"

Ryan grinned as he tossed a twenty onto the counter. "Any chance you'd give me the lady's name."

"None. But if you're really interested, she's got a show going up at a gallery in a couple weeks. If you're around that long, you could look her up then."

"Sounds good. Which gallery?"

"If you're still around, I'll tell you then."

"Fair enough. Something tells me she's worth sticking around for." He picked up two store business cards from the small seashell card holder on the counter and tucked one into his shirt pocket. He flipped the other over and wrote on the back, before handing it to Kimo. "If she happens to ask, will you give this to her?"

Kimo read the note on the card and looked back at Ryan. "Pretty confident, aren't you?"

"It never hurts to be optimistic."

The two men stared at each other for a moment, then Ryan tapped the counter with his camera and left the store.

He paused as the door swung shut behind him. *Worth sticking around for, huh?* Now wasn't the time to delve into that thought. Sliding his sunglasses back on, he scanned the street, then sauntered back to the 'Vette where AJ waited for him.

"Did he tell you anything?" She slid into the passenger seat and turned to face him. Her voice fairly vibrated with excitement.

As he sat next to her in the driver's seat, he noticed a lanky-looking man in an ill-fitting black suit leave the coffee shop carrying a small brown paper bag, but no coffee cup.

"Not much. You have a show going up at a gallery in a couple weeks." He reached for the ignition, but stopped with the key halfway in the slot. His yellow-alert status bumped up to red.

The coffee-shop patron was unlocking the passenger door of the navy sedan.

"My show? I'm having a show? Where? What gallery?"

Ryan watched the man get in and duck out of sight.

"Well now. Don't that beat all?" The man reappeared, got out of the car and locked the door.

"What?" AJ looked around. "What are you talking about? What's going on?"

Ryan nodded across the street. "Does the man crossing the street look familiar?"

AJ watched him tuck the brown paper bag under his arm and jog across the street to another nondescript sedan, this one a dark green. "No. Should he?"

"Tall, skinny, couldn't quite tell about his skin, but you must admit, that was one ugly tie."

She looked at him with wide eyes. "You think that's the man Uncle Kimo mentioned?"

"I'll bet dinner out they're one and the same. Are you ready for a little fun?" He smiled at her. The 'Vette's ignition turned over and the engine hummed to life.

"What kind of fun?"

"Keep an eye on Ole Slim." Ryan pulled away from the curb. "We're going to follow him for a tad and see where he takes us."

"Why are we doing that?"

He debated telling her for a moment. The stakeout might be totally unrelated to her situation. Or she may know exactly what it was all about. Either way, it wouldn't hurt to let her know he was aware of what was going on around them. "Well, I figure if he's interested enough in you to stake out the lab, then we should be interested enough in him to see where he's heading."

The sports car responded to his gentle nudge on the accelerator and leaped forward. Within a few blocks they'd caught up with the sedan. Only one car separated them. Ryan followed the sedan through several intersections and around a couple turns, letting other cars come and go between them.

They headed through downtown and into an industrial-park section. Ryan muttered to himself. Rather than enjoying the thrill of the chase, he was more worried about being made. Tailing someone in a cherry-red 'Vette wasn't exactly inconspicuous. The other driver hadn't given any indication that he'd noticed them. Yet.

Traffic thinned and the last car between them turned onto a side street, leaving them with no cover. Whatever the guy's next turn was, they'd have to continue on. He memorized the sedan's license plate. Later, he'd have the Bureau run it, see if it provided any useful information.

"Time to call it a morning." Ryan tapped the blinker

lever to take the turn at the T-intersection they were approaching. He stopped to let the oncoming traffic clear out of the way.

The sedan continued through the intersection, turned in the opposite direction without signaling and drove through a gap in a high chain-link gate.

Ryan completed his turn, pulled to the curb and studied the rearview mirror. As soon as the sedan cleared the sidewalk, a gate rolled closed behind it. A large sign on the gate warned away trespassers and proclaimed the fenced complex to be private property.

Ryan twisted in his seat to double-check the cross street and verify the address. Excitement buzzed along his nerve endings. The Bureau could do a little property owner check at the same time they ran the sedan's plates.

As he turned back in his seat, AJ straightened. She'd been slouched down a bit to watch their six through the passenger side mirror.

"What do we do now?" She began nibbling on her lower lip.

"Now, we go shopping." He merged back into traffic.

"Shopping? But what about that guy?" AJ swung around to stare at him.

"Sugar, even if that gate is unlocked, you can bet there's going to be a guard close inside. And we're not exactly invisible in this toy of Jamie's. There's nothing more for us here. Not today."

"So we just quit?" She sank back onto her seat.

"No. But there are a couple other things that need to take priority right now. Like finding you something other than my jeans to wear, running Slim's license plate, deciding where we're going to have dinner. If we're lucky, maybe we'll find your memory in the process."

He began compiling a mental list as he negotiated his way through the light traffic. The first chance he got, he'd be making a call into the Bureau, get them working on a bit of fact-finding. He'd have to talk to Jamie, too, about switching to a different car, something a little more common for the neighborhoods they'd be driving around.

The gallery lead would take a little more time to follow up. A few phone calls and they should have her name, presuming she wasn't showing under an alias. From there, it would be relatively simple to find more details. If they were lucky, with all the information flowing in, her memories would begin resurfacing.

At some point, regardless of AJ's reservations, they would have to go to the local police. The gun she had tucked in her camera bag raised a few too many questions not to. He added checking the gun's serial number and running it through the database to his task list. It might prove interesting to see if the gun was registered and who the owner of record was.

Traffic halted at a stoplight. He turned to her, ready to start making the case for going to the police. The words died unspoken.

AJ huddled in her seat, hugging herself, one hand covering her mouth. The unmistakable sheen of tears robbed her eyes of all color. He'd been so wrapped up in planning his investigation, he hadn't noticed her silence.

While he was enjoying the challenge of what lay ahead, she was grappling with problems the likes of which he hoped never to face. The look on her face left no doubt of the struggle she was having.

"AJ?" He tucked a strand of her silky hair behind her ear.

"Who were they, do you suppose?" AJ's voice broke. She took a shuddering breath then continued. "The men Uncle Kimo mentioned, David and Justin."

Her voice seemed to caress the men's names. Whether or not she remembered the men, the very manner in which she spoke their names told of some deep emotion tied to them. The stab of jealousy lasted only a second, long enough to register, short enough he could ignore for now.

"Who do you think they were? What do you feel when you think of them?" The light changed. He forced himself to look away from her and turn his attention back to driving.

The ring on her finger tingled in the silence as she rolled it back and forth over her knuckles. The action seemed to help her formulate an answer to his questions. After several long minutes, she finally answered. "Loss, loneliness. Fear of getting lost."

The short phrases gave Ryan a very strong sense of her emotions. She maybe couldn't put it into words, but she needed this David and Justin, and they weren't there. They were failing her.

He wouldn't. This time, he'd succeed.

"I wish I could go home." Her whispered words were barely audible.

"I know, baby." He reached over and covered her white-knuckled fists with his hand. "I know."

Chapter Five

AJ stared at the chaos surrounding her. Clothes hangers were hooked everywhere and more clothes littered every available surface. She'd done nothing except try on clothes since arriving at the trendy little boutique an hour ago. Ryan had kept a steady flow of shorts, blouses, swimsuits, even lingerie coming through the curtains.

When they'd first arrived, all she'd wanted to do was avoid any more efforts to release the blocked memories. The constant activity had provided the hoped-for reprieve. Now she was exhausted and she just wanted to sit down, but the only open space left in the tiny cubicle was the floor.

"Your husband asked me to bring this back for you to try on." The floral curtains that passed for a dressing-room door parted and the salesclerk's arm invaded the space. A bright red slip dress dangled from the hanger in the outstretched hand.

Husband? AJ's heart skipped a beat. No. Ryan. She's talking about Ryan. She pushed a swallow past the knot in her throat and took the proffered garment.

"He's so sweet." The clerk, Cassie, peeked through the curtain. "Most guys can't get out of here fast enough, but your guy is like a kid in a candy shop."

"Umm, actually, he's not my—we aren't—we're—friends." AJ stammered through the explanation.

"Whatever he is, in my book any man who knows how to shop is definitely a keeper. Play your cards right and you'll have a whole new wardrobe before you leave." She stepped back and the curtains fell into place.

AJ stared at the swaying cloth. Cassie seemed to have a somewhat skewed idea of what constituted a good relationship.

While the clerk might think it was great to have someone else pay for a new wardrobe, AJ did not like the idea. Not one bit. She didn't know herself let alone Ryan, and, in spite of an undeniable attraction to the man, she couldn't feel comfortable with him buying her anything. Certainly not such a personal gift as clothes.

Had Justin or David taken her shopping? A sense of guilt threatened to intrude on her hard-found composure. She fought it back, pushing the emotion into a tight little box and forcing the box into the recesses of her thoughts.

Whoever they were, they weren't here. She was on her own and she needed to stand on her own two feet. Which brought her back to the condition of the dressing room.

Cassie's misperception of the situation was understandable. If AJ didn't make some decisions in the next five minutes, Ryan would have the store's entire inventory hanging in here.

She eyed his most recent selection. The red minidress looked outrageously short. Shorter than anything else she'd tried on so far. The fabric shimmered in the overhead light, practically radiating a heat of its own.

She slipped the dress over her head and sighed as the soft fabric settled into place. The silk caressed her body, bringing her senses to tingling alertness with every breath. Cool air from the store's air-conditioning washed over the expanse of skin left naked by the low-cut back.

For a moment, as she stared in the mirror, her mind's curtain parted and a phantom memory flickered into view. A man held her in his arms as they glided across a dance floor. She could almost hear the music and an echo of laughter as her partner spun her in a circle and caught her in his arms again.

"How're we doing?"

The image splintered and disappeared, shattered by the return of the saleswoman. AJ almost cried. So close.

Cassie peeked through the curtain before pulling it open. "I brought some cute little strappy sandals that would look absolutely fabulous with that dress."

AJ shook off her frustration. Maybe, if she could get rid of Cassie's constant distractions, the images would return.

Hope of a quick end to any discussion died when she spotted the sandals.

Little was the perfect description. Evidently the designer thought three narrow strips were sufficient to keep the wearer's foot in place atop the thin leather sole. The three-inch heels practically shouted "sprained ankle." She'd fall off them at the first step.

"I don't think so."

"They're really comfortable."

"I doubt that."

"Really. You'll be amazed. All you need to do is change your toenail polish from that pale pink you've got on to red. I think I've got the perfect shade on the display by the counter, and you're ready to go. And the best part is, they're on sale." This last bit of information was imparted as though it made all the difference in the world. "At least try them."

AJ gave in. She'd never get out of the shop if every accessory became a negotiation.

"Perfect." Cassie sighed. "You have got to show your

guy this one. It'll drive him wild." She grabbed AJ's hand and pulled her onto the sales floor.

Ryan looked up from the rack of dresses he was leafing through. He only stared for ten seconds before he crossed the store to stand in front of her. It seemed like hours.

Her skin heated at the intensity of his look. Breathing required conscious effort. So this is what it means to be devoured by a man's eyes.

"You look...." He stopped. His Adam's apple bobbled around a swallow. He turned to the saleswoman and handed her a credit card. "We'll take it. And whatever else she needs."

"Ryan, no. You can't—"

He turned back to her. "Sure I can, sugar." He ran his hand down her arm and a trail of fire followed the path of his fingers. Glancing at the saleswoman, he stepped closer. "You need something to wear until we get a few things sorted out and find your place." The caress in his low voice released an answering warmth deep inside. He took her hand in his and gave it a gentle squeeze. "Consider it a favor from a friend. Please?"

She nibbled at her lower lip for a moment, debating the wisdom of accepting so much from him. Finally, she nodded. "But only a few things and only temporarily. When we do find my place, I'll repay you."

"My mama taught me never to argue with a lady." He grinned a lopsided grin and winked at her. "Why don't you change and we'll head back to the cottage."

Cassie followed her to the dressing room and waited with outstretched arms as AJ made the final selections. She opted for the plain T-shirts and a couple pairs of the longer shorts along with a pair of plain white Keds.

Lingerie options in the boutique were a far cry from the serviceable cotton underwear she had on, but she needed at least a couple changes and there didn't seem to be any other choice. The wispy bits of silk joined the growing pile.

"I'll wait outside while you slip off the dress and shoes." Cassie waggled her eyebrows.

AJ dismissed the possibility of winning any discussion involving the dress and snapped the curtains closed.

By the time she re-dressed in her borrowed clothes and exited the dressing room, everything had been rung up. Ryan stood waiting for her by the door, holding two large shopping bags. From the satisfied look on the salesgirl's face, AJ suspected she'd find the red nail polish and who knew what else added to the day's purchases.

"You need these." Ryan pulled a pair of tortoiseshell cat's-eye sunglasses and a straw hat from one of the bags and handed them to her. He slipped his own black Wayfarers into place and pushed the door open. "It's mighty bright out there."

Her protest to the accessories faded to nothing. The bright sunshine provided more than enough justification for the additional purchase.

Ryan nudged her across the sidewalk. Awareness of him hummed through her body as they walked to the car. Tension and heat radiated from his hand where it rested at the small of her back. The incredible sensuality of that simple touch had her standing a little straighter, trying for a little distance between them.

His relaxed saunter fooled her for a moment. Then she caught the movement of his eyes behind the dark sunglasses. He constantly scanned their surroundings, holding watch over their path to the car.

A warning to stay alert whispered through her memory. As she slid into the car, she glanced over her shoulder, searching for anything that might seem out of place. She didn't say anything until they were back on the road, safe from any eavesdroppers. She checked the side mirror before turning to him and asking, "Are you expecting someone?"

A subtle change crossed his features. If she didn't make a living from noticing subtleties, she might have missed it. As it was, she saw it but didn't know what had prompted it or what it meant.

A few seconds ticked off before he answered. "I find it's usually best to expect the worst. That guy we followed could have taken our license number just as easily as I got his. Depending on when he made us, he could have someone following us. If he has the right connections there could be someone waiting at the estate entrance by the time we get there."

"Why would we be targeted for a stakeout? For that matter, why would anyone be watching Kimo's in the first place?"

"Now that is an interesting question. Do you have any idea why Ole Slim was looking for you?"

"I haven't a clue. I'm not even sure why you decided the shop was being watched."

"Let's just say I recognize the operating methods. But don't worry, sugar." His smile held a sharp edge, all boyish charm gone. "They may be good, but I'm better."

His statement sounded more like a warning than an assurance. An uneasy wariness scraped her nerves. The intensity of his expression, the certainty in his tone, even the way he drove, it all held a sense of familiarity. It was like looking at a photograph through foggy glass. The wrong face looked back, but too many other details matched. She pressed back into the leather car seat.

The familiarity didn't comfort her.

A QUICK CHECK DOWN THE HALL assured Ryan that AJ had entered her room to change and put away her new clothes. He dialed the phone, running through a series of numbers from memory. The line clicked through several forwarding relays while he began making some sandwiches.

"Kingston." A human voice finally came on the line.

"Miss Jacquelyn, shouldn't you be headed home by now?"

"Williams. You wouldn't be calling me if you really thought that was true. You shouldn't be calling at all." Special Agent In Charge Jacquelyn Kingston didn't hide her displeasure. "You're supposed to be on R and R. Why are you sending me e-mail and why are we talking on a secure line?"

"Well, I've got something of a situation here. I'm hoping you can help me out a bit."

A sigh came across the line. He could picture Jacquelyn, perfectly turned out in discreet good taste, leaning back in her chair, rubbing at the frown lines between her eyes. She always seemed to have frown lines when she talked to him. "What have you gotten into, Williams?"

"I've met a woman." He positioned the plateful of ham sandwiches in the middle of the table and added two plates and napkins to the arrangement.

"Nothing new there. What makes it a problem this time?"

"I think she's in some kind of trouble." He poured two glasses of lemonade and added them to the table setting, positioning them just so on coasters.

"Trouble. Wonderful." Another sigh. "What kind of trouble?"

"Don't rightly know just yet."

"Did you try asking her?" Jacquelyn's voice sounded tired.

"Yeah, well now, that's where it starts to get real interesting." Ryan tugged on his earlobe. "She's got amnesia."

"I suggest you take her to the police, then."

"Not an option. She's afraid of the police." He checked down the hallway to make sure AJ was still in her room. Once her fear had come out, there'd been no further discussion of going outside for help, and he wasn't sure how she'd react to him making this call. The Bureau was really just an extension of him, so she couldn't get too upset. Could she? Besides, he needed to tap into the Bureau's resources if he was going to discover who was watching the lab.

"That's rather convenient, wouldn't you say? You're sure about the amnesia?"

"There's no sign of injury, but so far, her behavior has been consistent with the information I found on the Internet. Jamie gave me a referral to a doctor who might be able to help. We're seeing him in a couple hours."

"What makes you so sure she's legitimate?"

Ryan didn't answer immediately. He didn't know, not really. He leaned against the kitchen counter.

"Williams?" Jacquelyn warned.

He'd recognize that tone of voice anywhere. It was the tone every mother figure in his life had used every time he stepped out of line.

"I admit, right now I don't have much solid to go on, but my instincts say she's telling the truth." Over the years those instincts had saved his behind more than once. His reputation was that of a man with rock-solid judgement, and Jacquelyn knew it. Silence hummed across the line as Ryan waited for her to make a decision.

"What do you expect us to do?" she asked.

Ryan pumped his fist in a small victory salute. She still hadn't agreed to anything, but she hadn't shut him down, either.

"I thought maybe you all could do a little checking with the locals. See if they have any missing-person reports, find out why there might be a stakeout on a little photo shop in an out-of-the-way Honolulu neighborhood?''

"Stakeout? Ryan, tell me you didn't interfere with a local police op.''

"Now, don't go gettin' riled. I don't know that it was official cop business.''

"Well, what do you know? Give me something, anything a little more solid than your instinctive reaction to a pretty face.''

"First off, she's more than a pretty face. She's…'' Ryan searched for some way to explain what he saw when he looked at AJ. "There's something in her eyes, something deeper….''

"Fine, she's not some beach bunny. Why don't we start with an easy question? What are her stats?''

"Age 28 to 32 years. Height about five-eight, weight about 130, straight black waist-length hair, gray eyes, a small mole below the right corner of her mouth, dimple in her left cheek when she smiles, no other visible marks. The initials *AJD* seem to be significant.''

"Do you think you could get a picture of her? Prints would be helpful, too.''

"I can't make any promises, but I'll see what I can do.''

"Details and facts, Ryan. There's not very much I can do without data. Such as how you managed to walk into a stakeout. Perhaps you could clarify that detail for me?''

He took a couple swallows of the tart lemonade as he raced through what he knew, how much Jacquelyn could use and how any of this was going to sound to his boss. Not much of it was going to sound good, but there was no avoiding it.

"She's a photographer and she had some exposed film with her. I figured it might be relevant. So we decided to get it developed.''

"How did you happen to pick that particular shop?''

"Every now and again, a spontaneous memory seems to break through. She remembered this place, so we went there. I didn't see any reason not to when we might find out something."

"Did you?"

"A little. The owner, Kimo Kealoha, recognized her, treated her like family."

"I'll run a check on him, see if anything turns up. What else?"

"He mentioned two other names. Justin and David. No last name. They may or may not be related to her. The film will be ready tomorrow at ten. If that gives us anything useful I'll let you know."

"Anything else about the shop I can use?"

"Not much. Their primary business is as a lab, processing film and custom printing. It didn't look like they were very concerned about catering to the tourist trade."

"And the stakeout?"

"An unmarked sedan was parked across the street from the shop when we arrived. Nobody was in it, but there were a few kid's toys on the dash. When we were about to leave, I observed a very non-daddy kind of guy get in the car. He disappeared under the dash for a minute, then left. I'm guessing one of those plush puppies hid a camera connected to a time-lapse tape deck."

"What else?"

"I've got a license plate and the address we followed him to. If you could run those for me, it'd help. That's about it."

Jacquelyn hummed in a noncommittal tone, a sure sign she was double-checking her notes, looking for holes or details that needed clarifying.

"Where did you say you met this woman?"

"I didn't. On the beach this morning during my run."

"On the beach?"

Ryan braced himself for the storm about to hit.

"Let me see if I have this right. You find a woman on a secluded, private beach. This mystery woman claims to have amnesia, refuses to go to the authorities but conveniently remembers a lab where the owner recognizes her. When you leave that lab, you spot a possible stakeout and tail someone long enough to get a plate and address you want me to check out."

"Yes, ma'am. That pretty much covers it."

Silence flowed through the phone line. When Jacquelyn finally spoke, her displeasure crackled through the phone earpiece. "Ryan, how many people know you're in Hawaii? Who knows your vacation regimen? Have you checked your enemies list lately? Do you have any idea of how many people would like to get payback on you? This whole situation reeks of setup six ways from Sunday."

He sighed and rubbed his eyes, pinching the bridge of his nose. "I know, I know. That's why I want you to check things from your end. See if you can find out who the players are and who's doing the watching."

"There's something else, isn't there? What haven't you told me?"

Jacquelyn read him too well, but there wasn't much time left. AJ would be returning to the kitchen in a moment. He turned his back to the hall doorway and lowered his voice. "There was some kind of code book hidden in her camera bag. I don't think she knew about it. If she is legit, she's going to need all the help she can get."

"So are you. Have you talked to McRobbie?"

"Yes, ma'am. He hasn't met her yet, but if he'd picked up on anything, he would have mentioned it."

"Well, that's small comfort."

"In the meanwhile, I'm better off keeping her close. If

she is a setup, she might let something slip. If she isn't…''
Ryan let the sentence hang.

Jacquelyn sighed again. ''I'll see what we can turn up
from here. And Williams?''

''Yes, ma'am?''

''Watch your back and don't play hero.''

He turned to find AJ standing there, her arms wrapped
around her waist, eyes wide as she stared at him.

Blast, how long had she been standing there?

''Williams?'' Jacquelyn barked in his ear.

''Yeah, I hear you. I'll call you later.'' He dropped the
phone back in its cradle without waiting for a reply and
took a step toward AJ.

She took a step back.

''AJ?'' He took another step. She turned and walked
away from him, her back straight as a preacher on Sunday.
He followed her into the living room. ''C'mon, AJ. Talk
to me.''

She whirled to face him. ''Keep your friends close and
your enemies closer, is that it?''

He jammed his hands into his pockets to keep from
reaching out to her. ''It's a sound philosophy.''

''Which am I?'' Her voice trembled.

''Friend,'' he answered without hesitating.

''And if you find out different?''

It took him a little longer to answer that one. ''Then I'll
deal with it.''

She blinked. '' 'Deal with it'? What does that mean?''

''I don't know.'' He sighed and brushed his hair back
from his forehead. ''Look, AJ… Right now we don't have
a lot of information, and we're both running on instinct.
My instincts say you're in trouble and need my help.''

''And that's why you called the police even though *my*
instincts say not to?''

''I wasn't talking to the police. That was my boss. I

needed to check in." His conscience twanged at the half lie, but Jacquelyn had been right. There were too many questions and until he had a few more answers he had to tread carefully.

Her shoulders slumped and she sank onto the couch. "You told her about me."

"She isn't local." Ryan needed to erase the look of betrayal from AJ's face. It hadn't occurred to him that letting her down would bother him so much. Not after knowing her for less than eight hours.

"Well, golly. I guess that must make it all okay, doesn't it?"

"She can access resources that aren't available to me here. Don't you want to find out what happened to you?"

"Not if it means involving others. I thought you understood." She shot off the couch and began pacing. "Too much is at stake, it's already cost too much—" Eyes squeezed shut, head held with fisted hands, she stumbled to a stop. Her entire body trembled as she fought some internal demon.

"What, AJ?" Ryan reached out but stopped, letting his hands fall to his sides without touching her. He was afraid to touch her, afraid she'd pull away from him. "What's already cost too much?"

"I don't know!" She glared at him with storm-colored eyes. "It's almost there, I can almost see it, see him, them, then it's gone, and the harder I try the worse my head hurts, and the heavier the curtain blocking whatever it is I can't remember gets, and I just want to go home, but I can't even do that because I don't remember where home is or if I even have a home."

Her voice cracked on the last desperate words. Ryan pulled her into his arms and cradled her against his body.

The intimate contact set his heart to racing. The instant physical response came as no surprise. He'd been physically attracted to her from the first moment he saw her on the beach.

What did surprise him was the emotional response she'd triggered in him. He wanted to shelter her from the pain, protect her from the frustrations life had heaped on her. He wanted her on a level beyond anything he'd ever shared with any other woman.

The realization had the same effect on him as a cold shower. He stepped back, holding her at arm's length.

But still touching her. Just until he knew she could stand on her own.

Yeah. Right. What have you gotten yourself into, boyo?

AJ straightened her shoulders and pulled away from his loose hold, turning her back to him, putting some distance between them. When she turned to face him again, her eyes had returned to their original pale gray. She seemed to have conquered her demon, at least for the moment. "Did she have any advice?"

He wished he could settle his. "Who?"

"Your boss. Did she have any advice for you?"

"The usual watch your six and don't be dumb stuff."

"Where do I stand while you're watching your backside?"

"Right beside me, sugar." Where I can keep a close eye on you.

His mama didn't raise a dummy. *Watch your six* was military jargon. Not exactly a common phrase for a civilian to be so easily familiar with. Another tip that AJ was more than your average Jane Doe.

Jacquelyn's warning came back. He did have enemies and some would stop at nothing to get revenge.

Chapter Six

The expression in Ryan's eyes shifted. The change was subtle, like a shadow slipping across a night sky, but AJ saw it. Unease crawled over her scalp. *What am I doing here?*

She brushed past Ryan, heading for the kitchen door and the beach. At least out there she could see what was coming at her rather than being ambushed by the vagaries of his distrust.

"Where are you going?" Ryan followed her through the guest house. At least he didn't touch her.

"You don't trust me." The kitchen door slapped open and she headed out onto the beach. She shouldn't care, but it hurt more than she could have imagined.

Beyond reason, from the moment he'd handed the gun back to her, she'd trusted him. She'd believed it was mutual. All morning there'd been an easy acceptance, concern even, on Ryan's part. Then one phone call and his attitude had changed.

"I don't know if I do or not."

"Then you don't. If you did, you'd know." At least he was honest. Although she wasn't so sure she wouldn't have preferred just a little dishonesty.

"AJ, stop."

"Why?" The loose sand shifted beneath her feet, slowing her progress. She headed for the harder packed sand near the water, all the time keeping her back to him. He appeared on the edge of her peripheral vision, keeping pace with her.

"You don't understand."

"No, I don't. How can I? Everything I need, everything I know is wrapped in black cloth ten feet thick."

"That won't last—"

"What, suddenly you're an expert on amnesia?"

He touched her, a soft brush of his fingers on her shoulder. Heat cascaded over her back and down her arm, chasing the anger, light after dark. Her body ignored her demands to keep moving, to pull free from the warmth of his hand. Instead she turned and faced him, knowing everything she felt, all her confusion about the situation, about him would be evident.

The pale green of his eyes reflected his emotions as well. She watched his dismay grow as he read her expression and guessed its meaning. *Now he'll let go of me.*

He didn't. He pulled her closer, wrapping his arms around her, cradling her head against his shoulder.

The contact shocked her. An image broke through her shrouded memory. Overlaying Ryan's embrace, the sense of another man's arms holding her, comforting her, shimmered into existence. The echo of a deep voice reassured her that she was safe and protected.

No. This can't happen. I won't let it happen, not again. The thought relit her anger. This time, when her brain demanded that she pull free, every muscle in her body responded.

"Shhh." Ryan's arms tightened just enough to let her know escaping from his embrace wouldn't be easy. "We've got company."

She stilled and his arms loosened. "It's Jamie." He

framed her face with his hands and looked into her eyes. "I think it's time you met him."

The last thing she wanted to do was meet another stranger. She wanted to say no but Ryan didn't give her that option. He brushed a flyaway strand of her hair behind her ear and turned her to meet their host.

Jamison McRobbie was still some distance from them. His slow approach gave her needed time to collect herself. Details of his appearance came into focus as he strolled toward them. He was well dressed for a casual walk on the beach. Actually he looked as if he'd stepped out of a Ralph Lauren ad. The elegant drape of his clothes spoke of quality tailoring.

Quiet strength was evident in his easy stride as he crossed the soft sand. He was tall, as tall as Ryan, and about the same age, but that was the end of any similarity between the two men.

Jamie was lean compared to Ryan's solid muscles. Ryan's short, light brown hair had been bleached to a pale blond by the sun. Jamie's hair was pure white, thick and long, held in tight check at his nape. The only evidence of its original color showed in a black shadow at his temples and in the dark eyebrows that slashed above his eyes—eyes of cobalt blue. Whether the color was natural or enhanced by contacts, she couldn't say.

It didn't matter. Jamison McRobbie was a striking man and her hands itched for her camera. She could already envision how she'd like to photograph him, his exotic looks framed by the exotic foliage of the Hawaiian Islands.

Ryan made the formal introductions, names only, leaving out any personal details for either of them.

"I am honored to have you stay on the estate." Jamie took her hand and held it between both of his.

The sensation of his elegant, long-fingered hands encompassing hers was one of warmth and security. She relaxed as the gentle comfort of his touch radiated over her, easing her tension.

She hadn't felt calm since she opened her eyes that morning and realized she didn't remember anything. Now calm settled around her, a warm cloak against the chill of fear.

A strong impression of familiarity came with the comfort as he held her hand. "Have we met before?"

"I think not." His voice held a hint of some unnamed accent. "I'm sorry to intrude, but I must have a word with Ryan. Will you excuse us for a moment?" The men walked a short distance away.

Exhaustion began gnawing at the edge of her awareness as she watched them. She'd been running on little more than fear since she woke up. The strange calm Jamie instilled had displaced some of that edgy energy.

She studied Jamie as he talked with Ryan. His expression remained smooth and calm even as tension clearly began building in Ryan. Only forty-five seconds elapsed before Jamie raised his hand in farewell to her. He made a parting comment to Ryan then began retracing his steps.

Ryan, hands jammed in his pockets, watched Jamie's departing figure then spun on his heel and returned to her side.

"What does Jamie do for a living? I know he said we've never met, but there's something so familiar about him."

A grin tipped up one side of Ryan's lips. "Well, now that's a more interesting question than you might imagine. Jamie…helps people."

The hesitation in Ryan's comment pulled her attention from the retreating figure of their host. "What kind of help? Is he some sort of philanthropic gazillionaire?"

"Not quite. He's a psychic." Ryan's grin developed into a full-fledged smile.

She waited for him to enlarge on his answer. No one

could make enough money to support an estate such as this by simply performing parlor tricks.

"As for seeing him somewhere, you mighta caught sight of him on the news at some point or other. He's worked with the police here and on the mainland on a number of cases."

Police. The mere word renewed the chill fear slithering down her back. Once more Ryan seemed to be pushing her toward involving the police and that was exactly what she couldn't do. She stepped back, trying to put some distance between them.

"They call him. He doesn't call them." Ryan matched her steps, keeping the distance between them consistent. "He also travels around to various universities and research centers to lecture on the topic. Sometimes private parties seek him out to help. And they pay him very well for that help."

"Is that what he's doing now? Consulting with you?" Disappointment sharpened her question. Ryan didn't trust her and it was becoming increasingly clear that she shouldn't trust him. She'd told him she didn't want to involve anyone, yet at every turn he seemed hell-bent to bring in yet another player.

"No." Ryan's single word slashed across her thoughts. He continued in a softer tone. "No. He came to apologize. The doctor he'd recommended won't be able to see you this afternoon, after all."

The tiny spark of hope she'd been hanging on to dimmed. She'd been counting on the doctor to provide some sort of direction for her, some instruction on how to go about pushing the blasted curtain out of the way of her memory. "What happened?"

Ryan shrugged. "Something came up and he had to cancel."

"When can we reschedule?"

"It doesn't sound like he'll be available again for some time." Ryan brushed a gentle stroke across her shoulder, lifting her hair and smoothing it over her back. "I'm sorry."

The entire day had been a roller coaster of emotions. Now the bottom dropped out from beneath her. Her shoulders sagged and she closed her eyes.

"Come on, baby." The gentle pressure of Ryan's warm hand against the small of her back guided her to the cottage.

"Now what?" The bleak question echoed her hollowness. She'd been holding on for so long, fighting against the blankness of her mind, struggling to understand what had happened to her. Arguing with Ryan had taken a toll all its own. Now this latest disappointment leached even more of her energy. She just wanted to go home. Wherever that may be.

"Now, we have a sandwich, some lemonade. Then, I think it's time you took a little siesta."

She didn't try to argue. Whether she liked it or not, whether he trusted her or not, he was all she had. It wasn't much, but it was more than when she'd awakened on the beach.

AJ ROLLED OVER AS SHE stretched, reveling in the soft comfort of the bed. She opened her eyes.

Nothing looked familiar. She pushed herself up and looked around. Her breathing quickened as panic began to worm through her thoughts. She swung her legs over the side of the bed and realized she was wearing nothing but a short nightgown.

She fought to remember something, anything.

Footsteps in the hall stopped outside the bedroom door. A soft tap on the door was followed by a man's voice. "AJ, you awake yet?"

Ryan. Her breathing slowed as calm returned. Memories of yesterday flowed back, filling the void. The trip into Honolulu, shopping, meeting Jamie. After their late lunch, she'd lain down for a short nap. Rousing long enough to change out of her clothes and brush her teeth had been a struggle. Exhaustion and denial had pulled her back to the blessed oblivion of sleep.

Now it was morning and Ryan was at her door. "I'll be right out."

"No rush, sugar." The door opened and he poked his head into the room. "I'm heading out for a run, shouldn't…"

His words stumbled to a halt and his gaze caressed her from the floor, up her legs, over the white satin nightgown she wore, before coming to rest on her mouth. Heat rose in her cheeks and warmed her middle. Her breathing quickened again, this time for an entirely different reason. She wrapped her arms around herself as awareness washed over her.

She remembered this much. Everything else remained shrouded in a black cloth, but this flaring heat and sharp awareness of his presence were familiar.

"Did you sleep okay?" Ryan's voice sounded rough.

All she could manage was a nod.

"Well," he cleared his throat. "I better get moving. I shouldn't be gone more'n an hour." He backed out of the room and closed the door.

She leaned over, hugging herself. This was insanity. How could she feel such complete and overwhelming attraction for a man who didn't even trust her? The conversation she'd overheard still haunted her. *I'm better off keeping her close. If she is a setup, she might let something slip.*

Did he really think she was faking the amnesia, that she

was some kind of plant? What could she possibly be involved in that she would do something like that?

Maybe he was some modern James Bond type who got the girl for the moment then walked away.

Why did that possibility hurt more than anything else?

The questions chased through her mind in an unending circle. Her head began to throb. The idea of crawling back into bed and hiding under the pillows tugged at her. *I just want everything to be normal. I want to know what normal is.*

She stood, gathered together some of her new clothes and headed to the shower. She'd felt better after a shower yesterday, maybe it would do the same trick today.

RYAN PUSHED HIMSELF, running harder than he had all week. He needed to keep in top physical shape for his work. He shouldn't slack off just because he was on two weeks of R and R.

He was not trying to outrun thoughts of AJ's long, long legs and short, short nightgown.

The nightgown he'd picked out for her.

The nightgown he'd fantasized stripping off her slender body.

He ran harder.

The estate's main house came into view and he slowed. A small stand of palm trees hid the guest house. Both houses had the illusion of complete privacy, yet only a short walk separated them.

As he neared the larger house, he spied Jamie on the patio and waved. Jamie waved back and motioned him over. Ryan hesitated, torn between wanting to get back to AJ and needing to talk with his friend. Need won out.

Jamie met him at the edge of the patio with a towel and a glass of fresh-squeezed orange juice. Ryan dried the sweat streaming down his face, hung the towel around his neck and downed the juice.

"Thanks." He handed the glass back. He paced the edge of the patio to cool down.

"Sleep well?" Jamie asked in what Ryan had dubbed the "professional soother" voice. The cultured tones could lull a body into all kinds of admissions if a body wasn't careful.

"Yep."

"Liar. Want to talk about it?"

"Nope." He met Jamie's cool blue gaze without flinching.

"Very well. How is your houseguest?"

Ryan wiped his face again, using the action to avoid answering for a moment. He didn't want to talk about AJ. Of course, refusing would be as good as admitting that thoughts of her sleeping across the hall from him had kept him up most of the night. He flopped into a chair. "How 'bout another glass of juice. Or coffee if you've got something decent."

Jamie filled a cup with a rich, fragrant brew, added two teaspoons of sugar and handed it across the glass-topped table. He relaxed into his own chair, leaning back and resting his elbows on the chair arms. His steepled fingers rested against his lips and he looked at Ryan with a steady gaze.

This was Jamie's tell-me-all-about-it-I'm-your-best-friend-in-the-world pose. Ryan sighed. It was no use trying to avoid the topic of AJ. Besides, he had a few questions of his own. "You canceled the doctor's appointment, didn't you?"

Jamie nodded but didn't add any explanation.

Ryan leaned forward and set his coffee cup on the table. "Why? She doesn't seem to take kindly to just sitting and waiting for something to happen. She was counting on getting some direction from someone who actually knows something about amnesia.''

"Once I met her, I realized it would not be of any benefit for her to see the doctor.'' Jamie's gaze didn't waver. "I created the excuse for the cancellation because I didn't think you'd want to lie to her.''

"I don't need you making those kinds of decisions for me.'' Ryan didn't like Jamie's presumption any more than AJ would like knowing how much the truth was already being bent.

"She didn't cope well?'' Jamie didn't react to the snap in Ryan's voice.

"What do you think? She slept all afternoon and through the night.''

"Sleep can be very healing.''

"It didn't do a lick of good.'' Ryan sank back into the cushioned patio chair. "I don't think she woke up remembering much of anything, otherwise I'm pretty sure she woulda said something.''

"How did you fill the time while she slept?''

"I did a little more Net surfing. There's a lot of information about amnesia out there and very little in the way of solid solutions. There's no guarantee she'll regain one-hundred percent of her memories and trying to hurry it along only gives her headaches.''

"What does Jacquelyn think of the situation? You have spoken with her?''

Ryan nodded as he fiddled with his coffee cup, turning it back and forth on its saucer. "She thinks I'm being set up.''

"Interesting. Why would she think that?''

"It goes with the job.'' He shrugged. "She's naturally suspicious.''

"That's the only reason?''

"No.'' A sip of his sweetened coffee burned a trail

down his throat. "I found a book hidden under a false bottom in AJ's camera bag. It's a record of some sort, near as I can tell. But it's written in some kind of code. The best I've been able to figure out so far is it documents payoffs and exchanges of some kind."

"Did AJ have an explanation for it?"

Ryan shook his head. "I haven't told her I found it." He paused for another sip of coffee. "I hoped to figure out the code by myself, but I'm gonna have to turn it over to the encryption boys."

"Would you like me to take a look at it?"

Ryan shrugged. "Sure, if you think you might pick up on something, it's worth a try."

"What else?"

"I'll need to switch vehicles for a while. We tailed someone yesterday. Much as I like driving the 'Vette, it's a bit too obvious if I have to do that again."

"Take the four-by-four. It blends in pretty well. What else?"

He shook his head and met Jamie's level gaze. "Nothing. Unless you've got any insights?"

"That would depend on what kind of insight you want."

"I'm flying blind here." Ryan cradled the delicate china cup in both hands. "At this point, I'll take anything you can give me. Your second sight is more reliable than many an eyewitness report I've seen."

"There isn't anything very concrete I can tell you."

"Then how about the nonconcrete. You don't normally go out of your way to touch someone, but you sure held her hand for long enough yesterday."

Jamie raised an eyebrow.

Ryan ignored the silent question. Jealousy was not a factor in his question. "You picked up on something, didn't you? She kept thinking she knew you from somewhere."

"I've never met her. However, if she is who I think she is, I have heard of her. She may have heard of me through the same channel."

"And that would be…?"

"A mutual acquaintance."

"Who?"

"A member of the police force who consulted with me on several cases."

"AJ refuses to go anywhere near the police. How do you see her fitting into this little scenario?"

"You did ask for nonconcrete." Jamie straightened his silverware. A frown shadowed his normally placid expression. "This is where we get into very nonconcrete. The detective made mention of a childhood friend, someone who had been in trouble."

"Trouble? What kind?"

Jamie puffed out a small sigh. "Justin didn't go into details. All he would say was she'd trusted the wrong people. He and his brother helped her get back on track. They were very proud of her photographic talents."

Justin. That was one of the names Kimo had mentioned at the photo lab. Ryan gently returned his coffee cup to its saucer and pushed it away. The rich brew had lost its flavor. "When was this?"

Jamie looked out across the beach, seeming to search the horizon for the answer. "The last time I consulted with him on a case…it was nearly two years ago."

"You haven't worked with this Justin again?"

Sadness darkened Jamie's eyes. "He was killed not long after that."

It was different when Justin was still alive. Kimo's words came back to Ryan. "What was the brother's name?"

"David."

"Justin and David." AJ had nearly swooned when the

lab owner mentioned those names yesterday. Ryan leaned forward, clasping his hands in a half-conscious prayer gesture. "What's their last name?"

"Angelini."

"And the woman?"

Jamie shook his head. "I'm sorry. He referred to her only as Alex, never a last name."

Ryan shrugged. "Nothing you've said explains why she's afraid of the police."

"That is a question only she can answer."

Ryan's chair scraped across the patio bricks as he stood. "Provided she ever remembers." He stepped off the patio and headed back to the guest house.

"Ryan," Jamie called.

He turned and looked back.

"Be careful. There's more at risk here than you know."

Ryan backtracked to stand in front of his friend. "Maybe you should tell me what else you know."

Jamie shook his head. "I really don't *know* anything. Just…be careful. Watch your back."

Chapter Seven

Watch your back. Folks seemed mighty fond of giving Ryan that particular bit of advice. He was getting mighty tired of it.

When he got back to the guest cottage, AJ was sitting in the kitchen, sipping on tea and nibbling a piece of toast. Her camera bag sat on the floor next to her.

A deep hunger tugged at him. The sensation was becoming habit every time he looked at AJ. There was nothing he could do about that particular appetite, so he ignored it.

The rumbling of his empty stomach left little doubt about another hunger, one that he could remedy. The OJ and coffee he'd had at Jamie's was fixing to eat a hole in his belly if he didn't get some real food soon.

"I don't know about you, sugar, but I'm hungry enough to start gnawing on that camera bag of yours. Why don't I get cleaned up and we can stop for some breakfast before we hit the lab."

"Okay." She didn't look up at him, just sat there hunched over, tracing around a pattern in the Formica tabletop.

Ryan stared at the top of her head, at a loss for how to break through her quiet. He wanted to take her into his arms and hold her, feel her pressed against him, smell the soft fragrance that clung to her skin. Every fiber of his upbringing demanded that he offer her some comfort. Every survival instinct warned him to tread carefully.

The morning continued downhill as he rushed through his shower and shave, nicking himself in the process. By the time they picked up Jamie's hunter-green Explorer and were headed for town, his nerves hummed right along with the tires on the road.

He checked in the rearview mirror, but their six was clean. No one had been hanging around outside of the estate gates when they'd left. There hadn't been another vehicle within sight for several miles. If they were being followed it would have to be by air, and, even at his most paranoid, Ryan doubted that could be the case. It was too early in the game for such extreme measures.

Beside him, AJ sat silent, her head turned away, presumably looking out the side window. His investigative training wanted to drill her about Justin and David, the trouble she'd been in, where she'd been, why she'd needed saving, why he hadn't been the one…no. *Wrong track, boyo.*

He glanced at her. Her knuckles showed white against the black nylon camera bag she clutched in her lap. He was beginning to hate that bag and the way she clung to it like a shield.

They rounded a corner in the road and the small breakfast joint they'd eaten at yesterday appeared. He pulled into the parking lot.

AJ dragged her attention back to her surroundings. "Do you always eat breakfast here?"

Ryan grinned. "If I did, I'd have to double my morning run. But it's comfort food."

"And you thought I could use a little comfort?"

His smile changed, softened. "Sugar, I figured we both could." He hopped out of the Explorer and crossed around to open her door. Before she could stop him, he tugged her camera bag from her hands. A moment of vulnerability flashed in her eyes.

His mama taught him to treat a woman with respect, to protect her. If she'd witnessed this little ploy, she'd'a given him what for. He was beginning to wonder if he needed to protect AJ from himself.

Before he repented, she accepted his silent challenge. Instead of reaching for her camera bag, she placed her hand in his and slid off the leather seat.

Never mind comfort food. The heat generated by the mere touch of her fingers held a whole other kind of comfort. He released her hand to lock the car door before settling his arm across her back.

One day and already he was accustomed to the feel of her, liked how the gentle curve of her hip fit the cup of his hand. This connection to another person answered a need he'd long ago denied.

Something small and painful lodged in his throat. He swallowed and ruthlessly beat the emotion back into its tidy little hole. Vulnerability he didn't do.

The restaurant door provided an excuse to break the physical contact. He pulled it open for AJ and breathed a silent thanks that he'd recognized the approaching danger before it was too late.

AJ RELAXED AGAINST THE BACK of the restaurant booth. Like yesterday, Ryan seemed intent on entertaining her with stories of his life.

The clatter and din of the diner faded to the background, the waitress's interruptions went unnoticed as she watched him, fascinated by the expressions and lightning-quick mood changes his face revealed. He only paused every now and then to push his sun-streaked hair out of his eyes. He seemed to need his hands to speak.

On impulse, she caught his right hand in hers. He fell silent as she turned it palm up, angling it to catch the light streaming in through the large window beside their booth. She brushed her fingers over the roughened skin of his palm.

He cleared his throat. "D'you see anything interesting?"

"Uh-huh. You've done manual labor rather recently. The calluses are still prominent."

"My last assignment." He pushed their empty plates out of the way. "I was on a ranch for six months."

"Ahh. A cowboy."

"It was just a role. And it doesn't take much of a palm reader to figure that out." A glint of humor filtered through some other emotion she couldn't quite identify in his glance.

She accepted his challenge with a smile and slipped into a role of her own. "Ahh. Come to Madame Alexandra. She sees all and tells some," she said in a thick east European accent as she began tracing the various lines and ridges of his palm. "In your hand I see character, strength, loyalty. You have a very long life line. And a strong heart line. You tend to fall in love easily. But when you finally love, truly love, it will be forever." She curled his hand into a fist and looked at the single line below his little finger. "You will marry, once only, and believe yourself to be lucky."

He tightened his hand, capturing the fingers of her left hand in his hold. Her breath caught in her throat. Where their skin touched heat sparked, sending a chain reaction chasing along her nerves.

His thumb brushed over the triple gold bands on her ring finger. "Is that how it is for you, Alexandra?" he asked, voice low and husky. "Do you feel lucky to be married?"

She stared at the ring on her finger. An ice-cold pain seeped through her heart and lodged in her throat. Breathing became a conscious effort. She leaned back, pulling her hand from Ryan's loose hold and tucking it into her lap. Shadows, faint as the first light of dawn, beat at the curtain drawn over her memory. Two figures silhouetted beside her, holding her, laughing with her.

She closed her eyes, trying to bring the images into focus, trying to see the faces hidden from her by the darkness.

Nothing.

Ryan stood, picked up her camera bag and held out his hand. "C'mon, AJ. Let's get out of here." He led her out of the diner to the Explorer, tucked her into the passenger seat and buckled her seat belt for her.

Neither of them spoke as they drove toward the city. Her head hurt from trying to remember and her heart ached for the unknown losses. After twelve minutes she couldn't stand the silence any longer. "Can we talk?"

"Sure." Behind his sunglasses, his glance flickered in her direction. "What do you want to talk about?"

"How about what just happened back at the diner?"

"You remembered your name."

She waved that away. "You think I'm married."

"Aren't you?"

She opened her mouth to deny it, but the words caught in her throat. "I…I don't know. If I am…" She shook her head and looked out the side window, not really seeing any of the scenery as it flashed by. "It seems as though, if I am married, I should feel something, some sense of urgency to get back. And I don't."

"So you're running from something. Maybe it's not a good marriage. Are you afraid to go back?"

"No." She shook her head as she searched the empty memories. "It's not that. Nothing like the idea of going to the police. The word marriage doesn't evoke any fear. It's more like…'' She turned in her seat to look at Ryan.

''Like what?'' His guarded tone hinted at some suspicion he wouldn't come right out and admit.

''Sadness. Like I've lost something and I'll never find it again.''

Ryan slowed, then pulled to the side of the road. He held on to the steering wheel as though it were a lifeline. Just then, that's pretty much what it was. His tight grip was the only thing that kept him from reaching out to her.

But he knew that sadness too well. The echoes from his childhood pried his hands from the wheel. He could no more ignore the pain in AJ's voice than he could stop the tide from rising. He turned in his seat, taking off his sunglasses to finally look her in the eye.

At the diner, he'd watched the blood drain from her face when he'd asked about marriage. He'd wanted to pull her into his arms then, to apologize for the pain his question had brought. He still wanted to. The need to protect her kept growing.

All he would allow himself was a touch. Only one touch. He tucked her hair behind her ear and traced the line of her jaw with the tip of his finger. The velvet softness of her skin sent a bolt of desire crashing headlong into his best intention to keep his distance.

Damn. For all they knew, she could be married. Maybe to the presumably dead Justin. Maybe to the other brother, David, presumably very much alive. Ryan didn't mess with married women. That was just plain wrong. He fought the urge to pull her closer. He lost the battle an inch at a time.

He cupped her cheek in the palm of his hand and leaned closer. The distance between them narrowed. He zeroed in on her lips as they parted slightly on a quick-drawn breath.

She let it out in a rush as he paused a hairsbreadth from actually kissing her.

Her warm breath triggered the heat of a desire he knew he should deny. ''This is probably a bad idea,'' he whispered, his lips barely touching hers as he formed the words.

Her eyes drifted shut. ''You're probably right.''

He inhaled, savoring the sunshine scent of her. Desire unfurled, reaching deep, pulling him tight in an iron-fisted grip. ''We probably shouldn't even consider this.''

The moment stretched into an eternity as what he wanted came head-to-head with what he knew to be the right thing to do.

She was attracted to him. There was no question about the attraction being mutual. All he needed to hear were the right words from her.

Her warm sigh flowed over his skin, sending another wave of heat straight to his core. ''Probably not.''

That's all she said. Two soft words.

The wrong two.

For a heartbeat he considered ignoring the one rule he'd held to for his entire adult life.

If she'd been willing, he might have succeeded. But she wasn't.

It wouldn't be right.

Disappointment replaced want as he straightened away from her, putting much-needed distance between them. His sunglasses added another small barrier.

Not until they knew who she was, what was going on and if there was a husband somewhere waiting for her to return. Once they knew that…

He pushed the accelerator and the tires spun on the soft shoulder before grabbing and pulling them back onto the pavement.

As they neared Kimo's photo shop, he pushed thoughts

of desire for AJ to the back of his mind. Time to switch to agent mode. When all was said and done, that was better, safer than allowing himself to feel for her.

He began scanning the area. The streets were filled with a variety of cars, Jeeps and trucks. They weren't nearly so obvious in the dark green four-by-four as they had been in the cherry-red Corvette. The occasional full-size sedan stood out, registering on his awareness. For the most part they seemed harmless enough.

Except for the unmarked car staked out across the street from the shop. Ryan drove by, glancing at the driver of the car and getting a good enough look to know it wasn't Ole Slim from yesterday.

AJ touched his arm. "Something's wrong," she whispered.

He drove down a couple blocks and turned around. On the next pass, Ryan looked through the shop windows. He couldn't see much, but what he did make out sent a shiver down his back.

Kimo stood behind the counter with his hands raised in the air.

"Blast it to hell." His grip on the steering wheel tightened. "Is there a back door to the shop?"

She nodded. "There are a couple parking spaces behind the lab. Kimo usually leaves the back door propped open."

He took the corner into the alley with tight control. "When I get out, you slide behind the wheel. I'm going to go in. If anyone other than me or Kimo comes out the door, you take off."

"But…"

"Head back to the estate. Go to Jamie. You'll be safe there."

"What about you? I can't sit and do nothing while you get yourself shot." Her voice cracked. "I won't do that again."

Her words sent a chill down his spine. What the devil had she witnessed? He backed into one of the empty parking stalls, positioning the Explorer so she'd have an easy getaway if it came to that. He hoped it wouldn't.

When he turned to face her, her gray eyes shimmered with tears. He brushed a finger across her cheek, wiping away the single tear tracing a path over her smooth skin. The urge to hold her swelled up again, but there was no time. "AJ, I need you to promise that you'll stay in the car until I come for you. I can't help Kimo if I have to protect you, too."

"But who'll watch your back?"

Watch your back. Jamie's warning echoed in his mind. He ran through his options. None held much promise.

"Here's what you can do. Keep an eye on the door. If anyone else goes in, lay on the horn. That's all the warning I'll need. I promise you, it'll be okay."

He hoped he hadn't just lied to her. He slipped out and pushed the door shut with a soft thud.

The back door of Kimo's shop stood propped open. At least there wouldn't be any squeaking hinges to give away his entrance. Crouched low, he paused inside the door to slip off his sunglasses. As his eyes adjusted to the dim light he surveyed the back room. A work island stood in the center of the space. Shelves, stacked high with photography equipment and supplies, lined the wall beside the door. To his left, a matte black revolving door led into a windowless room. A large machine extended from one wall of the room. A long, shallow metal sink and more shelves, these stocked with jugs of chemicals, filled the wall to his right.

The doorway leading into the shop stood in front of him, a little left of center. Long strings of shells provided a curtain of sorts. From his position, he couldn't see Kimo, but he could hear voices.

He reached to the small of his back where his gun nestled against his spine with reassuring weight. He'd clipped on the holster almost without thinking as he'd dressed after his shower. Jamie's warning had kicked the old instincts into gear and he hadn't questioned the habit. His loose Hawaiian-print shirt hid the holstered gun from view, so he hadn't needed to explain its presence to AJ. Now he was glad to have the handy little Walther PPK in his hand.

He crab-walked closer to the front of the store, still keeping low, every sense on high alert. As his position changed, he could see farther into the shop. Kimo still held his hands in the air. From the tone of his voice, his patience had reached its limit.

"I already told you. I don't know what you're looking for. Why don't you just take the money and go."

"Listen, old man," the gunman's voice sounded as if he gargled with drain cleaner. "It's not money I'm interested in. I want the film. You give it to me and you won't get hurt."

"Which film? Take your pick, color, black-and-white, prints, slides. I'll get a bag, you can take it—" Kimo's words were cut off as the gunman grabbed the front of his shirt and pulled him part way over the counter.

"Don't be stupid," Drano-voice growled. "I want the film the girl dropped off yesterday."

"Which girl? I got over a hundred orders waiting to be picked up. Give me a name, I'll find it for you, you can have it." Panic laced Kimo's voice.

If this didn't end soon, someone would get hurt. Ryan didn't want it to be AJ's friend. Leaning against the wall next to the door, he slowly stood up, all the time watching the two men as they moved down the counter. They stopped at the bins where orders were stored.

"I need a name."

"She came in here yesterday morning. Long black hair in a braid. A man came in right behind her."

"Alex? Why would you want her film? She's an artist...that's it, isn't it? You know she's good and want to sell her stuff on the black market."

"Get the film," Drano-voice barked.

Kimo jumped. "It...it's in the back room."

"Well then, let's go get it." The gunman vaulted over the counter and jerked his head toward the back room. "Lead on, old man."

Ryan slipped behind the work island and ducked down as they entered. The surface of the sink acted as a mirror, providing him with a distorted reflection of the two men as they moved into the room. He shifted his position, slowly circling the work island to get behind the gunman.

Kimo led Drano-voice to the film processor. "Alex's stuff won't be coming out for a while. It's still going through the machine."

"How long?"

"Twenty-five, maybe thirty minutes."

Drano-voice cocked his revolver. "I'm not a patient man. I suggest you figure a way to hurry it up a bit."

Kimo waved his hands in front of his chest. "There's nothing I can do. Once the machine starts processing the film, it's all automatic."

"Wrong answer, old man. Try again. What are those handles for?"

Kimo glanced at the machine, then back at the gunman. His eyes widened. "Those are for maintenance. When I clean the machine, I have to take out all the gears and rollers."

Drano leveled his gun at Kimo's chest. "Bloodstains are hard to remove, I've been told."

AJ, sugar, what's on that film to make it worth murder?

Ryan shifted into a better position to tackle the gunman.

He'd only get one chance to take him down. He better get it right, or Kimo would pay the price.

A bell jangled out in the shop. Someone had come in from the street. Ryan ducked back around the work island as Drano turned to look over his shoulder.

"Hello? Anyone here?" a child's voice called.

Kimo stood frozen, his eyes wide.

"Uncle Kimo? Where are you?" The voice came closer to the back door.

Drano swung around, the barrel of his gun digging into Kimo's chest.

"She's my niece."

"I don't care if she's Princess Kaiulani herself. Get rid of her." He waved Kimo to the curtained doorway.

Kimo scurried out of the back room. Ryan couldn't see anything from his position crouched behind the work island. He checked the reflection in the metal sink and nearly cursed. He could clearly see Drano's reflection. Same as Drano could see Ryan's if he happened to glance that way. Fortunately, Drano was more interested in what was going on in the shop.

Kimo's voice carried clearly to the back room. The shop owner answered his niece's many questions about film speed and light. Finally the overhead bell jangled again, signaling the little girl's departure.

"Don't even think of trying to call the police, old man," Drano called out. Silence answered the implied threat. The curtain shifted and Kimo returned to the back room.

He looked directly at Ryan. What little color was left beneath his dark complexion drained away.

Ryan motioned him to keep silent, praying that Kimo would recognize him as a friend and not give away his presence.

Kimo looked back at Drano, saying nothing. Ryan let out the breath he'd been holding.

"Now, old man. About that film."

Kimo walked back to the machine, drawing Drano with him.

Ryan sent a silent thanks to the old man. He shifted back around the work island. He stopped when he was directly behind Drano.

"When will that film be out?"

Kimo shook his head slowly from side to side. "I told you, maybe another twenty minutes yet. It depends on where it is among the other customers' rolls."

"What about those doors on top? Why don't you open one of those, pull out the stuff I want and we'll be done."

"If I open those doors now, all the film will be ruined."

"I suppose I could ruin your shirt instead."

"We'll never be able to tell which is Alex's or what is on any of the film."

Drano swore. "That'd suit me fine, but my boss has other plans. I guess you and me are just going to wait."

Ryan rose behind Drano and jammed his gun into the man's back. "I have a better idea. Why don't you give your gun to Uncle Kimo, here? Then you and I can discuss your manners like proper gentlemen."

Drano spread his arms out to the sides. Kimo took the gun and stepped away, putting the work island between himself and the other two men.

"Now then." Ryan tucked his own gun back into his holster and began patting down Drano. "Didn't your mama teach you that it's not nice to take what don't belong to you?"

Drano let loose a string of four-letter words.

"Tsk, tsk. Such language. My mama always said profanity was symptomatic of a poor vocabulary." Ryan pulled a switchblade knife from Drano's front pocket and dropped it into his own.

"Too bad she didn't tell you it's not smart to stick your nose in other people's business."

"She did, she did." Ryan finished searching Drano, without finding any more weapons. He pulled his gun from his holster and turned Drano around to face him. "But you see, this is my business."

A movement in the doorway caught his attention. He shifted his hold on Drano and swung his gun around to aim at the new threat.

AJ stood silhouetted in the door, the Glock clutched in her hands.

Ryan let loose with a choice few words of his own. "Kimo, get her out of here."

The damage was done. AJ's distraction was enough for Drano to land a punch to Ryan's stomach. The blow didn't pack much of a wallop, but it was enough to make him lose his hold on Drano's shirtfront.

Ryan swung a counterpunch and the fight was on in earnest. Drano was bigger and heavier, but Ryan was faster. Both rained blows on the other. Ryan managed to block more punches than Drano landed. It was a dead heat until Drano's ham fist glanced off Ryan's chin and landed a solid punch to his throat. It was a lucky punch, but it was enough to send Ryan to his knees.

Drano barreled through the doorway into the shop. He leaped the counter and headed for the door to the street. The overhead bell jangled a cheery farewell before Ryan could vault over the counter. By the time he reached the door, Drano and his buddy in the stakeout car were disappearing around the corner.

Damn. This is not good. The adrenaline surge began to fade. He leaned against the doorway wishing he could go someplace and regroup.

The soft clacking of the shell curtain warned him that he wasn't alone.

He looked back over his shoulder. Kimo and AJ stood in the doorway staring at him.

"I thought I told you to wait." Anger propelled Ryan back across the store. He ignored the various muscle groups already protesting the abuse they'd just suffered.

"Are you all right?"

"I told you to wait." He glared at AJ as he tested his jaw. That last punch might have done a lot more damage if it hadn't slipped.

"It took so long. I thought something happened, that you might need help."

"Not that an empty gun would do much good."

"I'm sorry. I…" AJ stammered to a stop. "Are you okay? Do you need to go to the hospital?"

Ryan didn't answer. He wanted to shout at her, but couldn't. She stood her ground in spite of the fear in her eyes. Fear for him, not of him.

Kimo watched the exchange then turned to AJ. "You know this man?"

She nodded. "We met yesterday."

He turned a narrow-eyed stare at Ryan. "You didn't waste any time, did you, *haole?*"

AJ laid a restraining hand on the older man's arm. "It's all right, Uncle. He's…" She faltered, casting a look at Ryan for some direction.

"Let's go in back." Ryan rounded the counter and held the curtain out of the way. "We need to tell him, AJ. For his own safety, he needs to know."

"What's he talking about?" Kimo asked as they retreated to the cool dimness of the back room.

AJ looked from one man to the other then dragged three high stools from the storage room and arranged them around the work island. Ryan eased onto one. Kimo took the stool across from him. She pulled bottles of water from a small refrigerator and placed one in front of each of them.

The plastic seal on her bottle cracked open, sounding loud in the silence. Pacing the width of the lab, she sipped water and avoided looking at either of them.

''Alex?'' Kimo prompted her when she failed to start her explanation.

Ryan nudged the third stool with the toe of his Top-Sider. She accepted his silent invitation to sit and settled on the edge of the stool. His hand closed over hers, stilling her fingers before she completely shredded the water-bottle label. ''Would you like me to tell him?''

Kimo was bristling with protectiveness. He deserved the truth. It would be better coming from her, but Ryan would do his best if she wasn't up to it.

The tightness around her mouth gave a hint of how much she wanted to have this conversation. Ryan couldn't blame her. How could she explain with any sort of logic what she didn't know, who she didn't know and why she didn't know any it.

She shook her head, took another swallow of water and began. ''I seem to be in something of a fix, Uncle. And I seem to have dragged you into it. I am truly sorry.''

Kimo waved off her apology. ''Don't worry about that. Tell me what's happened and why this one is with you, and not David.''

She did her best to explain what little she knew, beginning with waking up the previous morning with no memory. She told how Ryan had found her. Why they'd pretended not to know each other when she'd dropped off the film. Who they'd followed after leaving.

Ryan watched and listened. Kimo reacted much as one might expect upon hearing such a story. Ryan wanted to believe it was because everything AJ said was true, Kimo wasn't involved in any way and there was no setup against either of them.

"I'm so sorry I endangered you." She brushed her hand over Kimo's where it lay on the tabletop. "If I'd had any idea someone was after my film, I never would have brought it to you."

Kimo patted her hand. "You did the right thing—you trusted your instincts when they told you to come here. But you haven't explained who he is and why he has a gun."

Kimo fixed his dark-eyed gaze on Ryan.

Ryan shifted on his stool, grimacing as sore muscles protested the movement. He pulled his ID wallet out of his back pocket, opened it and laid it on the table in front of Kimo. "FBI. I'm between assignments at the moment. What I told you yesterday about staying with a friend on the north shore is the truth."

Kimo examined the ID with admirable thoroughness, even pulling it out of the case and checking for signs of tampering. He put it back in the case and slid it across the table to Ryan.

He didn't try to return the case to his pants pocket. Instead, he slipped it into his shirt pocket. "If AJ was going to be found by someone who didn't know her, I'm probably the best person."

"What about David?" Kimo looked at AJ.

She closed her eyes and massaged her temples. "Who is David?"

Kimo stared at her for a moment. "David Angelini. You have no memory of him?"

AJ shook her head.

"And Justin?"

Again she shook her head, never opening her eyes. "Every time I hear their names, I just feel…sad."

Kimo looked at Ryan. "How could this happen?"

"We don't know. We may never know, unless she recovers some of her memories. Some things have come back to her. That's how we found you yesterday. There's a chance she'll remember more as we find more familiar surroundings."

"Like her home?" Kimo asked.

AJ's head snapped up. "Yes! Please, Kimo, tell me where I live. I need to know at least that much about myself."

Kimo gave them an address in a middle-class area not far from the lab. "That's where you've lived ever since the brothers brought you back."

AJ opened her mouth, but Kimo waved her question away before she could ask it. "There are details only David can tell you. I don't know them. But I'm thinking, if you never remember that time…maybe that's not such a bad thing."

There it was again, the reference to AJ needing rescuing. Ryan resented not being the rescuer. Curiosity and jealousy took turns poking at his conscience. The Angelinis, whatever else they were to AJ, had been the ones to rescue her.

Ryan walked across the room, as much to get away from the unwanted emotions stirred by AJ's situation as to loosen his stiffening muscles. The large processing machine drew his attention. "We were hoping the film we brought in might give us some more clues."

He checked his watch then verified the time with the wall clock. More than an hour had elapsed since the confrontation with Drano. Pointing at the wire basket hanging from the end of the machine he asked, "The processed film comes out here?"

Kimo nodded. "Yes. If there were any film in the machine to be processed."

"Perhaps you better spell it out for me. You told ole

Drano-voice that AJ's film would be coming out in twenty-five minutes. It's looking to be about forty minutes late. You said there were other rolls in the machine, too. I'm not seeing anything. Did the machine malfunction?''

"Yes."

Chapter Eight

"No." AJ's whispered cry cut to Ryan's soul. There was no mistaking the pain in her voice. The anguish revealed how much she'd been hoping to see the film. He couldn't blame her, he was mighty curious himself to see what she'd taken pictures of.

Kimo took both of her hands in his. "Not with your film in it. Alex, look at me." He waited for her tear-filled eyes to focus on him. "I never run your film through the processor. You know that. I was going to develop your film last night, but the machine broke down. So instead of processing your film, I had to work on the machine. I finally got it running this morning. I haven't even had time to run a test strip. If you want, I can run your film as soon as I know the processor is running properly again."

He looked from Alex to Ryan. "To be honest, I'd feel much better if we still ran it by hand. But I won't be able to do that until this evening."

Ryan nodded in agreement. "I think you're right. Do it by hand. We can get it tomorrow."

AJ pulled her hands free of Kimo's hold and commenced pacing again. "No. We need to see what's on that film today. I can't wait. I need to know...."

Ryan crossed the room and gathered her into his arms. "I know, baby. I know." He pressed a kiss to AJ's soft hair. When he looked up, Kimo's knowing expression had him grinding his teeth. Let the Hawaiian think what he would. He was wrong. Ryan was being nothing more than considerate of AJ's needs. Right now she needed to be comforted.

He loosened his hold and forced her chin up so he could look in her eyes. "We've got plenty of ground to cover now that we have your address. Maybe we can even track down David."

That last bit left a sour taste in his mouth. The last thing he wanted to do was turn her over to another man. A man who, by all indications, held great importance in AJ's life. Ryan forced himself to continue. "The film can wait a little longer. I'd rather know Kimo is doing it by hand and we're safe from mechanical breakdowns."

Small tremors racked her body. He rubbed his hands up and down her back. If he thought it would do any good, he'd suggest that she stay at the lab and process the film herself.

The idea had some merit. He wasn't sure how many more shocks she could endure. The idea of taking her to an unknown location without some assurance that she wouldn't be hit with yet another disappointment sat like a mess of week-old grits in his belly. While she was busy in the lab, he could execute the initial recon of her home without having to keep an eye on her. Then, whatever he found, he could prepare her.

Besides, he worked best alone.

On the other hand, there was also the chance that Drano might return to the lab with reinforcements. Ryan looked at Kimo. "If you have any more trouble—"

"I don't think he'd be so foolish and come back here. What he wanted was the film and he's gonna figure you have that now. By this time tomorrow, you will."

Ryan nodded. Whoever was searching for AJ, he preferred to keep their attention focused in one direction. That would be the best protection for AJ's friend.

Ultimately, keeping AJ with him was her best protection, too. At least physically.

When it came to the emotions, he was really concerned they'd both wind up getting hurt. His own pain he could deal with. He'd been doing that since he was knee-high. Where AJ was concerned, he might not be able to protect her from everything the world kept throwing at her, but he damn well refused to be the cause of any hurt.

AJ PULLED HERSELF TOGETHER, second by second. Falling apart was a surefire way to end up in worse trouble. She might not remember the exact details of why she knew that, but the knowledge flared in sharp contrast to her curtained memory.

Since leaving Kimo's shop, Ryan hadn't pressed her for any information or details she may have remembered. She appreciated the space he'd provided so she could begin to function as something resembling a sane person.

Rather than focusing on everything she couldn't remember, she needed to work from what she did know. Such as the fact that she wasn't alone. She had Ryan on her side. And Kimo. Jamie. Three strong men who seemed to accept her without qualifications.

That realization eased her fears enough that she could take stock of her surroundings and pay attention to what lay ahead—her home.

The neighborhood changed in subtle ways as they neared the address Kimo had given them. The houses were smaller, older, with more yard and taller trees. She searched for something she could identify with a bit more certainty than a vague sense of familiarity, but nothing stood out.

Ryan pulled to the curb. The hope she'd been tending

so carefully began to deflate. She turned to Ryan. "This isn't right. It can't be."

"It's not." He lifted one hand as though he was going to touch her, then stopped himself. He curled his long, lean fingers into a tight fist and pulled back a bit farther. "We're still a couple blocks away. Considering what we ran into at the lab, caution seems like a good idea."

She nodded. "What do you want to do?"

"Take you back to the estate." He raised a hand before she drew a breath to protest. "You asked what I wanted to do. But that's not going to work. So, we're going to drive these last couple blocks in red-alert mode. We're both going to watch for cars that look like they don't belong. Cars like the ones we saw outside the lab."

She nodded. "Then what?"

"Then, if there's an alley, we're going to drive down that. Once we've covered all the approaches, and I'm reasonably sure we've ID'd any possible stakeouts, we're going to park around the corner and talk a bit more."

AJ wanted to protest the caution, but the bruise darkening along Ryan's jaw kept her silent.

They followed the plan exactly as Ryan outlined it. The height of the Explorer gave them the added advantage of being able to look down into some of the vehicles parked along the street. None were nondescript sedans with stuffed animals on the dash and no child seat in the back. Everything looked clear.

The alley was narrow with garbage cans lined up like neat little pillars at the end of each driveway. Everything appeared as it should.

They left the alley and Ryan pulled to the curb a block away. She clung to the camera bag to keep herself from opening the door and leaping out. She'd spotted the house number, her house number, painted on the driveway. The only thing she wanted to do now was run back down the alley, caution be damned.

Ryan's hand closed over hers. She clung to it like a life preserver.

"Everything looked clear. We're going to walk back down the alley. When we get to the house, I want you to stay behind me." He gave her hand a soft squeeze. "Ready?"

The simple question ignited a firestorm of emotions, most prominently fear. What if she didn't recognize anything?

She fought off the doubts and nodded. As they walked down the alley, her hand brushed Ryan's. He slipped his over hers, cradling her fingers in a gentle embrace. He also kept his right hand on the pistol tucked against his back.

They crossed the driveway and continued on into the yard. She pretended this was exactly how she always came home.

The lawn needed mowing and a few weeds mingled with the flowers. Nothing about the yard seemed extraordinary. She searched the house for something that would trigger a memory but the black curtain still held the details swathed in darkness.

Then she heard it.

A small cry.

Ryan heard it, too. He pulled her behind him, released her hand and drew his gun, all in one smooth motion. They stood still, silent, waiting.

The wisp of noise came again, sounding suspiciously like a cat's meow.

A memory sneaked out from beneath the curtain. AJ almost shouted with joy. She stepped around Ryan. He tried to stop her, but she avoided his outstretched hand and headed for the house.

"Ansel. Where are you, sweetie?" She crouched to look beneath the lanai and called again. "Ansel, come on out."

She sat on the ground and waited. From the corner of her eye, she could see Ryan inching his way around her. She waved him off and he froze. She called again. "Ansel. Come out from under there."

A small black, white and gray bundle of fur ran out from beneath the deck and leaped into her lap. She scooped up the young cat and nuzzled the soft fur. Laughter and tears mingled. "I remember you," she whispered. "I remember. What are you doing out here?"

She stood, cradling Ansel in her arms like a tiny baby, tickling his tummy. For the first time in two days the hope that her life would return to normal seemed attainable. She turned to Ryan. "He must have slipped out when David came home."

Ryan caught his breath. AJ's eyes glowed with happiness. The smile lifting her lips was nothing short of angelic, the elusive dimple in full view. Want for a taste of that kind of joy tightened a knot in his belly.

"Maybe David's still here." She turned and headed for the back door. "He's probably going crazy, wondering where I am."

Ryan followed her, all his senses on alert. He scanned the yard and what he could see of the neighboring houses. As much as he'd like to believe Angelini was inside, all the evidence indicated otherwise.

This was the only house without a garbage can sitting at the end of the drive. None of the windows in the house appeared to be open. No lights shone. The house had a decidedly empty look from the outside. If anyone was in there, they were keeping real quiet about it.

He watched as AJ tried the door. Hope that she wouldn't be disappointed, that he was wrong and she would find

David home ran up against the desire to keep her to himself, just for a little while longer.

The door didn't budge. She knocked and stepped back, peering through the closest windows as she worried the triple bands over her knuckle. When there was no sign of movement from inside, she knocked again, a little louder, a little longer.

The desperate tattoo echoed in his chest, calling up an image he'd relegated to the farthest reaches of his memory a long time ago. A dull ache took up residence in the vicinity of his heart.

She looked at him, the pleasure in her expression fading. "He must have gone out again."

"AJ." There were no right words for him to say, nothing that could ease the disappointment. It was too late anyway.

She brushed past him and he followed. She shifted the cat to her shoulder. The animal was purring loud enough for Ryan to hear it three feet away.

He'd never had a pet when he was a child. There'd been dogs and cats in the homes he'd stayed in. But he'd moved too often to risk getting attached to any of them. The entire concept was foreign to him. He watched AJ smooth a hand over the cat's fur, and his fingers itched to share the contact, to feel that connection to another living creature that accepted without question.

AJ pointed to a small, colorful glass globe hanging from a low branch of one of the trees. "There's a key in there. Could you get it, please? I kinda have my hands full."

Ryan reached over her head, tipped the globe and a key tumbled into his outstretched palm.

"Be sure to put the stick back in the doorway."

He stared at her. She'd changed in the few minutes they'd been in the backyard of the house. Some of the tension had left her expression and the dimple reappeared every time Ansel the cat gave her a lick with his little pink tongue. Even knowing she would be entering an empty house, she was home and she clung to that joy with a nearly palpable determination.

She picked up the stick that had fallen to the ground when he retrieved the key. "It's a fairy house. You need to put a stick in the doorway so they have something to sit on."

She balanced the stick in the opening, then headed for the back door. She would have pushed into the house without hesitation except he still held the key. And his gun.

"AJ."

She stopped.

He walked around her and slid the key into the lock. "Is there any kind of alarm system?" He turned to her, waiting for her answer. She chewed on her lower lip. Her hair rippled as she shook her head.

"Please." Her plea was nearly drowned out by Ansel's contented purr. When she finally looked up at him, his heart nearly broke for her. He recognized the look in her eyes. Not from the outside, but from the inside. It was the emotion he'd felt after his mother left him with the first of many relatives. He'd been six.

All she wanted was to be in her own home.

He should make her wait outside while he searched the house, but he couldn't do that to her. He pressed a kiss to her forehead and swallowed around the growing ache in his chest. "Let me go first. Stay behind me. Okay?"

She nodded and he turned the key in the lock.

The door swung in on silent hinges. He pushed it completely open, then stepped into the entry. Plants hung in front of each window, trailing vines and flowers. AJ stepped in behind him and he motioned for her to close the door.

He moved into the next room, the kitchen. A flour-sack

dish towel draped over a drainer filled with clean dishes, a second towel puddled on the floor beneath a hook. A cookbook lay open on the counter. A row of herbs in small clay pots lined the wide kitchen windowsill. A teakettle and a coffeepot sat side by side next to the stove.

A soft thud warned him an instant before the cat brushed past his feet. AJ's pet made a beeline for the water and food bowls tucked in a corner beside the cupboards.

Ryan continued through the house. Each room was neat yet lived-in. Bookshelves lined the walls of the living room. He glanced at the photographs mingled with the books and trinkets on the many shelves. Most of the pictures were candid shots. AJ appeared in a few. Ryan didn't allow himself to study the images too closely. There'd be plenty of time for that once he was sure her home was secure.

He moved from room to room, checking behind doors and in closets, looking for signs that someone had been there.

One of the bedrooms had been converted into an office. The room was an interesting mix of mess and neat. Two desks snugged up against opposite walls. A sea of papers, mainly printouts from various stateside law-enforcement agencies, from the look of it, covered the surface of one desk, barely leaving room for the computer. David would appear to have been something of a slob.

The other desk held a scanner and the latest Mac, a tidy stack of files fanned out next to it. Ryan's quick glance at the file contents confirmed this pool of tranquility to be AJ's desk.

File cabinets and bookshelves formed a dividing line between the two work areas. Nothing seemed out of the ordinary.

David's bedroom resembled his desk. A king-size bed dominated the room. The lightweight quilted bed cover dragged to the floor on one side, the other side was caught beneath the mattress. On the bedside table the latest Turow novel lay next to a simple picture frame. The photograph showed AJ laughing with her arms around a dark-haired man who looked at her with an expression of complete indulgence. Ryan turned away from the display of such obvious affection.

He held his breath as he opened the closet door. A quiet sigh of relief escaped as the door swung open to reveal nothing but men's clothes. The closet floor doubled as a laundry hamper. Jeans, shorts and T-shirts piled next to running shoes. Empty hangers poked up between dress shirts fresh from the laundry.

On the tall dresser a handful of coins, a pair of cuff links and a triple band ring lay spread out next to a wood-framed picture of a trio of kids. The colors had faded and from the clothes it was clear the snapshot had been taken some years ago. Even so, it was easy to recognize a much younger AJ standing between two dark-haired boys.

Ryan poked at the ring, turning it until light caught on the inscription. *Remember.* An emotion he refused to name twisted the ache in his chest a little tighter.

He moved to the last bedroom. This one had a decidedly feminine flavor. A chair in one corner was piled with a stack of neatly folded clothes. Mystery, romance and science-fiction paperbacks shared space on the bedside table. The dresser in this room also held pictures. Individual photos of grown-up versions of the boys flanked a duplicate of the kids' photo. He turned his back on the happy images of the past.

When he opened the closet, the scent of sunshine and ocean breezes surrounded him. He didn't allow himself to linger.

This was a home. AJ's home.

The home she shared with someone else.

Ansel wound around his legs, but AJ had stopped following him before he got to the bedrooms. He missed her presence and hurried down the hall, back to the living room. That's where he found her, standing in front of a bookcase, holding one of the picture frames. She turned when he entered. Tears streamed over her cheeks, an expression of loss and devastation clouded her features.

He recognized that look, too. He'd felt like that the day he'd been moving to yet another relative's home. It was the day he finally realized his mother wouldn't be coming back for him.

It was the day he'd decided he didn't want to have a home. It hurt too much to want what he could never have.

He'd been ten.

AJ TURNED AWAY FROM the sympathy in Ryan's face. She didn't deserve it. Shame at all the betrayals squeezed her heart so tight she wondered if it would ever beat a normal rhythm again.

She placed the photo back onto the shelf, turning it so the afternoon light would catch it. *It's all my fault. Because of me, they're dead.* She traced the features of the men staring back at her with laughter in their eyes. "I recognize them."

Sadness welled up, closing her throat, forcing her to swallow around the pain. This was how it felt when the last vestige of hope withered and floated away on an arid breeze.

She glanced toward Ryan, but couldn't look him straight in the eyes. "I remember. Some of it. There are still holes. But I remember them."

He came to stand beside her and looked at the picture. She wanted to reach out to him, to have him hold her, tell her it would be all right once more. But that would be a lie and the solace, which she didn't deserve, would only be temporary.

"The Angelinis?" He waited for her to fill in the information.

"Justin and David." She wiped nonexistent dust from the frame. "My guardian angels. Except now they're gone and I don't know how to go on without them even if I want to."

Standing so close to Ryan became unbearable. She moved across the room.

Memories she'd just as soon never recover took over her thoughts. The vague fears she'd shoved to the background pushed forward, demanding her acknowledgement.

It was her fault. March fifteenth, the day they'd brought her back to Oahu, was supposed to mark a fresh start. Instead, it was the day their lives had begun to deteriorate. They'd tried to hide it from her, but she'd known then and remembered now.

Trouble had followed her from L.A. and landed hard in this island paradise, right on the Angelini doorstep. They'd paid the ultimate price for believing in her.

Now Uncle Kimo had been dragged into the mess. And Ryan.

She scrubbed the tears from her face and pulled her shoulders back. With each deep breath she took, calm settled a little more within her. She knew what had to be done. This had begun with her and she would be the one to end it.

First, she had to tell Ryan the truth. She couldn't do this alone, and he was her best bet. But only if he understood the situation and knew what she was.

It shouldn't be so hard to tell him. They'd met only yesterday. Ryan would be leaving soon to return to his duties. He wasn't looking for an involvement. Neither was she.

So the only thing at risk was respect. A small price to pay for avenging the Angelini brothers' murders.

She wiped away the last tear and turned back to him. "I'm sorry. That was a bit melodramatic, wasn't it?" She tried to smile.

"Understandable, considering the circumstances." Ryan brushed his thumb over her cheek, drying the last tear track. "Can you tell me what you remember about them?"

That was the last thing she wanted to do. She sank onto the large couch. Extra long to accommodate the Angelini boys' height. Ansel hopped into her lap. He curled into the crook of her arm, just like always, and promptly fell asleep.

With the cat's soft purr lending an odd counterpoint, she began telling a carefully edited version of the bare facts. Ryan prowled the room, studying the various books and photos as she talked.

"Mostly, I remember when we were kids. We met in grade school, David and I were in fourth grade, Justin in fifth. From the first day, we were best friends. They were the brothers I never had. We liked the same books, the same games, same music. We were the three peas in a pod.

"Then, shortly before my fifteenth birthday, my family moved back to the mainland. The picture you're holding was taken on our last day together."

Ryan returned the picture to the shelf. "Did you lose touch with them?"

"Not right away. For a while, we were pen pals. I'd write long, rambling letters about what it was like in L.A. They'd write short letters about how nothing changed on the island. After a few years, my letters got shorter and theirs became rarer."

"You never saw them?"

"Only once. When my parents were killed, they came

to the funeral. They wanted me to move back here, but I was stubborn and determined to make it on my own. I did pretty well, too. For a while.''

''What happened?'' Ryan settled on the far end of the couch. Even that far away, his attraction pulled at her.

She wanted so badly to find shelter in his arms. But she wouldn't make the same mistake a second time. Even with the sure knowledge that Ryan was different from the devil of her past, the end result would be the same. She couldn't risk that kind of pain again.

She shrugged. ''Growing pains, learning a few of life's harder lessons.'' No need to tell Ryan the dirty details about her addiction and what she'd done to survive. Kimo had been right. There were some memories she would have been happy to leave behind the curtain.

She left the details to Ryan's imagination. Any scenario he came up with would be better than the truth.

She couldn't look him in the eyes, knowing how misleading this version of her life was. Ansel grumbled at the disruption when she stood and laid him on the couch. He stretched, walked over to Ryan and promptly curled in the crook of his crossed arms.

Ryan's startled expression as he looked at the pile of fur in his arms gave her five seconds of relief from his scrutiny. She escaped into the kitchen.

The refrigerator was well stocked with bottled water. She pulled out one for each of them. When she bumped the door closed with her hip and turned around, Ryan was standing in the doorway, his steady green eyes watching her. Ansel, still snuggled in his arm, purred in contentment as Ryan kneaded his fingers through the cat's glossy coat. ''When did you come back to Hawaii?''

She wished she'd never started telling him any of this. As tempting as it might be, she refused to use the amnesia to avoid answering his questions. She'd answer his questions with as few details as possible, but she wouldn't lie to him.

"About three years ago, for some reason they never really explained, Justin and David flew to L.A. one more time. They found me, packed up my pitiful life and hauled me out of there."

He accepted the opened bottle she held out to him, then followed her back into the living room. "They brought you here?"

She nodded. "They gave me a place to stay, helped me get my life back on track. We made a home for ourselves. Along the way, I discovered a knack for photography." She crossed the room and picked up one of her earliest attempts. The composition and lighting were terrible, but the brothers' expressions were so vivid, she could still hear their laughter.

The memory of that day squeezed her chest into a tight knot. They'd tolerated being her guinea pigs/models until she realized her true talent lay in nature photography.

Ansel's purr warned her of Ryan's approach. "What do they do for a living?"

"Justin, that's him on the left, was a police officer. He made detective a couple years ago. He loved his work."

"And David?"

"FBI. Undercover." Sadness washed over her in a wave. Something had happened to David. She knew it in her bones, even if she couldn't remember the details. She sank into her favorite overstuffed, oversized chair-and-a-half.

"Which one did you marry?"

She hadn't expected that question. A startled laugh escaped her tight throat. "Neither."

Ryan visibly relaxed at her answer. He returned to his corner of the couch and settled against the cushions.

"Or maybe it'd be more honest to say both."

He sat up straighter. "You lost me there, sugar. Maybe you could explain it a little more?"

"We, none of us, were interested in changing our relationship. We were too good at being friends to ever risk losing that to become lovers. Even if I'd been interested in getting married, I certainly couldn't have ever picked one over the other."

"What about the brothers?"

"They dated, but really, if there was any kind of marriage, it was between them and their careers. You can understand that, I'm sure. We all had our own careers and we had our home. Everything seemed to work with the three of us. We didn't really need any others."

"Do you remember what happened to Justin?"

Another of the memories she could have lived her life without ever recovering. Even after two years, the pain washed over her in a strong wave. Time might heal, but this particular wound went too deep for an easy recovery. "He was working a case, something for Internal Affairs. One night, he never came home. He just…disappeared."

"The police—"

"'HPD is not in the habit of commenting on open investigations and the disappearance of Detective Justin Angelini is so designated.' She parroted the official statement.

"The living hell of limbo."

She nodded. That put the situation in nice sharp focus.

"How is David handling it?"

It would be simple enough to tell him everything. But she couldn't, not without knowing him way better than she did. "How would you handle a situation like that?"

Every trace of the sympathetic listener disappeared in a flash. Ryan's jaw tightened, his lips thinned, his eyes narrowed. Before he spoke a word, she knew there'd be little trace of his soft southern drawl.

"My entire career is based on bringing traitors to justice."

The plain statement exposed the truth so carefully hidden under the guise of the southern gentleman Ryan liked to perpetuate. Just like that, she knew everything she needed to know about Ryan Williams and the kind of man he was.

She could so easily fall in love with him, she was halfway there already. But it would be futile.

In the end, enlisting Ryan's help would cost her any hope of a future with him. But if it meant bringing justice to the Angelini brothers' killers, she wouldn't hesitate to pay the price. The cost to her friends had been so much higher.

"Then you understand exactly how David handled it."

Chapter Nine

"Every spare moment David had, he dedicated to tracking down those responsible for Justin's murder."

"What did his SAC say about that?"

AJ shook her head. "I doubt David ever even mentioned it to the Special Agent in Charge. Would you tell your boss if you were engaged in a personal vendetta on the side? Or would you just use every resource you had available to track down the—" She stopped.

Her shoulders sagged and she leaned back against the cushions. Exhaustion dragged at her, in spite of all the sleep she'd had last night. It hurt so much to keep remembering and know she was still forgetting...something.

She could feel Ryan's steady regard. The silence stretched between them, interrupted only by Ansel's constant purr.

"How much did David tell you?" His quiet question didn't surprise her.

She wondered the same thing. "Very little, I think."

"You don't remember?"

She sat up a little straighter and thought. "I'm not sure. We used to discuss their cases all the time, bouncing theories off each other, trying to make sure they'd covered all the angles. I remember that." She raised her hands, helpless, frustrated with the shroud that still clung to some memories. "I don't think Justin ever talked about the Internal Affairs case. At least, not with me, maybe because it was IA. David didn't tell me anything, either. Not until…" She kneaded at her temples, trying to force the memory free.

"Not until when?" Ryan set Ansel on the ground and leaned forward.

"It's so close. I can almost see it…."

"What?"

"I don't know. Something about one of the other agents in the office, the police, there's some connection." Her hands fell back to her lap. "He shouldn't have been so damn secretive." Anger pushed her out of the chair and sent her pacing along the bookshelves and around the borders of the room.

Everywhere she looked, another shadowed memory hinted at what she'd forgotten. She stopped at a grouping of photos hanging on one wall. "I remember every detail of taking these shots a year ago, the location, time of day, selecting the crop, even picking out the frame and mat. Yet all I can recall about what I shot for David is that it was night."

She nudged one of the frames back into alignment and continued skirting the sisal rug covering the hardwood floor.

Ryan rose from the couch, turning to watch her progress around the room. Awareness of him and a longing to lose herself in the comfort of his arms lit a need she wouldn't allow herself to explore. Not now, not yet.

She moved to David's bookcase. His collection of Stephen King paperbacks triggered another memory. "We always argued, rather energetically, about whose favorite author was the better writer." Sliding her fingers over the book spines snugged the occasional book tighter into the row but did nothing to release any more information.

"You keep referring to David in the past." Ryan took a step in her direction. "You think he's dead, don't you?"

She nodded and crossed to Justin's bookcase, restoring some of the distance between her and Ryan.

"Why?"

She pushed a boxed set of Mozart CDs back against the bookshelf and stereo system. "Because, I think I saw him killed. I was there. I think."

Ryan came up behind her. She didn't turn to face him. If she did that, she'd fall back into the old weakness and want him to hold her and take care of her.

"What the hell were you doing there?"

It would be so easy. Ryan, by every action, had shown himself to be a natural protector. She could lean on him, just a little. Just until they knew the truth. Then there'd be plenty of time to be strong by herself. She tapped the cover of an inlaid, wooden box back into place.

Ryan swore under his breath. He caught her hand as she reached to straighten a picture.

"Never mind. You can tell me later." He wrapped his hand around her arm and pulled her down the hall to her bedroom. "We need to get out of here. Pack some clothes. Whatever you need for the next week or so."

"What, are you crazy?" She pulled away from his warm hold. "I'm not leaving when we've just found my home. What if there's something here, some clue that will trigger the rest of my memories?"

"Use your head, sugar. If you think you witnessed a murder, so does someone else. That's why they tried to get their hands on your film. That's why this whole house has been tossed." He shook his head. "All the signs were there. I shoulda seen them when we first walked in."

"What signs?" A feeling of dread curled around her stomach. "What are you talking about?"

"Someone searched this place, top to bottom."

"How can you say that? Everything's fine, it looks like it did the day before yesterday when we left."

"Then why have you been straightening books and pictures all over the place? We should count ourselves lucky. If they'd been really good, you'd never have known they were here."

"You can't know that for sure. Not really." Nausea seeped up the back of her throat. She wanted to deny it, even though some unconscious awareness had been warning her.

"Don't forget the cat." He wouldn't let her deny it, either. "You were surprised to find him outdoors. If this is the first time you've been here in about forty-eight hours and David hasn't been here, how did Ansel get out?"

She scooped up the young cat, hugging him close. Someone had been in her home, touching her belongings. A shudder rolled across her shoulders. "Why?"

Ryan opened her closet door and pulled a small suitcase off the shelf. "I'm thinking they were looking for something."

She sagged onto the edge of the chair, a growing fear robbing her of the ability to stand. "My film?"

"They sure covered their bases on that one, staking out the lab and searching here." He tossed her suitcase on the bed.

She stared at it, not really seeing it as she searched for some image just out of range. "There's something else. What?"

"I was kinda hopin' you would tell me." Ryan squatted in front of her. He covered her hand with his, interrupting the flow of her ring back and forth over her knuckle.

She squeezed her eyes shut, trying to see, struggling to focus on the form that refused to take definite shape. All that came to her was her camera bag. But that made no sense. They'd found nothing out of the ordinary when they looked through it.

"Whatever they're looking for," Ryan continued, "they didn't find it here, they didn't get it from Kimo. That leaves one option. You. Until you come up with the mystery item they'll be dogging your heels."

Her home should have been a sanctuary, but the knowledge that someone had gone through it once, could return at any time, destroyed any chance for peace of mind.

"Time's a-wasting, sugar. Start packing." Ryan pulled her to her feet.

As she tugged open drawers, images of a stranger going through the same motions assaulted her. She dropped a pile of clothes on the bed and headed into the bathroom. The intimate confines of that room were no easier to bear, and she fled with a minimal supply of toiletries.

When she returned to her bedroom, Ryan was lifting Ansel out of the suitcase. He packed the last few items of clothing with a practiced efficiency. The young cat immediately jumped back in, curled into a small open space and looked at him with wide eyes.

The tears she'd been fighting for the past hour threatened again. She sank onto the bed, pulled the young cat into her lap and looked at Ryan. "When will I be able to come back?"

"I wouldn't want to venture a guess."

She swallowed and hugged Ansel closer. "I can't leave him. He's not an outdoor cat. He can't fend for himself."

"The neighbors?"

She shook her head.

Ryan sighed. "Does he have a suitcase?"

Some of the tightness eased from her chest. Being able to take Ansel along made her feel a little less alone, a little less lost.

RYAN CHECKED THEIR SIX as he made another lane change. He drove with the tight awareness of someone expecting to be followed. So far no suspicious vehicles had turned up. Not that that meant a whole hell of a lot.

The cat had stopped yowling after a few minutes in his carrier. Now he seemed content with the occasional growl, just to let them know he was still there and not very happy about it.

AJ didn't have much to say, either. There were still holes in her story and, presumably, in her memories. He had a strong feeling that some of what she'd told him had been as carefully sanitized as the stories he'd told her.

He didn't like the idea that she might be hiding something. The brief glimpse of her, when they walked into her backyard and she first began remembering had been like seeing magnolia blossoms after a ten-month winter. He wanted to see that joy return.

But that wouldn't be possible until they sorted out the details of where David Angelini was and what had really happened to him. Painful or not, she had to start answering some questions.

"When do you think David was killed?"

"Two days ago, the night before..." Her voice faded.

He waited for her to continue.

"The night before I woke with no memories."

"Amnesia can be caused by emotional trauma. Seeing your best friend killed would probably fall under that heading." He tugged on his earlobe. "What I don't understand is why were you there in the first place."

Her answer came slowly and was a question of her own. "He needed a witness?"

"Okay, that seems plausible. But why *you?* Why not someone from the Bureau."

"You mean a professional who could have provided some real backup instead of me who's afraid to hold a gun, much less shoot one?'' Bitterness edged her words. ''If he could have done it completely alone, he would have been more than happy to leave me out of the picture, as well.''

Realization seeped in, sending a chill down his back. ''Pictures.'' He glanced at her. ''If he wanted a record of what happened—''

''Who would be better at documenting a clandestine meeting in the middle of the night than a professional photographer who knows how to take pictures under the worst of conditions? Who else would have the equipment readily available?'' She leaned her head back against the headrest and closed her eyes.

Ryan reached across to brush her arm. Just a soft touch to comfort her when what he really wanted to do was pull her into his arms.

''The Bureau has camera equipment. And at least one of the agents would know how to use it.'' Angelini should never have involved her. She didn't have the background or training to help her handle the situation she'd been dragged into.

''You have to trust the person at your back.'' AJ looked at Ryan, her eyes shadowed with doubts. ''If David thought there was a connection between Justin's police investigation and someone at the FBI…''

''He wouldn't have gone to any authority until he had all his evidence in place.'' Ryan knew how that type of game played out. The possibility of a traitor in the Honolulu office gnawed at him.

''Paranoia is probably a healthy frame of mind for some agents.''

''I've always found it a good idea. So long as it doesn't get in the way of doing the job right.'' Ryan looked away, unable to meet the question in her eyes.

"All we needed was the one shot. Then we'd have the goods and could bring the SOBs down."

"There's got to be something more." Ryan shook his head. "It takes more than just a picture to convict someone." *Something like a record of transactions.* He wanted her to remember the book, to trust him enough to tell him about it. "There's a chunk of something missing."

"Yeah, my memory." Her ring rolled back and forth, jingling together in the pause. "I should have stayed at the lab and processed the film myself. Then we'd know for sure."

"Know what?"

"If I really did get it all. The meeting, David's murder, who pulled the trigger. Then we'd know." She turned and looked out of the side window.

Ryan didn't press her for any more information. To do so would have been beyond cruel. While the amnesia had taken a toll on AJ, the recovery of her memories had brought with it another kind of devastation.

As much as he might want to bundle her away and keep her safe from still more pain, that wasn't likely to happen anytime soon. If he was really going to be honest, it wasn't ever likely to happen with him anywhere in the picture. It simply wasn't in his nature to take on that sort of responsibility.

The more important issue at hand was to come up with a game plan. It was time, whether AJ liked it or not, to have a little come to Jesus and pull in the full strength of his connections.

It didn't take long for Ansel to make himself at home when they got back to the guest cottage. Once he knew where his food and litter box were, he curled up on AJ's bed to watch her unpack.

Ryan envied the cat. If he had his druthers, he'd hang

out with AJ, too. First, though, there was business that needed doing. If he put off making the call to Jacquelyn any longer, he'd have to wait until tomorrow. That didn't seem like such a good idea, given the circumstances.

There was a message waiting when he picked up the phone. He called the voice-mail number and listened to the recording. It was from Jacquelyn, "suggesting" that he call her. ASAP.

Ryan placed the call, running through the secured lines.

"Kingston." Jacquelyn answered on the first ring.

"Miss Jacquelyn, don't tell me you miss me so much you just had to hear this good ole boy's voice."

"It's about time you called. Where have you been?"

"Following up on a few leads."

"This wouldn't happen to pertain to your amnesiac houseguest, would it?"

"Yes, ma'am. We've had something of a breakthrough. She's regained some of her memories."

"So happy to hear it. Are you free to talk?"

"She's just down the hall unpacking."

"I thought you said she'd regained her memory?"

"Some of her memory." Ryan tugged on his ear. "The situation has gotten a bit more complicated. It seems like a good idea to keep her here for a while, until I can check out a few details of her story."

"That's all well and good, Williams, but you'll have to put your good Samaritan impulses on the shelf for a while. You're going back on duty."

Ryan bit back the protest he wanted to make. Instead, he asked, "When?"

"Now."

"Where?"

"Right there in your backyard."

He didn't like the tone in his supervisor's voice. "What's going on?"

"It seems there's an FBI agent missing in paradise. The SAC doesn't want that to become common knowledge so he called us and we've picked up the ball."

"How long has the agent been missing?"

"One day."

"That's not very long. If they're calling in OPR, there's got to be more to it. What's got their boxers in a bunch?"

"The AWOL agent has been behaving rather erratically lately. He asked for a day off, then never bothered reporting back in. They've been unable to contact him. There's no answer at his home which leads the office to think something's happened."

Premonition set his nape hairs on end. "Who's the agent?"

"David Angelini."

Ryan hung his head and swore.

"Williams?" Silence flowed over the phone line as Jacquelyn waited for him to elaborate.

"You're in luck. It looks like I'm already in the game."

"You know Angelini?"

"Friend of a friend."

"Not the amnesia case?"

"AJ. Yes, ma'am."

Jacquelyn muttered a very unladylike phrase of her own. "All right, Ryan. I think it's time for something resembling an official report."

"Yes, ma'am. Why don't we start with the facts you have on record."

"Angelini left a message for his SAC that he was working on a personal project and needed a day off. The rest is what I've already told you—erratic behavior, failure to report in. He's not returning their calls. A unit was sent to the house, but there was no sign of him."

"Did they search the house?" Ryan hoped they had. That would mean he'd jumped the gun and there wasn't someone else looking for AJ, her film or the mysterious little notebook.

Over the phone line, he could hear paper rustling as Jacquelyn leafed through her notes. "They did a drive-by, then knocked. No answer. No search. Why?"

"When we got to the house—"

"Wait a minute." Jacquelyn cut him off. "What were you doing at Angelini's house?"

"AJ is Angelini's housemate."

"Interesting. How long has that relationship existed?"

"They've known each other for years. She moved in with Angelini and his brother about two years ago."

"Cozy."

Ryan could picture Jacquelyn jotting that little fact in her notes. The innuendo set him to AJ's defense. "Don't be jumping to conclusions. They've been friends since childhood. That's all they were. Friends."

"Ryan." Jacquelyn tsked at him. "If I didn't know better, I'd think you were jealous."

"The house had been searched, my guess, within the last twenty-four hours." He wasn't about to dignify the dig. Sure, he cared about AJ, but jealousy meant a whole different kind of emotion. It couldn't be that. He'd never allow it.

"Any idea why someone would want to search the house?"

"Several, actually. There may be some photos documenting an exchange of information." He slid open the towel drawer, lifted the corner of the neatly folded cloths. The codebook, still sealed in the sandwich bag, lay undisturbed. He closed the drawer.

"What about the notebook you found? How does that figure into this?"

He started. For an instant it had seemed almost as though Jacquelyn had looked through the phone lines and over his shoulder. "Give me a little more time. I need to verify a few details."

"Don't take too long. The SAC left me with the distinct impression there was some concern about Angelini and his loyalties. If that's the case and he has turned, you need to pull damage control and pull it fast. What has your house-guest told you?"

"She claims Angelini is dead."

"If David Angelini went underground, having someone claim that would certainly help cover his trail."

"Is there really any evidence of that?"

"Nothing concrete, no. There was mention of a brother who also disappeared under mysterious circumstances. The implication is that dubious behavior may run in the family."

"That's using a pretty broad brush, don't you think?"

"All I have is general information, which makes it difficult to see anything other than a big picture. If you've got something specific, feel free to fill in the details. I'd like nothing better than to prove Angelini is one of the good guys. But if he's not, you are to find him and remedy the situation."

Ryan didn't care for how this was shaping up. AJ was not a traitor. He couldn't believe that of her. If anything she was the victim in this.

Jacquelyn continued. "I want to know who this woman is and what is her real relationship with the Angelini brothers. How well does she know them? If she was a regular part of Angelini's life, why wasn't she mentioned in the request from the Honolulu office? Use that legendary charm of yours and get some answers."

That didn't sit well, either. "She's already told me some of it. But there are still some things lost to the amnesia. They may never come back."

''That's just the problem. All you know is what she's told you. It's too convenient. I don't like convenient.''

''Convenient' as in 'setup'?''

''What does your experience tell you?''

No. Not AJ. The sour taste of the idea sent him in search of some lemonade. On one hand he wanted to know everything about AJ. There was nothing she had to hide from him.

The counterbalance to that was that he didn't want to cause her any more pain than she'd already suffered. If the last few memories were too difficult, he'd rather she never remember.

And over it all was the possibility that his gut instinct was being drowned out by a piece of his anatomy a little lower in the ranks.

''This is messy, Ryan.'' Jacquelyn sighed. ''I don't like it, not one bit. The woman is involved somehow.''

''She's involved because Angelini pulled her in and I don't believe he told her the full story.''

''I'm not buying that.''

''You don't have to.'' He took a breath and booted down the anger. ''Jackie, I'm here. I've watched her. I've seen the look on her face. She's hurting too much to be faking it.''

''You really believe her?''

''She's told me everything she can.''

''That's not a real answer.''

''I know. Can you trust me on this?'' If she didn't, she'd pull him off the case. She'd probably pull him back from Hawaii, too, to eliminate any chance of him interfering with the next agent she sent in.

''She's too much of a question mark for you to risk your life. First she shows up on your beach, now she's linked to a missing agent and we're no closer to knowing who she is than the last time we talked.''

"What do you want me to do?" Ryan watched the seconds tick off on the kitchen clock as he waited for his boss's answer.

"Report to the Honolulu office. The SAC is expecting you and maybe he can fill in a few more details. And get me this woman's fingerprints. I want to see what kind of hits we get on her."

Chapter Ten

AJ tucked the faded T-shirt back in the dresser drawer and pushed it closed. She really didn't need to keep folding and refolding her clothes. Everything had long since been neatly stored away.

Hope that having her own clothes, items that were familiar to her, that she'd found in her own home, would trigger more memories faded. No more memories had returned, no matter how many times she looked at or touched the items she'd brought from her home.

Sadness rippled through her at the possibility she'd never be able to complete the collage of images tumbling through her mind.

Too many holes still riddled her memories. On top of not knowing what still lay buried behind that curtain, there was no knowing if the information was important.

Obviously someone thought she knew something or had something of importance. Why else would they have searched her home?

As much as she might want to, there was no denying that someone had gone through the small house. A shiver swept over her. What would have happened if she'd been there? Would she have disappeared too?

She scooped Ansel from his perch on the end of the bed

and hugged him close. He licked her chin with his rough tongue then squirmed to get down.

AJ opened her arms and Ansel leaped to the floor to head for the door. He looked over his shoulder at her and meowed.

She smiled at the cat's insistent tone. "What? You don't need me to follow you to the kitchen. You know where your food is."

He meowed again, twitched his tail and walked down the hall.

Her smile faded. Sooner or later, she was going to have to go out there herself and face Ryan. She couldn't keep avoiding him, which was what she'd been doing. She wandered across the room to the window. Just now though, she couldn't face him and the questions he'd want to ask.

Questions she couldn't answer, not with any real certainty. Random memories kept popping up, but everything was such a jumble. Nothing seemed to be related to anything else. Some of the images were so confused, so hazy, it was like looking through a lens smeared with Vaseline. The scenes were more like dreams than actual events.

A light knock at the door pulled her away from the window. Ryan stood in the hall, his hands jammed in his pockets. He'd changed from his shorts and wild Hawaiian shirt to more conservative khaki pants, fine-knit shirt and navy blazer.

With his sun-bleached hair and pale eyes, he looked exactly the opposite of the dark-haired, dark-eyed Angelinis. Underneath the surfer good looks, though, he was the same type of man, honorable and protective of those around him. The combination was wreaking havoc on her nascent desire for self-sufficiency.

"All settled in?" He nodded in the direction of her suitcase standing on end by the dresser.

She nodded. "I thought I heard you on the phone."

"There was a message while we were gone. I need to head back into Honolulu for a couple hours."

She nodded again. When she started across the room he held his hand up to stop her.

"There's really no need for you to come along. In fact, it'd probably be better if you didn't."

That surprised her. Up to this point, Ryan had seemed reluctant to let her get too far away from him.

Up to this point, she hadn't fought the idea because his presence had been the only constant in her life since waking with no memory.

Ansel returned and brushed against Ryan's ankles. He reached down to pet the cat, seeming almost relieved for the excuse not to look at her as he continued. "There's some business I need to go deal with."

She studied Ryan as he crouched to scratch her pet under the chin. He was hiding something from her. His answers were less than informative, almost evasive. After keeping her close, he was suddenly drawing away from her.

The sense of desertion squeezed in her chest. It shouldn't matter so much that he was leaving her behind. She'd come to rely on him too much to fill the hours of the day. The awareness of that dependency didn't sit well. Neither did idleness.

What did matter was having a couple hours to herself.

New insights had a way of working their way into her consciousness while she was distracted with her camera. For the first time since he'd found her yesterday morning, she'd have a chance to escape into the healing of her photography.

That more than anything eased the tightness. Looking through the lens, focusing outward rather than inward had saved her sanity on a number of occasions, especially when she was first learning her craft. Perhaps, when she packed her equipment away this time, she would discover a new order to the jumbled memories that kept appearing.

Ryan turned to leave, then stopped. "When I get back...I don't want to just sit around the kitchen table eating potpies for supper. Let's go out. I know a private little place we could go to."

"I'd like that."

"Good. I've been dyin' to see how you look in the red dress with your toes painted to match." He winked and disappeared down the hall.

Oh. My. Tension of a completely different nature washed over her. Memories of the heat in his eyes when she'd tried on the dress sent tingles chasing from her fingertips to her toes. She looked down at her bare feet. The pale pink polish looked so innocent.

She shook herself free of the red silk images and trailed after him. "While you're gone, I think I'll wander around a little. I haven't seen much of the estate."

Ryan paused by the front door as he slipped on his deck shoes. His glance skittered away from her and he gave a quick nod. "Good idea. My mama always said a body should take at least an hour of fresh air every day. I've never found fresher than what's outside this door."

"Is that why you make your home here?" The question slipped out before she realized she was going to ask it.

"This isn't my home, baby." He looked at her then. Only for a moment, but it was long enough for her to see a wishful loneliness in his expression before he looked away. "It's just a place to hang my hat on occasion. That's something very different and I never mistake the two." He stepped outside and closed the door behind him, shutting her in and him out

His meaning wouldn't have been any clearer if he'd thrown a klieg light on it.

CAMERA IN HAND, AJ WANDERED around the estate for several hours. It didn't take long before her photographer's eye became enchanted. Rock banks marked what she presumed were the boundaries of Jamie's property. On one end of the estate she discovered several tidal pools. In short order, she filled a roll of film with shots of the various sea creatures held captive until the next high tide.

On the other edge of the property, waves crashed against a high escarpment. She picked her way over the wave-worn rocks and discovered a level outcropping with an unrestricted view of the horizon. From there the endless expanse of blue ocean reached out and touched the sky in a long curve at the edge of the world. She filled another two rolls.

The unending variety of scenes fired her artist's vision. The camera, film and lens selection, plans on how to crop the finished photo, every detail absorbed her complete concentration. The process was familiar, comfortable. Safe.

All too soon, the time she'd allotted for her escape passed.

Her determined focus on nothing but the scenery faded as clouds gathered over the sun. The light flattened, removing shadows and robbing details from the landscape. She repacked her equipment and headed back to the guest house. Worry needled at her every step of the way.

Her path led her by the spot where Ryan had found her. Such a short time ago. The reality of all that had elapsed since then pushed forward, forcing her to consciously consider her situation.

She'd developed a certain amount of independence in the past two years. At least, she thought she had. But now, returning memories revealed that independence had been little more than an illusion. Like a child learning to ride a bicycle with daddy at her side, AJ's confidence had been based on knowledge that the Angelinis were always in the background, ready to catch her if she began to fall.

A soft breeze carried the ocean's scent to her. She closed her eyes and savored the salt tang in the air. Her sense of independence may have been as ephemeral as the breeze, but it had served a purpose. She'd learned to enjoy solitude. She liked being alone, it was safe. Trust wasn't an issue.

Another memory shifted into place. The ease with which she'd accepted Ryan's presence set off an alarm. She could see the behavior as one that had gotten her into trouble in the past.

She'd been so hungry to create a home for herself after her parents' deaths she'd made a similar mistake, trusted the wrong person.

With the exception of her childhood friends, she'd established a pretty abysmal record when it came to trusting.

When Ryan left, she'd return to the house in Honolulu. She should be happy that she'd be back in her home. But the fact that she would be alone and there was no safety net this time filled her with dread.

Memories continued to filter through the disintegrating curtain of the amnesia. Chances were pretty high she'd be dead right now, if it hadn't been for her guardian Angelinis coming to the rescue.

Instead, David was dead. She could feel it in her soul even if she couldn't remember the exact images.

With him gone, there was no one else for her to turn to, no one to keep her on track, to protect her from herself.

Certainly not Ryan who refused to maintain a home anywhere. He'd made that abundantly clear with his parting remark. His presence on Oahu, and in her life, was temporary only.

The one person who would rescue her was herself. Fear cascaded over her, leaving her chilled. Would she ever find the balance between home and independence, trust and seclusion?

She spun on her heel and headed for the guest house at a faster pace. The added speed didn't help. There was no eluding the harsh truth. She wasn't strong enough to save anyone, least of all herself. If she had been, maybe David would still be alive.

When she pushed through the kitchen door, Ansel greeted her with a scolding meow. He sat on his haunches and reached for her with his front paws. She scooped him into her arms and buried her nose in the soft fur. He was easily appeased when she opened a can of his favorite food.

If only her fears were so simple to resolve. A good meal, someone to hold her…

The coming evening held promise for the good meal, at least. The rest she would have to deal with eventually. But not tonight.

Tonight she wanted to pretend life could be normal. Just for a little while.

THE SHOWER COMING ON was her first indication Ryan had returned from his errand. She'd focused so completely on painting her toenails that she missed his quiet tread down the hall.

The boutique clerk must have conned Ryan into buying the bottle of polish. The crimson lacquer gave her toes a happy, sexy look. She couldn't begrudge Ryan the added expense any more than she could keep from smiling every time she looked down. Especially not when she remembered his teasing comment.

The shower stopped. Three-and-a-half minutes.

If he held true to his earlier routine, he'd be rapping on her door in another three-and-a-half minutes.

Anticipation and maybe a little trepidation warmed her cheeks.

She checked her reflection in the full-length mirror and her blush deepened. The fire-red dress hugged her body, the modest scoop neck giving no hint of the deep *U* that bared most of her back.

The one thing the boutique clerk hadn't provided was a bra that would work with the dress style so the only item of lingerie between her and the heavy silk was a pair of black silk thong panties. All in all, the sensations teasing her skin were decidedly erotic in nature.

Maybe this isn't such a good idea. She finished braiding her hair with practiced speed, but before she could pull a more modest clothing option from the closet, Ryan knocked.

With a deep breath and one last glance in the mirror, she turned as he opened the door.

Her pulse skipped at the vision he presented. He stood framed in the doorway looking like the latest hot model straight out of *GQ*.

He actually wore a suit. The ebony fabric lay in sharp contrast against a crisp white shirt. That's where conformity ended. The top two buttons of his shirt were left open. He wore no tie. And no socks or shoes.

His low whistle ignited another wave of heat in her cheeks. The flock of butterflies residing in her tummy took flight at his appreciative smile and heat pooled low in her belly.

"Sugar, you better come out or we may never make it to dinner."

She scooped the high-heeled sandals from the box sitting on her bed and hurried from the room.

Ansel followed them down the hall to the back door where he flopped onto his back at their feet. AJ crouched down. "Be a good kitty while we're gone." She gave the exposed white belly a good tummy rub before standing.

The green fire in Ryan's eyes sent spirals of desire cascading all the way to her toes.

"It just don't seem right to be jealous of a cat." He plucked the sandals from her loose hold, threaded his fingers through hers and led her out the back door.

Rather than heading for the garage where Jamie kept his collection of cars, Ryan set off across the beach.

Light from the waning moon reflected off the sand, providing some illumination for their walk. He followed a barely perceptible path through the narrow palm grove. When they emerged from the trees, Jamie's house stood before them, alive with white bee lights and warm candle glow.

"I hope you don't mind. I asked Jamie if we could join him this evening. It seemed…safer."

"Safer?"

He studied her face with such intensity it seemed almost like a physical caress. "Someone's looking for you, baby." He gave her hand a squeeze. "Until we know who or why, we're better off keeping a low profile."

She nodded in understanding and pushed away her disappointment. Under normal circumstances, she'd been free to go anywhere she chose at a moment's notice. It wasn't unusual for her to disappear for long periods of time, returning home only to clean up and get more supplies. Even though she'd roamed freely around the estate today, she'd been constantly aware of the limitations of her range. The constraints chafed.

He tugged on her hand and she followed him onto the smooth terra-cotta tiles of the patio floor. A small table stood on one corner of the expanse. A pair of black leather slippers was tucked underneath it, on top was a pile of neatly folded hand towels. He shook out one of the towels and brushed the sand from his feet, before stepping into the slippers.

"I wondered about your bare feet."

"Jamie is a very accommodating host." Ryan held up a fresh towel. "May I?"

He squatted in front of her before she fully realized his intention. With great care, he brushed the sand from her left foot, paying particular attention to her now red-painted toenails.

She'd never realized how sensitive her feet were until that moment. The butterflies took flight once more and breathing became a conscious effort of slow inhale, slow exhale. Tiny shivers chased over her skin.

Ryan looked up. Even in the low light out here he could see every detail of AJ's expression. The dilation of her pupils, the rhythm of her breathing, spoke volumes. All the signs confirmed his hope. She wanted him.

This had nothing to do with Jacquelyn's suggestion to "use your charms." He didn't share her suspicions of AJ.

Guilt by association just didn't fly. Not in this case, not with AJ. Even if there was evidence against Angelini, which there wasn't. At least not yet. What the SAC had given him was circumstantial and Ryan had a whole lot of digging to do before he'd buy what amounted to speculation.

No, this had nothing to do with the assignment.

They had eliminated the possibility of a husband waiting somewhere for her. Which meant all bets were off and he could loosen the tight rein he'd been holding on his libido.

No, this heat flowing between them had everything to do with a mutual attraction he intended to explore to the fullest extent.

He slipped her sandal into place, relishing the soft texture of her skin. When he lifted her right foot to repeat the process, she rested one hand on his shoulder to steady herself.

Her gentle touch set off a chain reaction of sensations from his shoulder to his groin.

He stood in one smooth motion, capturing her hand and cradling it against his chest. She seemed frozen in place, her eyes, startled and round, hinted at the dawning realization of what she read in his expression. Her lips…he nearly groaned.

She'd used the red lipstick the sales consultant had recommended he buy. At the time the suggestion had seemed innocent enough.

Now he wanted to kiss the deep cherry color off the lush fullness of her lips and never stop. He leaned closer. Her silk-clad breasts brushed against his shirtfront.

Sweet heavens, no bra.

Blood beat a fierce trail to his belly and lower. Muscles he had no control over tightened to attention.

Her tremulous sigh fanned the flames.

The towel he still held fell to the patio floor. He pulled her closer, smoothing his hands down her bare arms, breathing in deep. Sunshine and sea. Light and innocence. Her delicate fragrance blended with the salty evening air.

He closed his eyes, savoring the feel of her skin beneath his hands.

This woman drew him like no other ever had. Maybe it was the mystery that surrounded her. The need to protect her, keep her safe from more pain had him holding back questions that wanted asking.

Maybe it was purely physical. Right now, he didn't really want to examine the why.

He just wanted. His fingers brushed across the naked expanse of her back as he slid his arm around her waist. Shock waves set his heart to thudding with a heavy beat.

She moved against him, and he tightened his embrace,

running his hand down her spine, pressing her silk and heat closer. She shifted again, fitting herself in his arms, her soft curves against his hard muscles. From chest to thigh, they touched.

A sigh trembled between them and Ryan would have been hard-pressed to say whose it had been.

He wound her braid around his free hand, tilting her head back with a gentle tug. Her lips gleamed in the soft patio light.

Desire threatened to blaze out of control. If he didn't kiss her—

A light flared on in the breakfast room beside them. AJ stiffened in his arms.

The patio door slid open and Jamie stepped out. Ryan made no effort to disguise his frustrated groan.

"Am I interrupting?"

"Yes." Ryan drew a deep breath and contented himself with kissing AJ on the corner of her lips, right where her dimple appeared when she smiled.

"Later." He whispered the promise as he released her.

She blinked and bobbed her head in the smallest of nods.

Amusement danced in Jamie's eyes. "My apologies, however the wine is breathing and dinner is ready to be served."

AJ welcomed the momentary distraction. *If that's what it's like to be almost kissed by Ryan...* Heaven help her if they ever actually progressed to the next step. The timely interruption had kept the situation from flashing out of control.

Jamie turned to AJ. "Welcome to my home. Now that I've rescued you, for the moment, from Ryan's ardor, won't you come in?"

She gathered her shredded composure enough to follow their host through the breakfast room into his kitchen.

A work island with stools along one side dominated the well-appointed space. Jamie held out a stool. "Have a seat while we finish the salad."

She sank onto the cushioned seat with silent relief. High heels may look sexy, but they were better for sitting than moving, especially for someone more accustomed to flats. The short walk from the patio had tested her already compromised sense of balance.

Ryan finished the salad greens as Jamie stirred together a balsamic vinaigrette dressing. They moved about the kitchen with an easy camaraderie reminiscent of the Angelini brothers. Ryan relaxed, his smile came easier, the tension lines around his eyes and mouth lessened. His trust in Jamie lit their easy banter.

That, too, reminded her of the Angelinis.

To distract herself from that train of thought, she looked around, taking in the layout of their surroundings. Noticing there was no clear view of the patio from anywhere in the kitchen she turned back to Jamie. "How did you know we were here?"

He looked from her to Ryan and back. "Let's just say the glass doors are poor insulation against certain types of energy."

"Oh." Heat bloomed in her cheeks as his meaning registered. She knew what she'd been feeling as Ryan played Prince Charming to her Cinderella. She risked a sideways glance at him. A dull red crept up his neck. He busied himself at the counter cleaning up nonexistent spills.

Jamie cleared his throat. "Shall we go into the dining room?" He led the way to an elegant room softly lit with candles. Windows comprised an entire wall, offering a spectacular view of the night.

"I hope you don't mind the candles." Jamie held a chair for her. "I find them much more conducive to relaxation than artificial light."

"They're lovely. The scent is intriguing."

"A friend makes them for me with specially distilled oils. Tonight we have lemon and rosemary for memory."

"For my benefit?" She smiled at Jamie. In this light particularly he appeared very mysterious.

He chuckled as he took his seat. "For Ryan actually. In an effort, futile I am certain, to help him remember to behave."

Ryan bristled at the implication. "I don't need some New Age hocus-pocus to remind me of that. My mama raised me to be a gentleman."

"Would that have been your Mama Ellie? Or Mama Dorothy-Ann?"

Ryan shook open his napkin, ignoring the question.

She studied his shuttered expression, curious about what he wasn't saying.

Jamie didn't seem bothered by Ryan's silence. He handed her a plate filled with salad. "How was your day? Have you made any progress in remembering?"

"Actually, yes." She swallowed a bite of the delicious salad, surprised by her hunger. "We found my home and my pet. I hope you don't mind that we brought Ansel back. He's barely more than a kitten. I couldn't leave him again and Ryan wouldn't let me stay there."

"Why is that?" Jamie turned to Ryan.

"Because someone had searched the place very thoroughly and very carefully. It's not safe."

"You can't be certain—"

"Yes I can." Ryan cut her off. "We both saw the signs. And we both saw what went down at the lab."

"I know, it's just that…that was my home," she whispered.

"If having Ansel makes your stay in the cottage a bit more comfortable, he's more than welcome, AJ."

"Thank you." She relaxed against her chair back. "I've

also remembered my full name—Alexandra Justine Davidson. Alex to my friends, although I've come to like AJ.''

"Why didn't you tell me?" Ryan's sharp question had both Jamie and her looking at him.

She couldn't read the expression glittering in his narrowed eyes. For an instant it seemed to be mistrust, then he blinked and the impression disappeared.

"I didn't think it would make a difference. There were so many other things…besides, you usually call me sugar.''

"Alexandra's a lovely name." Jamie's comment smoothed over the tension before it could fully develop.

"When I was in elementary school, my name led me to my best friends. Or rather," she smiled at the memory, "led them to me. Justin and David decided I belonged to them because of our shared names. Once the Angelinis laid claim to something, they never let go. Even after my family moved to the mainland, they kept the connection alive. They are…were…'' Her throat tightened.

Ryan brushed her hand with his, lingering just long enough to pull her back from sadness. Renewed awareness of him warmed her cold hand. She took a sip from her water glass before continuing. "They *were* the best friends a girl could have.''

Jamie filled a wineglass with a deep red Merlot and handed it to her. After a taste of the fortifying alcohol, she chuckled. "Of course, having two such paragons at my back did make dating rather difficult.''

"They scared all the boys away?" Jamie handed her a plate of beef Wellington.

She tilted her head to the side. "No, it wasn't that. More like no boy or man could hope to compete with the brothers for my affection. So very few even tried.''

Ryan was the exception. She wondered if he understood that and glanced in his direction, catching his intent stare.

He looked away as he picked at his food. A tiny frown shadowed his face.

"I knew Justin." Jamie's revelation brought her attention fully back on him. "In fact I worked with him on several cases. The last time we consulted, he told me of his friend, a wonderful photographer. He was very proud of you."

"Thank you." She missed Justin. Memories of him seemed easier to recapture than those of David. Tears stung her eyes.

"I never understood what happened, why he disappeared."

"He was murdered." The hard word stuck in her throat, stealing her appetite. "He'd gotten too close…" She looked at Ryan and stopped.

"Too close to what?" he asked. "Do you remember?"

She bit her lip to keep the tears at bay. "I don't know."

"I've always been interested by how the mind works." Jamie again turned the conversation from an awkward moment with a change of topic. "Would you mind telling me more of your amnesia, what's happened, what triggers the memories."

For twelve minutes they talked about the process of regaining her memory. All the while, awareness of Ryan, of his steady gaze watching her, stole a little of her breath.

"Has there been anything you've known all along, that you haven't had to remember?"

"My camera. Holding it is like breathing for me."

"Did Ryan tell you I have a darkroom?" Jamie shifted the topic with masterful ease. "I keep it stocked, but seldom have time to put it to good use."

Details of her upcoming show bubbled to the foreground of her memory. They chatted on about her photography preferences.

"I don't normally photograph people." She eased into

the request she'd wanted to make since meeting Jamie. "But I'd love to shoot a portrait of you sometime."

"I'm flattered." Jamie smiled at her. "Unless, of course, you think you'll capture spirits floating around my head or some other such nonsense."

"Tropical plants were more what I had in mind." She studied him for a moment. "Or, with your eye color, perhaps the ocean and sky."

"Actually, you'd be doing me a tremendous favor. I'm to be a guest lecturer at university for a term in the autumn and need a new photograph. I'll give you whatever time you need and free rein in the darkroom."

"It's a deal." The new project would provide a welcome, if temporary, distraction. "Whenever you have time, let me know."

"Would tomorrow be acceptable? I'm not working on anything at the moment."

"Ryan hasn't asked you to consult?"

The men exchanged glances. Ryan shrugged.

"I've offered my services." Jamie said.

"Has he accepted?"

"'He' is in the room," Ryan reminded her. Not that she could have forgotten. The soft touch of his lips still tingled on her cheek. Every time he moved, she was aware of him, aware of the strong attraction between them. She also was aware of the fact that he hadn't said anything about his errand to Honolulu.

"Have you accepted Jamie's offer?" She turned to Ryan.

"I believe in using every resource available." Ryan stood and gathered their empty plates.

"I see."

"No, I don't think you do. I've been called back on assignment." He carried the dishes to the kitchen.

"Oh." She'd known this would happen, sooner or later.

Later would have been so much better. "So you'll be leaving," she said when he returned.

He sighed. "No."

"Your assignment is in Hawaii?"

Ryan kneeled on one knee beside her chair. "Did David ever tell you about his undercover assignments while he was on them?"

She frowned. An inkling of where he was leading glimmered into existence. "Sometimes, when things were wrapping up or the case had gone cold."

"Then you understand that I can't talk to you about an active case just now." He took her hands in his and squeezed. "I'm sorry, baby. I wish it could be different. On the upside, I'll be staying here for a good while longer."

"What happens to me in the meantime?"

"You stay with me. I'm not abandoning you." He raised her hands to his lips and brushed a kiss across her knuckles. "You don't get rid of me that easy."

She relaxed with his reassurances. A little warning light blinked on in the back of her mind.

Even if he was staying longer than he'd anticipated, he would be working. Their time together would be limited.

And, when it was all over, he would still leave.

Then she'd be alone, without anyone to lean on. She needed to prepare for that.

Recovered memories of the Angelinis had provided her a certain amount of strength. Perhaps, if she could store away enough memories of her time with Ryan, she would be strong enough when he left.

He stood and helped her to her feet. "Come on, sug— Alex. We've both got work to do tomorrow, we better head home." He tucked her hand into the crook of his arm. Beneath her fingers, his muscles flexed with a subtle strength, rekindling the awareness that had been simmering since their almost-kiss on the patio.

Home. She liked the sound of that. What would it be like to have a home with Ryan?

The warning light grew brighter.

Chapter Eleven

Ryan rested his hand on AJ's back as they strolled along the path to the cottage. The skin left naked by the low back of her dress felt satin cool to his touch. Her long braid brushed the back of his hand. He wanted to play with her hair, free it from the confining style, feel the silken strands sift through his fingers.

He wanted to concentrate on all the sensations her proximity generated. Instead, an uneasy mix of feelings plagued him.

On the surface was jealousy. Ryan acknowledged the emotion for what it was. Plain old green-eyed jealousy would have been bad enough. Worse, this was jealousy of two men who were, near as he could figure, both dead.

From everything AJ had said, the relationship with the Angelini brothers had never been anything other than platonic. So there really was no competition, nothing for him to be jealous of.

Nothing, except for the fact that AJ had relied on them. They had saved her from some hell she refused to tell him about.

Ryan glanced at her. Moonlight edged her hair with a subtle glow, giving her the appearance of wearing a halo. The fanciful image forced a smile from him.

Whatever she may have been involved in, it couldn't be

as bad as she believed. He'd glimpsed the real person, before memories had started returning, weighing her down with life's guilt and disappointment. Whatever she'd done, it hadn't been of her own free will.

While it was true she shared a history with the Angelinis, he had her present. He hoped that would be enough. He could offer her sanctuary for now but he could never offer her a future. Not now, not here. Not in his line of work.

That work brought in another factor of his discomfort. Layered with the jealousy was a certain distrust. The meeting at the Honolulu office had raised a lot of questions. David Angelini's recent actions appeared highly suspect.

By her close association, she fell under some of the same suspicions. Regardless of his personal feelings toward her, professionally, he had to follow where the evidence led.

Being attracted to someone in collusion with a traitor didn't sit well. He had no doubts that the woman he'd come to know understood the importance of loyalty and honor. What he didn't know was where her loyalty lay.

Maybe he just didn't want to see what would be clear to anyone else.

Maybe being half in love with her was blinding him.

Half in love? That realization sent dread crashing through him. In Montana, he'd seen what being in love could do to an agent on assignment.

There was no room in his life for that sort of emotion. Love meant caring for someone, belonging someplace, feeling connected.

The way he felt with AJ.

"You had more than one mother?"

Her question caught him off guard. He would have welcomed the distraction from his thoughts if it had been any other topic.

''No.'' He brushed his hand down her back, caught and slipped off the ruffled elastic holding her braid together. ''Only one mother.''

''Who were Mama Ellie and Mama Dorothy-Ann?''

Ryan considered not answering, but he owed AJ better than that. He owed her an understanding of why he could never be the man for her. ''When I was young, my mother...became ill.'' That was one way to put it. ''She left me with an aunt of hers for a time.''

''How old were you?''

''Six.''

''So young.'' Her soft words were nearly lost on the breeze.

He looked straight ahead, unwilling to see the sympathy in her expression. If it hadn't been for him, his mother probably would have coped with life just fine. The burden of a child, of him, had been too much.

''How long was it before your mother came back?''

''I stayed with the first aunt for a year. Then I moved on to the next relative's. There always seemed to be some aunt or other who was willing to take me in for a time. When I hit eighteen, I entered the navy.''

They walked in silence for a few steps, the soft sand giving beneath their feet, the waves whispering secrets against the shore. ''The aunts were good women.''

''They must have been, to help out a niece and raise her child.''

Ryan shrugged. He brushed his hand across her back and a couple twists in her braid came undone. ''I took to calling each one 'Mama.' It was simpler than 'Great-Aunt whoever.' Each one of those ladies taught me something important about life.''

''So, all this time you've been referring to them. How many were there?''

''Enough to provide a well-rounded education.'' One

lesson he'd learned from all of them was the nobility of doing the right thing. If they could see him now they'd be fixing to tan his hide.

His intentions toward AJ were anything but platonic and not particularly noble. What he wanted with her was the impossible.

He would be leaving when he completed his assignment. While he would come back whenever he had an opportunity, that wasn't the kind of relationship AJ deserved.

No. Not AJ. Alex.

Another reminder that he seemed more focused on his own agenda. When the memories had begun to return, he'd never even thought of asking her name. That failure, as much as anything else, proved he was far from what she needed.

Time for a change of subject, before she asked any more questions and he came face-to-face with more of his short-comings.

"While you're working with Jamie tomorrow, I need to head to the Field Office for a while." He ran his hand down her back and managed to undo a little more of the braid. "I can stop at Kimo's lab to pick up the film."

She nibbled her full lower lip. Most of her lipstick had worn off through dinner. Ryan wondered if she'd still taste of the wine they'd drunk with the meal. A twist of desire razored straight to his groin. He held back a groan and concentrated on her answer, watching with intent concentration as her mouth formed the words, her lips shaped each syllable.

"I'd hoped we could do that before…" Her voice trailed off as they stopped at the back door of the cottage. She turned to face him. "I suppose it makes more sense for you to take care of it on your own."

"I promise not to peek at anything until I get back."

He brushed his hand across her shoulders and more of her braid loosened.

"Fine." She smiled up at him. "I'll check Jamie's darkroom in the morning. If I need anything, could you pick up some supplies while you're at the lab?"

"Yes, ma'am, my pleasure." He took a slow, deep breath. Her delicate scent teased his weakening control.

She shook her head. A frown pinched between her eyebrows as she swept her hair forward over her shoulder to discover his handiwork.

He held up the coated elastic, rather pleased that he'd managed to undo most of the braid before she caught him. He winked at her.

"How'd you manage to do that?" A smile lifted her full lips, revealing a hint of the dimple. She reached for the hair tie, her elegant fingers lingering for a moment against his hand before drawing back.

"Tsk, tsk. Never expect an agent to divulge his methods." He held the door open for her. As they stepped into the kitchen, a low growl came from the direction of the living room. The cat crouched in the doorway, his back hairs standing in a stiff ridge along his spine and his tail at full bristle.

Adrenaline buzzed through his veins, washing away any aftereffects of the dinner wine.

"We must have startled him." Alex took a step forward.

He stopped her. "He's looking the other direction." He pulled his gun from his back holster.

Alex drew back. Dread overlaid surprise. Even dining in his friend's home, Ryan had been armed. Was it habit or did he really expect to need a weapon?

"Stay behind me," he directed in a low voice.

She followed his movements as he edged around the kitchen. He picked up a flashlight from the counter and positioned himself beside the open doorway.

In one smooth motion he swung through the door, gun and flashlight covering every corner of the room.

Her heart pounded. She held her breath, half expecting to hear a shot. Instead, there was the soft click of the light switch.

The warm glow of the table lamps revealed everything in neat order. Ryan eased his way down the hall.

She scooped Ansel off the floor and followed, keeping some distance between them, but not letting Ryan out of her sight. Their cautious inspection ended in her bedroom.

The overhead light revealed the room much as she'd left it. Ryan holstered his gun and turned to her. She pointed at the bed. "My camera bag," she whispered. "When we left, it was on the floor."

"You're certain?"

She nodded and handed Ansel to him. The sharp click of the quick-release snaps sounded in the room. She folded the lid back, her heart thumping in her throat.

"Is everything there?" Ryan asked.

"Yes, but it's not right." She laid camera bodies and lenses on the bed, opened film canisters, dumped them out. "It's all jumbled up. Nothing's in the right place."

"You're sure?"

She turned to Ryan. "Who did this? How did they get in here?"

"Both very good questions."

"I thought you said I'd be safer here."

"I thought you would be."

"If I'd been here alone…" The words caught in her throat.

"You weren't. And going forward, you'll be with either Jamie or me." He handed Ansel back to her and headed to the kitchen.

She set Ansel on the bed and stowed her camera bag before following Ryan. He spoke on the phone with Jamie, alerting him to the intruder and asking him to check the security system.

The call complete, he pulled her into his arms, cocooning her in his strength. "You're safe here, I promise, baby. Whoever it is, they're looking for something. Do you have any idea what it might be?"

"I want to remember, really I do, but..."

"Shhh, it's going to be all right." He stroked a soothing hand down her back, then threaded his fingers through her hair, releasing the final few twists of her braid. "I've wanted to do this all evening."

She searched his face, memorizing the play of light and shadow on his features. She'd wanted this all evening, as well. In spite of the amnesia, or maybe because of it, this man had captured her heart. Without the protection of her memories, she'd begun to fall just a little in love with him.

With the return of her memories, she understood the futility of the situation. Their worlds were not really so different, but their methods for dealing with life were as opposite as night and day.

She wanted the security of a home. Ryan held himself separate from any such permanence.

Depending on others came all too easily for her. He relied only on himself.

The contrast was inescapable and none of that mattered. Before she realized it, before she had even thought to create a defense against him, it was too late.

She wasn't just a little in love.

He drew her closer. "There's something else I've wanted to do all evening."

Her eyes fluttered shut. Other senses took over, casting vivid images in her mind's eye. His heat and pure masculine scent surrounded her in a blanket of desire. The first caress of his lips against hers was soft as the dawn light. He cradled her head in one hand. With his arm around her waist he drew her closer still. His teeth grazed her lower lip, nipping and tugging with soft insistence.

She'd lost so much. The thought of pulling away from Ryan, of denying what was about to happen between them, grew unbearable. For better or worse, for however long this connection existed between them, she would accept what portion of himself Ryan was willing to share.

Fear and anticipation mingled, squeezing her chest with an aching tightness. She drew a quaking breath. Ryan took full advantage of the opportunity and deepened the kiss, his tongue delving in to tease the soft flesh of her inner lip.

She thrilled at the sensations his touch set off. His hands warmed the naked skin of her back. Heat uncurled and spread from where his hand pressed against her spine through her entire body.

Fear melted. Tomorrow would be soon enough to pick up the pieces.

A long-dormant hunger developed into full-blown urgency. She opened her mouth, welcoming the touch and taste of his kiss.

She wound her arms around his neck, snugging herself as close to his hard-muscled body as she could. The silk of her dress rubbed across her sensitized skin, adding to the myriad sensations clamoring to overwhelm her. Ryan's low groan triggered her own instant response.

She wanted to be closer, to feel every breath he took, to pulse with every beat of his heart.

He swept her off her feet and carried her down the hall, never breaking their hungry kiss as he turned into his bedroom. The stained-glass table lamp next to his bed threw shards of color around the room, lighting their way.

The support of his arm beneath her legs shifted. The skirt of her dress rode up as he lowered her feet to the cool wooden floor. His hand followed the fabric's journey, tracing a path of fire until he encountered the tiny scrap of her panties.

He curled one finger in the thong's waistband and tugged, sending her heart chasing to new heights. Her moan escaped with the last of her breath.

Still they kissed. His hot mouth trailed a path from her lips across her jaw, stopping for a moment to nibble at her earlobe. Each tiny nip sent jolts of excitement straight to her belly. The assault on her senses robbed her legs of any ability to stand. Coherent thought faded.

Ryan paused at the pulse fluttering madly at the base of her throat. The shoulder of her dress impeded any further progress of his mouth against her skin. He slid the offending fabric out of the way and continued exploring the taste and fragrance of her.

With one shoulder freed, he brushed the other red silk shoulder down her arm. He held her too close for the dress to just fall away, but he couldn't bring himself to loosen his hold. He contented himself with running his hand through her hair and using the ends to tease over her naked skin.

She moaned as his hand slipped inside her dress and smoothed along her delicate rib cage, not quite reaching the curve of her breast. She pushed at his shoulders.

For one instant he thought she'd changed her mind, that she wanted to stop. Then he realized she was as busy with his clothes as he was with hers. She managed to undo his shirt buttons and push the fabric open. All that stood between them was the heavy crimson silk of her dress.

The tight beads of her nipples brushed across his chest in an erotic caress. It was his turn to groan as desire lanced through him, pulling him tighter, ratcheting the hunger even higher.

He shrugged out of his jacket and shirt, tossing them aside as he reached for her once more. He brushed his hands down her arms, pushing the dress free until it pooled at her feet. She stood before him, her long hair draped over her shoulder like a cloak.

She looked like a work of art. The colors from the lamp painted her pale skin with soft color. The ebony fall of her hair alternately hid and revealed, teasing him with glimpses of her curves.

Hunger unlike any he'd ever known ripped through him. He'd been without a woman for too long, but that didn't explain this response. No other woman had set his hands to shaking as they shook now.

He ran his fingertips over Alex's hair from shoulder to waist, teasing it open to reveal her beautifully rounded breast. He stooped to gently take the taut peak into his mouth and suckled.

Her moan echoed to his core. He'd never felt so moved by a woman before. He'd never wanted to please a woman as much as he did Alex.

The realization stabbed through him. Alex was different. She deserved better. She deserved more than he could offer her. But God help him, he couldn't help himself.

He sank to his knees, trailing kisses over her belly, exalting in every ripple and shiver that followed his touch. His tongue dove into the cleft of her navel as he eased her panties down her thighs.

Before he could move his ministrations lower, her hands threaded through his hair and she fell to her knees, her lips covering his mouth in a ravenous kiss, unlike any he'd tasted before.

He held her tight, chest to breasts, thigh to thigh, skin to skin. They were both on fire. He wanted nothing more than to sink into her and forget all of his pain, make her forget all of her pain.

He stood and pulled her to her feet.

"What?" She looked at him with wide, startled eyes.

Her pupils were so dilated with desire the gray irises were virtually nonexistent.

"Our first time isn't going to be on the floor. We're going to do this properly." Further conversation was impossible, so he kissed the questions from her lips.

He stripped the comforter from the bed and laid her in the middle of cool sheets covering the king-size mattress. He shed his pants and briefs and sat on the edge of the mattress. From the dresser drawer, he pulled a foil packet.

His rapidly weakening control took a direct hit when she rested one hand on his thigh. He rolled the sheath into place, then stretched out next to her.

"If I were more of a man, I'd tell you we can stop if you have any doubts about this." He dipped his head and kissed her collarbone, tracing the fragile line to the pulse at the base of her throat. The heady fragrance of her stoked the blaze of desire racking his body. "But if we were to stop now—" he forced himself to stop, to look into her eyes and will her to see what he couldn't say "—I think I'd probably die."

She smiled and trailed her fingers over his cheek in a soft caress. "So would I. Please, let's…" Her eyes drifted shut as he ran his hand down her torso.

He needed no more than her soft moan to know he was lost. He moved to cover her slender body with his, fitting himself to her curves and hollows, sliding into her heat.

She wrapped her legs around his waist, holding him deep inside. For a heartbeat they lay without moving, breathing and sighing as one. Desire built until he had to move, to pull out and bury himself once more in her intimate embrace. She rose to match him, move for move, touch for touch, kiss for kiss.

She became the center of his world, the sole focus of his being. His only goal was bringing her the ultimate joy.

He framed her face with his hands, threading his fingers

into her hair. Their gazes locked, the nonphysical contact as strong as the physical. He lost himself in the depths of her eyes, reading there what he desperately needed to find.

Tension spiraled with each move, each touch, each soft cry.

When her release finally took control of her body, he followed her on the journey. The world disappeared and he found what he'd never let himself seek. He found a place to belong, heaven on earth. He found home.

It could only mean one thing.

He was heading straight into hell.

Chapter Twelve

Ryan didn't want to wake up. Not yet. He needed at least a decade before he'd be ready to face Alex.

In spite of his determination, the sound of rain beating down and a low rumble of thunder pulled him from sleep.

He shifted a little, just enough to discover the empty space next to him. A moment of relief did little to ease the remorse lying heavy on his chest.

Making love had never felt so right or been so wrong as last night with Alex.

He pried one eye open and registered the bright sunshine bathing the room.

Sunshine and rain? Something's out of whack.

He forced both eyes open and looked directly into Ansel's dark amber stare. That explained the rumble and a little of the weight on his chest. The cat licked Ryan's nose with a sandpapery tongue then yawned, showing every one of its razor-sharp teeth.

"I'll be takin' that as a threat." Ryan lifted the cat off his chest and rolled to a sitting position. Alex being in the shower accounted for the "rain". And the empty bed beside him.

He didn't like admitting it, but he was grateful for the momentary reprieve.

"Come on, cat. Let's feed you before you decide I look

like breakfast.'' Ryan pulled his running shorts on and padded into the kitchen. He wasn't trying to avoid Alex. He was doing her a favor and feeding the cat.

Liar, his conscience whispered.

He busied himself putting fresh water out for the cat, starting the coffeepot brewing and putting a kettle of water on for Alex's tea. Then he consulted with Ansel on which can of food to open.

None of the tactics worked to keep his conscience quiet. He wouldn't deny that making love with Alex had been the most pleasurable experience of his life. From her response, he was pretty confident she'd enjoyed the encounter as well.

None of that excused the fact that he'd made love to her under false pretenses at a time when she was vulnerable.

She deserved someone who would be there for her for the long run, someone to help her through all the minefields that were sure to crop up. Especially if she never fully recovered her memories.

Amnesia left her exposed. She needed protection and he wasn't the man for the job. No way in hell could a short-timer like him do much more than add on a heap more hurt.

A gentleman didn't take advantage of a lady like that, no matter if the pleasure was mutual. Whatever else his failings, he tried to live up to certain standards.

Just now, he figured his mamas, all eight of them, would be mighty ashamed of him.

THE SCENT OF FRESH COFFEE filled the air, drawing Alex to the kitchen. That's where she found Ryan. The morning sun streamed over his sculpted body, a corona of gold rimmed his sleep-tousled, sun-bleached hair. He leaned against the counter, arms crossed over his chest and Ansel at his feet, happily scarfing down a plate of food.

She wavered between wanting to capture the image of him on film and wanting to drag him back to the bedroom.

Last night had opened her eyes to what could exist between a man and a woman when they cared for each other.

Loved each other.

That understanding had finally pushed its way to the foreground where she couldn't deny what existed for her. Ryan hadn't said anything, but his actions spoke volumes. The combination of what she knew and what she believed developed into a contentment she hadn't felt in far too long.

He looked at her and she read the regret in his expression. All it took was that oh-so-brief glance to douse the pleasant glow she'd held close since waking.

She strolled across the kitchen, opened a cupboard only to realize Ryan had set out everything she needed to make tea. Maybe she was mistaken. Had she misread the look in his eyes?

Perhaps it was just a matter of getting past the awkward first morning-after jitters. To break the ice she offered a cheery "Good morning."

"Mornin'." Ryan mumbled his response. No welcoming smile, no reaching to pull her into his arms, no what-took-you-so-long kiss.

Disappointment at his response overshadowed the hope she refused to release. The two emotions congealed into a thick lump in her stomach.

"You beat me out here." All she needed to do was act normal, pretend nothing had changed between them. He'd realize there was nothing to regret.

"Your cat threatened to eat me for breakfast." He didn't even glance at her.

She died a little and welcomed the excuse to reframe her attention. "He is at that awkward age when he's more legs than sense and hungry all the time."

Ryan watched the gangly, adolescent feline lick the plate clean. She watched Ryan. He never glanced her way, not once.

He didn't need to. His feelings were abundantly clear. For him, last night had been a huge mistake.

Regret of her own wormed around her heart. Wishful thinking had taken her down the wrong path. Again.

At least she seemed to be learning. This time she'd realized her mistake quickly enough, before she'd allowed her imaginings to fully develop.

She was a big girl. She could handle this. It didn't have to disintegrate any further.

The shrill whistle of the teakettle broke the silence. Ryan had already filled her mug with hot water so it would be warmed for brewing her tea. The gesture, small and insignificant, had her eyes stinging with tears she wouldn't allow to fall. *So much for being a big girl.*

She emptied the mug and dropped a tea bag in. Maybe he couldn't admit it, but he did care about her. Just a little bit.

As she poured boiling water over the bag she glanced at Ryan. "Are you running?"

His head snapped up and he finally looked at her. "What do you mean?"

She focused on swirling her tea bag through the hot water. If she could tolerate weak tea she would have fled the kitchen right then. Instead, she poured a cup of coffee and handed it to him. "I meant, are you going for your morning run?"

"Oh." He glanced at the clock on the wall, a slightly hunted look on his face. "Yes."

She searched his face but his features had settled into a mask, eliminating any further clues to his thoughts. "What did you think I meant?"

"Nothing."

"Ryan." This hurt, more than she had imagined. "About last night."

He took a swallow from his cup, grimaced and set it aside. "I'm sorry about last night."

Not exactly the response she'd expected or hoped for, but at least he was talking to her. "I'm not."

"I took advantage of you."

"I don't see how." She doctored her tea with milk and sugar, took a bracing swallow and turned to face him. "As I recall, I was a willing participant through the entire process." *That's right. Keep the focus on the physical.*

"You deserve better."

Better? "Let me see if I have this straight. We had mind-blowingly wonderful sex, and I deserve better." She took another sip of tea. "Okay. When can we try for that?"

He actually blushed at her teasing. "You know that's not what I meant."

"No, I don't suppose it is." The brief moment of humor faded out. "Perhaps you should explain exactly what you're thinking."

He pushed away from the counter and paced to the other side of the kitchen, putting all the distance between them that he could achieve in the confined space.

She wrapped both hands around her mug, clinging to it like a shield.

"The situation has changed. I'm not on leave anymore, and I can't help you as I'd intended." He avoided looking at her. "I've been assigned to track down a missing agent."

A chill seeped over her in spite of the warm mug clutched against her chest. She didn't really need to ask the question, but she did anyway. "It's David, isn't it?"

Ryan nodded. "I shouldn't say anything to you, but

you'll find out soon enough. The SAC has some concerns about how he disappeared.''

"I should hope so. Doesn't the Bureau always 'have concerns' when one of their agents turns up missing?''

"Particularly in a case like this. They don't know if he's dead. What they do know is that he's been behaving rather erratic lately. He asked for a day off and hasn't reported in since. That sort of thing tends to alarm the Bureau.''

"But you know different.'' She took a step toward him, one hand outstretched.

He held his hands up and took a step away from her. "I know what you've told me.''

"I see.'' The hope she'd clung to dimmed. Ryan didn't believe her, didn't trust her to have told him the truth.

"I'm sorry, baby. There are so many holes in this case it's looking like well-aged Swiss cheese. I have to investigate everything. That includes anything you've already told me and anything you can add.''

"So you can clear David and disprove the Bureau's suspicion? Or so you can disprove what I've said?''

"It's not that easy.''

"Of course it is.''

"Alex.'' He took a step toward her. "Last night…''

Comprehension hit her with the brilliance of a thousand-watt flash. "I'm so stupid.'' It was her turn to step back, putting distance between them. "I should have realized. This is just an assignment for you. I'm a part of the assignment. And a good agent, which you are, will use any means necessary to obtain the information he needs.''

She forced down another swallow of tea. The rest she dumped down the drain. "I'm sorry if your fact-finding efforts fell short last night. Perhaps next time you'll have greater success if you stick to traditional interrogation methods.''

She left the kitchen to retrieve her equipment from her bedroom. When she returned, Ryan hadn't moved.

"Last night wasn't about information. Believe anything else about me, but not that." His words left an ache in her throat.

"Whatever your intentions may have been, the moment you accepted your assignment, all I could be to you is an informant." She headed for the door. "If you believe otherwise, you're only kidding yourself."

"Where are you going?"

She stopped but didn't look at him. "I will be scouting locations for Jamie's portrait for approximately one half hour, during which time I will remain on the estate. Then I will meet Jamie on his patio. When we've completed our shoot, I'll come back here.

"Unless," she turned to face him, "you prefer that I stay in his custody until your return."

He couldn't look her in the eyes for very long. "Jamie probably wouldn't mind if you borrowed one of his cars and ran to the lab for your film."

"That won't be necessary. No need to tie up an agent's time with following me. Besides, I'm sure you'd much prefer to be the first to look at the film so you can be reasonably certain there was no tampering involved."

She paused for a moment, hoping he'd deny anything, if not everything she'd just said.

He didn't.

A piece of her heart died. Blinking back a film of tears, she left the guest cottage.

RYAN SHORTENED HIS RUN by half so he'd have time to talk to Jamie before leaving for the Field Office. He jogged up to the patio.

Jamie, with his usual uncanny timing, slid open the patio door and leaned against the doorjamb. "Good morning."

"So I've been told." Ryan picked up one of the towels at the patio edge. Images seared his memory. Alex, her toenails painted crimson, the moonlight silvering her hair, the soft velvet of her skin against his.

"Something's happened, I take it?" Jamie asked.

"I need your help, if the offer still stands." Ryan scowled at the towel, damning the harmless fabric for prompting memories that only led to pain. "I've got a real bad feeling about the situation with Angelini. The agent in charge has his take on things. Alex has hers. Nothing matches up very well and I'm finding it mighty hard to maintain any kind of neutrality."

"I see."

In more ways than you're telling me, I bet. "I need to run Alex's prints. Did you remember—"

"Your request that I not wash the wineglass she used? Of course. I sealed it in a clean plastic bag and have already put it in the Explorer for you."

"Thanks." The order to get Alex's prints was pretty standard. Even so, handling it this way seemed underhanded. He should have just asked her outright to give him samples before he reported to the Field Office yesterday.

Now it was too late. Making the request today would only reinforce her belief that she was under suspicion.

"What else would you like me to do?"

"What you always do. Listen, watch, perceive. Find out the truth."

"Truth can be elusive. Especially when it doesn't look the way you expect." Jamie crossed the patio to stand beside him. "I'll do what I can but I can't guarantee any specific results."

Ryan nodded. "I know. There's the damn notebook, too. It might not mean anything."

"Or it could mean a great deal."

"I'll bring it by later, maybe you could take a crack at it?"

"Certainly."

"If you find out anything while you're working with Alex…" He pushed his hair away from his face. Asking Jamie to do all this didn't sit well. The whole situation smacked of distrust. He sighed. "We'll talk later."

"Am I to focus strictly on the Angelini case?"

Ryan didn't respond. The implications of his answer would reveal too much to Jamie. And to himself.

"Ryan, is the nature of your inquiry FBI business?" Jamie wore his time-to-face-the-truth expression. "Or is it personal?"

"Yes." He turned to leave and spotted Alex coming around the corner of the house. He turned back to Jamie. "No. It's business, strictly business. Anything else would be…it's business. That's all it can ever be."

"If you believe that, you're going to lose the one thing you've always wanted."

"Thanks for the warning, but you're too late." He watched Alex approach. "I've already lost," he whispered

"Am I interrupting?" She stopped a few feet back from the patio border, a guarded look on her face.

"I was just leaving." Ryan stepped off the patio, realized he still held the unused towel in his hand and hesitated. He held the towel out to her, wondering how much she hated him.

Alex accepted the towel, taking care their fingers didn't inadvertently touch.

For an instant, she held her breath, wondering if he'd reach for her. Then his hand fell to his side. Disappointment and relief overlapped, creating an uneasy mix of emotion.

Ryan turned halfway back to Jamie. "I'll swing by later this afternoon."

Since he didn't seem to be addressing either of them directly, she didn't try to formulate an answer. He walked by without sparing her a glance. She watched him leave then turned to find Jamie watching her.

"Won't you come in?" He stepped back to allow her room to pass. "I was just brewing some tea. Would you like some?"

Tension ebbed from her shoulders. "Yes, I'd like that very much. Thank you."

She sat at the kitchen counter and watched Jamie prepare a light breakfast. Today he had dressed all in black, the clothes tailor-made and striking with an understated elegance.

Over toast and juice, they discussed possible locations around the estate to use as backgrounds for his portrait.

She immersed herself in their project, blocking out any doubts of Jamie's intention for wanting to accomplish the shoot today. The timing was coincidental and had nothing to do with him keeping an eye on her while Ryan was occupied elsewhere.

For three exhilarating hours, she focused on Jamie and capturing a shot worthy of his presence. When she hit the end of the tenth roll of film, she stopped. "Thank you, Jamie. I needed this—" she held up her Nikon "—more than I realized."

She clipped the lens cap back in place and busied herself stowing her equipment back in the bag.

When she stood, she realized Jamie hadn't moved from his last pose, his eyes seemed fixed on some point behind her.

She glanced over her shoulder but didn't see anything other than rocks and sky. She looked back. "Jamie? We're done."

He closed his eyes and gave a little nod, then looked at her. "Finished already?"

"Three minutes ago. Did you…" She didn't know how to finish the question.

"I feel in need of some refreshment. What about you? You've been working very hard, you must be exhausted."

Photography never tired her. The excitement of creating energized her rather than drained her. The same couldn't be said for Jamie. He'd cooperated with her, humored her, provided her with distraction. Now it was past time for her to let him resume his normal activities.

They returned to the house and Jamie excused himself for a few minutes. She spent the time sorting through all the film she'd shot. When he returned, he'd changed into a light colored shirt and shorts. It was the most casual she'd seen him.

"I hope you don't mind." He gestured at his clothes. "It's refreshing to relax a bit. I never would have guessed posing could take so much attention and concentration."

"I hope you didn't find it too arduous."

"Not at all."

"You sort of…disappeared for a couple minutes, as we were finishing."

Jamie nodded.

"What happened?"

He studied her for a moment with those eerie blue eyes. "I'm not sure you're ready."

She stiffened. "What do you mean?"

"I apologize." He held up his hands in a placating gesture. "A poor choice of words. I think you are ready for the message, rather the timing is not optimal. But then, it seldom is."

"Message?"

"I'm not sure how familiar you are with psychic abilities. I'm primarily clairaudient, I hear things. Sometimes, though, I will see images as well."

Up to this point, she hadn't spared a great deal of

thought for Jamie's talent. His statement piqued her curiosity. Now she was left to wonder if how much credence she gave to the messenger would depend on the message.

Jamie brought out a pitcher of iced tea and filled two tall frosted glasses. He handed her one, capturing her with his steady gaze. "I've sensed a presence about you since we met. Today I saw him, which is some indication of how insistent he was for me to acknowledge him."

"Him?" Her mouth went dry and she took a sip of tea.

"Justin."

She sank against the counter, gulping more of the cold liquid to wash down the lump in her throat. "What did he want?" *What did she believe?*

"He wanted you to know that David has joined him and they are all right. That everything will work out." Jamie sighed. "He said that, above all else, you should trust yourself."

Her head jerked up at that. "Trusting myself has seldom proved to be the wisest choice."

"Nevertheless, that is Justin's message."

"Just like that, I'm supposed to trust myself and everything will be okay?" Her hand shook as she set her glass on the counter. "You were right. I'm not ready for that message."

"I didn't say you would like it, but you are ready."

She stared at her half-emptied glass, wishing the answer would appear among the crackling ice cubes.

"Follow your heart," Jamie said. "When the time comes, you will make the right decision."

"Is that Justin's recommendation or yours?"

"Justin's, however I wouldn't be honest if I were to say I didn't concur."

"And Ryan?" She'd followed her heart into Ryan's arms and bed last night. Look where it got her—the head of his suspect list.

That whole fiasco was still too fresh for her to believe Ryan's friend with blind faith. "How much of the 'message' is influenced by your friendship with Ryan? Did he…" She searched for the right words. She didn't want to insult Jamie, but she needed to know. "Did Ryan suggest some portion of Justin's 'message'?"

"Ryan is an honorable man. He has challenges of his own that he needs to overcome. But he would never suggest that I falsify information." Jamie refilled her glass. "Nor would I, if he had."

"I'm sorry, Jamie, but I had to ask."

He nodded acceptance of her apology. "I do understand."

Neither spoke, each lost in their own thoughts. A clock in the living room chimed the hour, breaking the spell.

"Enough contemplation." Jamie smiled at her. "Tell me, what is the next step in our photographic project. I'm quite anxious to see the end result."

"As am I." She waved a hand over the array of film canisters. "Which means developing the film is next."

"Would you like to use my darkroom?"

"Yes, please." Excitement thrummed along her nerves.

Jamie laughed. "You look like a small child on Christmas morning."

"I feel like a kid at Christmas. Whenever I can, I talk Kimo into letting me do my own processing and printing." She ran her fingers across the canisters. "Working in the darkroom for me is a vital connection between the first glimmer of an idea and the final piece. You're really okay with letting me use your darkroom?"

"Right this way." He led her through the house. "I just restocked the chemicals and laid in a supply of paper, so you should have everything you need for black-and-white or color."

He showed her around the small room and helped her

organize the necessary materials. The metallic tang of the chemicals acted as a balm, making her feel at home with each breath. She soon lost herself in the chemistry of film development and never noticed him leave.

She didn't take a break until she completed developing all the film. When she finally left the darkroom she found Jamie relaxing in the living room. The scented candles flickered and filled the air with their exotic aromas.

He rose to his feet as she entered. "Are you hungry?"

She shook her head, but didn't sit down. Instead, she paced the width of the room. "This is the hardest part. I can see the images but can't do anything until the film is dry."

"Ah, yes. 'Patience is a virtue.'"

"One of which I'm in short supply."

Jamie chuckled. "Nonetheless, it is well past lunch and you've eaten nothing since that meager slice of toast this morning. I'm not about to let my resident artist faint from hunger. Come along, Alexandra." He crossed the room and led her out to the kitchen.

The instant she finished the salad he set in front of her, she excused herself. The negatives would be dry. The time had come to discover their secrets.

Chapter Thirteen

"Alex?" Ryan called out as he entered the cottage. Ansel trotted up to greet him, but there was no sign of Alex.

Ryan dropped the bag from Kimo's lab on the counter and walked through the cottage. A fear he wouldn't name grew.

There was no sign of her anywhere. Her camera bag was also missing. He stood in the door to her bedroom. The dress she'd worn last night hung from the closet door, the high-heeled sandals on the floor underneath. Other than that, there was little evidence of her presence.

An aching loneliness coiled in Ryan's chest. Every minute he'd spent away from her had crawled like a sinner headed for a prayer meeting. Only a couple days of knowing her and he missed her at his side.

Ansel stretched against his leg, reaching up like a child asking to be picked up. Ryan leaned down to pet the cat. "What am I going to do, Ansel? I think I really blew it."

Ever since she'd walked out of the cottage that morning, growing guilt and regret had gnawed at him. All day, everything he'd worked on reminded him of her, of the night before, of everything he'd never had and found with her.

He wanted that connection. He wanted to be needed by someone for himself, not for his job. He wanted to wake up in the morning in a home that he'd created with the woman he loved.

That Alex was that woman, not just a victim needing his help or a witness he needed to protect, had been abundantly clear. Once he forced himself to look he couldn't escape the truth. Even before they'd made love, there had been a connection beyond anything he could rationalize away.

She'd given herself to him completely, and he'd insulted her, doubting her and denying his trust.

"At least I can be reasonably sure she hasn't disappeared for good. As long as you're still here, I might have a chance." The cat flopped over onto its back in an unsubtle hint for a belly rub. Ryan complied. "I'm not quite sure how I'm going to fix things. I only know that this time, I can't fail."

He retrieved the coded notebook from its hiding place—another piece of business he should have been up front with her about. Giving it to her now would probably add another sin to the growing list.

Or…he could return it to the camera bag. If she hadn't remembered it existed yet, she wouldn't know it was missing.

The idea held some attraction, but it would be the coward's way out. He needed to be honest with Alex. She deserved more, but it was all he could offer her.

He scooped up the bag from Kimo's lab as he headed out the door for Jamie's.

THE PATIO DOOR SILENTLY closed behind him as he entered the main house. Alex's voice drew him toward the living room.

"My camera bag?" Panic laced through her words. An answering tension stabbed through him.

"In the kitchen, right where you left it," Jamie answered. "What's wrong?"

Ryan froze where he stood. Alex gave no indication of seeing him as she rushed past. Jamie stopped beside him, shaking his head in answer to Ryan's silent question.

Alex dropped some papers onto the table. Her hands shook as she grabbed her camera bag and laid it on its side. She began unscrewing one of the footpads.

You're damned for sure now, boyo. Ryan's heart fell someplace down around his knees.

"Alex." Jamie's soft voice had no visible effect on her. "Speak to me, tell me what's happening."

"Memories started coming back." She spared them a quick glance as she removed one pad and began on another. "Memories from three nights ago, when I went out with David."

The second pad came off and she set to work on the last two simultaneously. The excitement and fear coursing through her were nearly palpable. "I still don't remember everything. But I do remember he gave me something and told me to hide it. He didn't want to know where. He only needed to know it was someplace safe."

The final pads pulled free. Ryan wanted to stop her, tell her he already had the book, but it wouldn't do any good until they cracked the code.

She looked up as she pried the bottom off. "Whatever it is, I put it in here. It was the only place I could think of."

The bottom fell away from the bag, revealing the empty space.

She sank to a chair. Tears welled in her eyes and clogged her voice. "No."

Ryan kneeled beside her. He tucked a strand of hair behind her ear, cupping her face in his hand. Any lingering doubt about her knowledge of the book dissolved with her tears.

"It's got to be there." She looked at him finally. All of the pain and anguish in her eyes set off an echoing ache in his throat. "I didn't just imagine it. I know I didn't."

"You didn't, baby."

He pulled the sandwich bag containing the notebook out of the lab bag and laid it in her lap.

She picked up the bag, turning it over and over in her hands. "You had it?"

He nodded.

"You found this—" She frowned, her eyes narrowing as she looked from the bag to him. "Where? Where did you get this?"

"Right where you were looking. In the false bottom of the bag."

She leaned back in the chair. "How long?"

The anger behind her words had the same effect as if she'd shoved him away. He sank back to sit on his heels. At the time, his actions had been appropriate. At least he'd thought so. "Since the first morning."

"And you didn't say anything?"

He shook his head.

Pain darkened her eyes. "You hid it from me?"

"I know it looks like that, but—"

"I trusted you. All this time you've had something that might help me regain my memory, something that might help find David's killer, and you kept it from me?"

"I know, baby." He hung his head, unable to meet her accusing look. "I'm sorry."

"What were you going to do with it? Were you ever even going to tell me you had it?" Her words ripped through him.

He'd failed her. He should have shown her the book as soon as he'd found it.

But he hadn't. Added to his morning-after bad behavior…his own actions condemned him.

Nothing he could say would make up for his failure, but he had to try. "I thought it might give some lead to what was going on, what had happened to you."

"Did it?"

He shook his head. "It's in some kind of code. I was fixin' to turn it over to the experts in Quantico. They'll be able to figure it out, and then we can settle…" His words died in his throat.

She tore open the bag and pulled the book out. As she leafed through the pages, she read snippets of information.

Ryan stared at her, uncomprehending at first. The words broke through the confusion warring in his brain and began to make sense. "You know the code?"

She glared at him with icy gray eyes. "If you'd bothered to ask two days ago, I would have told you."

"If you'd remembered."

"I would have remembered. It's as familiar to me as my camera. We made this code up, David and Justin and I, when we were kids, so we could play spy and pass secret notes to each other."

"The two different handwritings?"

"This was Justin's book. We found it among his things after he disappeared. He was investigating a ring of corrupt law-enforcement officers. It was a small group, but it included both police and FBI. After he was killed, David took up the battle."

"With your help."

"For all the good I did him."

"You protected the evidence. You documented the meeting." Ryan leaned toward her. Maybe there was a chance yet. Maybe he could redeem himself. "If you translate the code for me, I can finish it. I swear to you, if it's the last thing I do, I'll find their killers for you."

He dumped the remaining contents of the bag on the table. "Kimo sent the film and contact prints. Show me David's killer."

"He's the one with the gun. That should be easy enough to figure out, even for someone with vision as narrowed as yours."

The dig hurt, but far less than he deserved. "I haven't looked at the film."

That got her to look at him. "Why not?"

"Because it's yours, and it's your choice whether or not I see it."

Alex pulled the sealed envelopes across the table. He'd told the truth. None of the envelopes had been opened. Later, she would try figuring out what it might all mean. Right now, she needed to see the film.

She pried open the flap on the first packet. Several sheets of contacts and sleeved negatives slithered onto the table. She glanced at the images, pushed them aside and opened the next envelope.

The fourth envelope produced contents that held her attention. She reached for the loupe she'd brought out of the darkroom and tilted the contact sheet toward the light to see better. David's image stared at her through the lens.

Words stuck in her throat as she gathered the contacts and film and stood.

Ryan rose with her. He would have followed her, she could see it in his eyes, but Jamie held him back.

The darkroom door closed behind her, sealing her away from Ryan and all the mixed-up emotions he stirred.

Printing Jamie's photos had held the comfort of routine. She convinced herself this session would be no different as the dim red safety light washed over the workspace. The illusion held all through the setup, the focusing and paper selection, the test print. Right up until she took in the negative image projected on the stark white photographic paper.

David, empty hands raised in a futile effort to stop the inevitable. Her throat closed on her silent cry, same as it had that night.

The muzzle flash of the gun as the fatal shot was fired. Her chest tightened, keeping her heart from falling into a million pieces.

The face of the shooter. Her tears blurred the details.

She let the emotions swamp her for the few seconds it took to expose the paper. When the light went out, she stared through the darkness, battling the pain.

Everything fell to her now. The pictures she'd taken held the only hope of bringing David's killer to justice. And Justin's. The two were related, they had to be. The notebook would prove that.

She slipped the paper into the developer bath and waited for the image of her nightmare to appear.

Murder.

Mechanics took over as she moved the photo through each step then hung it to dry. She turned back to the enlarger, adjusted the framing, cropping in tighter, blowing up the image, pushing the limits of the film and her endurance.

Tears cooled her burning eyes. Somehow it all tied back to her. If she could remember, she could get Ryan to believe her. He'd help figure it out. He had to.

She gathered the damp prints and returned to the bright sunlit kitchen.

''The images are pretty grainy from being blown up so large.'' She tossed the eight-by-tens on the table. ''We could run them through a computer program, make it easier to identify the men.''

Ryan poked at the sheets, turning them to get a better

look. "No need." He almost spat the words. "They're plenty clear."

"You recognize them?" She rested her head in her hands, too exhausted to sit upright.

Pointing at one of the men he said, "Meet Special Agent Tim Pela, of the FBI's Honolulu Field Office."

"FBI?" Her stomach did a slow roll.

He nodded. "I met with him today so he could fill me in on all the evidence that seems to be piling up against David."

"Then it's my word against a federal agent. No one's going to believe me, not once—" She took a shuddering breath. "With David unable to defend himself, there's no one to stop him."

"That's what he's thinking."

"They know about me. They must."

"Pela never mentioned you. My guess is he's fixin' to find you himself and tie up all the loose ends nice and neat."

"You didn't tell him about me?"

"No, I never got around to talking about what I was doing to keep busy. Besides which, I don't figure who I have as a houseguest is any of ole Pela's business."

She studied Ryan. Clenched fists and a cold glitter in his eye radiated his anger. There was no mistaking the fact that he believed what he saw in the picture.

A little of her tension eased. The photo provided some backup to what she'd remembered, and he was on her side. For the moment.

Would he have been so quick to believe her if she'd told him everything she'd remembered?

"That boy was a bit too nervous for my taste. It suits me fine if he thinks I'm coming on the case completely cold. Far as he's concerned, I don't know any of the people involved, I don't know you, I don't know about you."

"What about the other agents? There were a couple that David worked with on a regular basis. Surely one of them—"

"Pela kept me pretty isolated today. I haven't met any of the other agents yet. A few were out on assignment, the rest Pela did his best to keep me away from. He claimed it was to protect David's privacy, on the 'slim chance' that it was all a misunderstanding and David is actually innocent of any wrongdoing."

"Do you think Pela was the one to search my house?"

"Hard to tell. It might have been someone else in the ring."

"What about the man we followed from Kimo's? We saw him at the lab twice. He might have made the connection between us. Do you think he's FBI, too?"

"I don't know, baby. I'm working on getting info on the locals and trying to track down the owner of that address we followed the guy to. All that will add more pieces to the puzzle."

"But if he works for Pela, what if he's made the connection between us?"

"I don't think Pela's the leader. He strikes me more as a soldier in this than a commander."

"So we need him to take us to the head of the ring." Hope began to bloom, and she leaned toward Ryan, excitement thrumming through her veins. "We can set him up, just like he's trying to set up and discredit David."

"What do you mean 'we'?"

"We, as in you and me. You need me to translate the book."

Ryan nodded slowly. "Yeah, I got that. But that's the end of your involvement."

"Not by a long shot." She stood, confronting him. "They, whoever *they* are, know I have something. I'm the only one who can deliver it."

"Oh, no. You are not going in harm's way. I won't allow it."

"'Allow.' She raised an eyebrow in disbelief. "You don't have any choice. It's me or no one. You can't do it yourself and until this is cleaned up, you don't know who to trust."

"I'll know as soon as you translate that book for me."

They stood across the table from each other, mirror-image poses with their hands on their hips and their feet braced apart.

Ryan looked the most intimidating, but she wasn't going to give in to him. The risks were too high. "Without the codebook, you have nothing."

"With the codebook, your life is in danger."

"Not if they think there's more to it."

That got Ryan's attention. "What else is there?"

"Nothing. But they don't need to know that, do they? I give them a partial of the book, but make it clear there's more. They won't dare hurt me until they're certain they have everything that might be incriminating to them. Especially if they think it's possible the entire translation could go out in the open."

"I shouldn't involve a civilian. That sort of thing never ends well."

He was weakening, she could tell. "I'm already involved. Face it, Ryan. No matter which way you try to come at this, you need me."

HE NEEDED HER ALL RIGHT. But not out in the field where she could get killed.

She'd been busy writing out a translation of the book all evening, making a list of people involved, payments, dates, information transferred. With each name she added, the scope of what they were looking at grew. As it stood, the situation was well beyond what he could handle on his own.

He needed reinforcements, but they would have to be from the mainland. He couldn't risk any of the local agents, or anyone from the police.

He checked his watch. It was 8 p.m. Hawaiian standard time, which made it 2 a.m. on the East Coast. Jacquelyn wouldn't be in the office for another six, maybe seven hours. Making it three in the morning on Oahu.

No problem there. He'd set the alarm and start calling until she got in. He'd arrange with her for the right people to be sent. Then there'd be another delay while she assembled the team and they were transported.

Any way he looked at it, it'd be a couple days before they would have all the players in place. He scrubbed his face with both hands, trying to eradicate the impatience pushing him to take action now.

Planning the course of action in any detail would be impossible until the team arrived. He couldn't help Alex with the translation. There was nothing for him to do.

He looked at Alex, hunched over the table in the guest cottage kitchen. The instant they'd gotten back, she'd started transcribing. She paused in her writing to shake out her hand.

Correction. There was one thing he could do.

"That's enough for now, sugar." He crossed the room and took the pen from her resistant grip. "I don't know about you, but I'm near to starving."

"Have some cookies." She grabbed the pen from his hand.

"Alex, you've been working on that for hours now, and you need to take a break."

"It's only been two hours and twenty-three minutes. I'm barely started."

"Baby—" Ryan took a deep breath and let it out

slowly, then crouched beside her chair. "How long is it going to take you to transcribe that entire book?"

"I'd be a lot further if I'd started two days ago."

He didn't flinch from her anger.

She leafed through what she'd completed and her shoulders sagged. "It's taking longer than I thought it would. I'll probably need a couple days to do the whole thing. Maybe more, depending on how often I'm interrupted. But I'm getting faster as I go along, so it could be less."

"Don't rush. It's more important that it get done right, than fast."

"Maybe I should skip to the last section in David's handwriting." She began to flip pages in the notebook.

He rested his hand over hers. "Do the whole book. It'll be safer that way. We'll have a better idea of who all the players are."

She pulled away from his touch and nodded. He couldn't resist brushing his hand through her long hair, smoothing it over her shoulder and down her back. She shifted in the chair, leaning away from him.

He'd have to be a complete idiot to miss the signals her body language was sending. She wasn't about to forgive him.

He wasn't about to give up. "By my reckoning, it'll be a good four days before we can put that information to use. Which means you have time to take a break for a sandwich and a walk on the beach."

"Are sandwiches all you know how to make?" She didn't smile. But she didn't say no, either.

"They're quick, easy, portable. What more do you want from a meal?"

"Portable?"

"An important characteristic when the intention is to dine alfresco."

"I see." She looked back at the codebook.

He could almost read her mind, the expression on her face was so transparent. "Tell you what. You keep translating. I'll prepare the food. When I'm done, you take a break. Deal?"

She nodded, still reluctant, but at least she'd agreed.

No doubt about it, he admired her determination. But determination wouldn't keep her safe when it came down to guns and traitors.

That thought sent a chill running through his bones. He'd promised to catch the Angelinis' killers but he wouldn't risk her life to accomplish it.

Sometime during the next few days, along with forcing her to take breaks, they were going to have a session on gun handling.

Chapter Fourteen

Jacquelyn sent three agents to work with Ryan. He met them at the airport thirty-six hours after he'd placed the first call. John Danse, the agent he'd met on his last assignment in Montana, came off the plane first.

"Jacquelyn gave me the report on your friend." He shook hands with Ryan. "We need to talk."

"You've read it?"

John nodded, his expression grim. "I haven't shared it with the others yet."

"But it doesn't look good?"

John shook his head. He seemed reluctant to say anything else.

Ryan turned away and watched as other passengers debarked from the plane. "A rap sheet doesn't always tell the whole story."

"True enough."

"How bad is it?"

"You'll have to be the judge of that." John pulled a file out of his carry-on bag and handed it to Ryan. "As team leader, it's up to you when and how much the others know."

He took the file but made no move to read it. The other two agents, Carly and Matt Adams came down the gangway. Normally, married agents weren't assigned together, but availability and their particular skills made them the best choice for this situation.

While the team claimed their luggage Ryan glanced through the file. The name and mug shot attached to the fingerprint search matched Alex, but the list of alleged offenses had to belong to someone else. An outstanding arrest warrant listed drugs, blackmail…his gut clenched in a sour knot.

He couldn't believe the woman he'd come to know would have willingly participated in these crimes. The pieces didn't fit.

Of course, how well did he know her? Based on the information in the file, he had to wonder just how far his emotions had led him astray.

His gut instincts had saved his behind on many an occasion. The possibility that he'd lost that edge didn't sit well.

There had to be more to the story. If there wasn't, the Angelinis were guilty of obstruction of justice at the very least. Was it the beginning of a pattern that had led to their deaths?

Ryan used the drive to Jamie's estate to explain the basic situation and fill in the team on what they knew so far, stopping short of reviewing the contents of Alex's file.

John didn't say anything about the omission. He didn't need to. Ryan read all sorts of meaning into the silence, knowing he would have thought the same if the situation were reversed.

He also knew how pissed off he'd be to discover this kind of information had been held back during a briefing. It wouldn't be fair to the team to keep them in the dark. But he couldn't bring himself to damn Alex in their eyes before they even met her. She deserved a chance to prove herself.

As they neared the estate, Ryan made his decision. ''We

ran Alex's prints and Jacquelyn sent the file.'' The fact that a file existed conveyed a certain amount of information. ''Once you've met Alex, we'll sort out all the information.''

''You want us to form our own conclusions?'' Carly asked from the back seat.

Ryan met her steady gaze in the rearview mirror. ''I need a fresh read on the situation.''

Carly didn't respond, but her raised eyebrows as she exchanged a glance with Matt hinted at her thoughts.

Way to go, boyo. Why not just flat out tell them you've fallen for her and have no perspective.

ALEX TORE ANOTHER SHEET from the tablet of paper and reviewed the information she'd translated. With each page, vague memories had come into focus. The transactions documented in the notebook revealed a pattern, one she recognized from her days in Los Angeles.

The return of Ryan with the newly arrived agents saved her from further contemplation of what the similarities could mean.

Introductions were completed and the usual polite travel inquiries answered. With the social niceties met, she turned over the pages she'd translated then disappeared into the guest bedroom where she could work without distraction.

While she continued decoding the book, the others tackled their own tasks. According to Ryan, Carly was a computer whiz, and she'd put her skills to work digging up material on each name decoded.

John and Matt were going to drive around the island, familiarizing themselves with the lay of the land and assembling the equipment they'd need for the operation.

Ryan reviewed the translations and Carly's printouts, assembling dossiers on each person named. He also forced Alex to take an occasional break. More than once, he'd taken the pen and paper from her hands and insisted she stop.

Even then, she took her camera along, still working, but at least it was on something different. Something that didn't remind her of her friends' deaths.

The camera also served as a barrier against Ryan. He seemed to know she was hiding behind it and set on a determined campaign to lure her out. Even so, the longest she stayed away from the cottage was an hour. Most breaks were shorter. The notebook dragged her back.

Evenings were spent lounging in the living room, reviewing information, discussing scenarios, options, resources. Time was too tight to bring in additional operatives. The small team would have to rely on themselves and all probable outcomes needed to be considered.

Two days after their arrival Alex entered the kitchen and laid another sheaf of pages on the table. "That's everything." Her voice was barely above a whisper. All conversation stopped as Ryan read the final list of names, then passed it to the others. He stood and pulled her into his arms. "It's almost over, baby."

The days had taken their toll on her. She'd barely slept or eaten. Exhaustion dragged at her, weakening her resolve. For a few precious seconds she allowed Ryan's embrace to comfort her.

She pulled away from him and glanced at the other team members who were all politely comparing notes and studiously ignoring them. "What's the next step?"

Her question seemed to startle them. They looked from Ryan to her and back.

Ryan cleared his throat. "Now that we know all the players, we set up the sting."

"I don't think you do know all the players." Alex put some distance between herself and Ryan.

"What do you mean?" He stepped toward her then stopped at the shake of her head.

This was the opening she needed to tell them the truth. If Casey hadn't already done so, it would only be a matter of time before she dug into Alex's past and discovered that she really wasn't very different from the scum they were trying to capture.

So much to lose. Her heart thudded in her throat. David and Justin had lost even more. She owed it to them to finish the investigation. To do that, she needed to be honest with Ryan's team. They deserved to know the truth and it should come from her.

She took a deep breath and started. "Before the Angelinis brought me back to Oahu, I lived in Los Angeles. I had gotten involved with…" The words stuck in her throat. She swallowed around the choking knot and continued. "There was a blackmail operation. I've remembered more details than I'd like to, but not everything. Just enough to know there were drugs involved. And other women. Some younger than me."

"Vulnerable, easy targets." Matt picked up his equipment and focused on making minute adjustments.

Casey gave a little nod. "It's an old story that never seems to end."

"I was in rather deep." She crossed her arms over her stomach, clutching her elbows in a vain effort to ease the building nausea. "Very deep. The man at the head seemed to take a liking to me and allowed me access to certain information."

"That's in the past, baby. You don't have to—"

"Yes I do." She held up one hand, stopping Ryan from coming any closer. "Because that operation ran an awful lot like this one."

"You think they're connected?" John asked.

She nodded. "I recognize a couple names from the L.A.

operation, the transactions are similar. When I add in how secretive David and Justin were, it all ties together.''

''Who is the leader?'' Casey looked up from her laptop, her fingers poised above the keyboard. ''Do you remember his name?''

''Frank Sullivan.''

The soft clicking of computer keys filled the background as she continued. ''You probably won't find much, if anything, on him. He had a knack for protecting himself. Others always took the fall, out of loyalty or expediency.''

Matt grinned. ''If there's a byte of data on the man, Casey will find it.'' He rubbed his wife's shoulder, and the gesture seemed to convey his pride and love all at once.

The interplay triggered a longing in Alex. Would she ever have a chance at that kind of closeness? Ryan had offered her a small taste of what it could be like. She savored every second of their nascent closeness, but what chance did that have of ever developing into a reality after all this?

The team's casual acceptance of her past gave her some hope. No one gave any indication that knowing her history affected their attitude toward her. She would do everything in her power to prove herself worthy of their trust.

''You think Pela knows about your connection?'' John asked.

''I'm not sure. If Sullivan is behind this, and if Pela is one of the higher-ranking members of his ring…'' She shrugged.

''What about David? Would he have said anything?''

''David never cared for Pela. Even if he had, my background isn't exactly the kind you brag about.''

''True enough.'' Casey smiled at her. ''It's also true that sometimes facts take on greater importance than they warrant.''

Was Casey trying to tell her it didn't matter? Alex

looked at the men. Their expressions gave no hints to their thoughts, but their bodies revealed a nearly imperceptible easing of tension. "We can use my past to your advantage."

"What were you thinking?" John leaned against the counter, his legs crossed at the ankle.

The casual pose didn't fool her. Ryan might be the team leader, but John was the skeptic. He was the one she needed to convince this was their best course of action.

"We play their game. They're blackmailing politicians and corporate executives to achieve their goal. So, we blackmail them."

"You were right about Sullivan being clean." Casey looked up from her computer. "I haven't found anything on him."

"Yet," Matt interjected.

Casey smiled, but ignored her husband's interruption. "How do you propose we blackmail him?"

"They're already looking for me so they must suspect I have information, either on film or in writing. I offer to meet with the leader, using the notebook as leverage."

"You really think that will work?" John made no attempt to hide his skepticism.

"Sullivan's pride will work to our advantage. He'll want to stare down anyone foolish enough to challenge him at his own game."

"Are you up to facing him?" Casey sounded genuinely concerned about her.

"I'll have to be."

"You can't be serious." Ryan looked at each agent in turn. "You don't have to humor her. She's done her part. Now it's up to us."

"We don't have time for humor." John pushed away from the counter and faced Ryan. "What she's proposing has some merit."

"No. She's a civilian." She didn't have the training to participate. Ryan paced across the room, stopping in front of Alex. "Your role is done. You've provided us with all the information we need. We'll take it from here."

He wouldn't put her at risk. Her friends had tried to protect her. He could do no less. "Just give us a couple more days, then you can get back to something a little more normal."

Normal. For him that had come to mean having her around. Normal meant her sleeping across the hall from him. Normal meant waking with her cat on the pillow beside his head.

He wanted normal to include her sleeping in his bed, sheltered in his arms.

In the short time he'd known her, he'd come to relish the stolen moments with her. But once they completed this assignment, he'd be returning to DC where normal didn't include a woman or her cat.

Who would take care of her then?

"If someone else shows up with this in their hand," Alex held up the notebook, "no one is going to believe it's the real deal unless they provide an on-the-spot translation. To do that, you need someone who can translate on the spot. The only person who can do that is me."

"No." He refused to endanger the woman he loved.

Love? That wasn't what he meant. His stomach rolled over before climbing up his throat and threatening to choke him. He cared about her, sure, but love? Love meant making a commitment, being there to take care of her. Letting her get closer to him than she already had, closer than he'd let anyone get since his mother deserted him.

Love meant sharing his days with her, sleeping with her in his arms. Waking up with a cat on his pillow. Love meant a shot at normal.

If he really loved her, he'd be doing everything within

his power to protect her. Which was exactly what he intended to do.

"She has a point." Casey looked up from her computer and pinned him with a steady look.

"That's one of the reasons why you're here, sugar. If we need a woman to go in, you can stand in for Alex."

"Don't 'sugar' me, Williams." Casey leaned back in her chair and crossed her arms. Her narrowed gaze warned he was close to crossing some line he hadn't been aware of nearing. "The only resemblance I bear to Alex is my eye color."

"We can pick up a wig."

"Which doesn't do a thing for the inches she has on me in height, or the pounds I have on her in weight. These people aren't stupid. If a woman has to go in there, we may not have any choice but to send Alex."

"Then we'll just have to make sure it's not necessary."

"Jacquelyn warned me that you wouldn't like working with a woman. After your last case, I can understand your hesitancy."

"You're right. I don't believe in putting a *civilian,*" he emphasized the word, "in danger if it can be avoided."

He looked to the men for support. "You can't condone using a civilian in a situation that puts them in danger. John, come on. You know better than anyone the risks involved."

John's last assignment had reunited him with his estranged wife, a woman he hadn't seen in eight years. She'd nearly died when the mission went south big time. Ryan had barely found them in time. "How is Tommi?"

"Mostly healed and driving me crazy. She wouldn't let me decline this mission, you know, not when she found out it was you needing backup." John went to the refrigerator for the lemonade pitcher. He refilled all the glasses on the table before continuing. "We all know the risks. I also know it sometimes can't be helped. Sometimes the mission has to take precedence over personal sentiment.''

Personal. That's what it had become. If he were honest with himself, that's what it had been from the first moment he clapped eyes on Alex. He'd immediately appointed himself as her guardian.

The role had come naturally enough for him. Now they expected him to just let that go? He'd sooner gargle with donkey piss.

Ryan looked from one team member to the next. Their expressions held varying degrees of sympathy. They all understood what he was going through, had experienced the same sort of impossible situation themselves at one time or another in their careers.

''Fine.'' Ryan nearly choked on the word. He really didn't have much choice. Their options were limited and the odds weren't exactly stacked in their favor. Each agent had a role to fulfill. If they had any chance of bringing down Sullivan and his ring, they needed Alex to play bait in their trap. ''We use Alex. But she doesn't go in alone.''

THEY MOVED THEIR BASE of operations to Jamie's house the next morning, needing more space for their planning and equipment checks. Even so, what they had seemed pitifully small, considering what they needed to accomplish.

Jamie gave them complete access to his office and anything else he might have that would be of use to their operation.

Alex photocopied the notebook and her translations. As a backup, Casey used Jamie's computer setup to scan in the documents. Each page was transmitted back to Jacquelyn. If the worst case scenario played out and they were all killed, the Bureau would still be able to follow through and put an end to the blackmail ring.

Matt and John visited a rent-a-wreck where they picked up a van. The next step required rigging the vehicle with the equipment that would make it their mobile base of operations.

An array of equipment was spread around the office, ready to be tested. The only way someone would be with Alex was via a two-way transmitter. Ryan picked up a tiny earpiece and called to her.

She looked up from the copier and his gut tied into a knot of longing. When she'd volunteered the information about her past, he'd nearly shouted his relief. She'd taken the risk, revealed her vulnerability to the team and proved herself worthy of their trust. The others maybe weren't completely convinced, but he was.

She'd been less aloof since then, and he used every opportunity to continue eroding her defenses against him. He wanted to regain the closeness he'd barely tasted when they'd made love. He wanted to protect her. He couldn't put her in danger. She'd been through too much already.

As she walked toward him, every fiber of his being refused to accept that he had to use her on this mission. Every fiber except those few brain cells that insisted on functioning in agent mode.

They needed her or the operation was guaranteed to fail. He had to use her. He knew it and it was killing him.

"Casey has the last pages for scanning." Alex stood in front of him. "What's next?"

A number of suggestions played through his imagination. Most required getting as far from here as possible. *Right boyo. As if running away has ever been an option.*

He held out his hand, the earpiece nestled in his palm. "Next is trying this on for size."

He brushed her hair behind one ear and instructed her in the proper placement. It took a few adjustments and every second of being so close to her was sweet torture. Finally, she had the piece securely in place.

"This will be your only contact with us. It's a two-way receiver. I'll be able to hear everything you say and you'll hear me."

"Got it." She sounded a little breathless. "Let's give it a whirl."

Ryan slipped on his headset. Before she reached the far side of the room, he flipped the switch and whispered in the microphone. "Okay, baby. You should be able to hear me inside your head."

She turned and looked at him, her eyes rounding in surprise. "That is a very strange sensation."

He'd had a similar reaction the first time he used this particular bit of technology. It had left him with a peculiar sense of intimacy with the person speaking to him. "I know. It's kind of like I'm inside you."

She blushed and the secondary meaning of his words hit him with a tidal wave of heat. *Inside her.* He pushed that thought away. As much as he might want to carry her back to the guest cottage and lose himself in making love with her, that would have to wait until later. Provided they had a later.

He cleared his throat. "Keep walking. Head out to the patio and tell me what you see."

For the next hour they tested the equipment, made adjustments and retested. Matt and John finished rigging the van and another round of testing began. There weren't any redundant systems, and Ryan was determined to make damn sure everything worked properly before putting anyone in the field.

While they worked on the equipment, Jamie kept busy cooking for them. Ryan insisted he join them at the dinner table. Jamie'd been around enough operations and had the security clearance to be included in the discussions.

Plus, any fresh insights he might be able to provide wouldn't hurt.

They settled into the now common routine of reviewing what they knew. The gravel-voiced man who'd roughed up Kimo was Sam Walker, a police detective. Pela was FBI. Each had recruited additional members for the blackmail ring. Ryan and Alex had followed one of them the first day.

"The building you tailed him to belongs to a shadow corporation." Casey flipped through sheets of paper as she verified the details. "Which belongs to a holding company which is a subsidiary of another company. After a lot of digging, the trail of ownership led back to Pela and Walker." She frowned. "If Sullivan is involved, he's hidden it very well."

"There has to be another person higher up?" Jamie set a small tea service next to Alex and poured her a cup of tea. He then moved around the table with a coffeepot, filling everyone's cup with a fragrant brew.

John pushed his empty plate away. "An organization like this, with two leaders, would have imploded long before now."

"My mama always said if you play with pigs, the stink's gonna stick to you. We just need to find the sty this Sullivan has been hiding in."

"Based on what?" Alex's teacup rattled against the saucer. "All you have is a book decoded by me and my less-than-stellar memory."

"Sugar, once we get everyone into custody, somebody'll roll over and spill."

Alex shook her head. "He'll get away somehow."

"There's no place he can go that we won't find him." John's slight grin hinted at how much he'd enjoy the chase.

"So," Matt chimed in, "we just need to make sure this Sullivan character shows."

"Do we really think he'll come when he's been so careful to keep separate from the ring?" Casey sipped from her coffee cup. "We can't prove his involvement."

"No, we can't. Not yet." John's eyes glittered with deadly cold intent. "But he doesn't know that. By the time he realizes what's happening, it'll be too late, because we'll have the goods on him."

"Will a tape of our conversation be enough?" Alex leaned back in her chair, massaging at her temples.

"It'll be enough to start." John's tone commanded attention. "You're our ace, in more ways than one. Without you, we have no case and a snowball's chance of making one."

"There's really only one question." He turned to face her, looking her straight in the eye. "Can you do it, Alex? Will you help us take down the people responsible for killing Justin and David?"

Fear flashed through her. Could she? She didn't know. All this time she'd been insisting that she be involved. When it came to the critical point, would she be strong enough?

She swallowed, nearly choking on the bitter taste of her doubts. Ryan and his team were ready to put their lives on the line all because of information she'd provided. They deserved her honesty.

"I don't know." She folded her napkin and placed it on the table as she stood. "But I have to try."

Chapter Fifteen

Ryan found her near the water's edge, tracing lines in the damp sand with her bare toes. A soft ocean breeze lifted strands of her hair, giving the illusion of living ropes of silk dancing in the night sky. He stopped beside her. Much as he wanted to, he didn't touch her.

"You don't have to do this, you know."

Alex nodded, but didn't answer.

He tilted his head to get a better look at her face. "Are you sure?"

She turned away from him and nodded again.

"No, you're not. But you're going to try anyway, aren't you?" He made no effort to hide the resignation in his tone.

She nodded a third time.

"Why?"

"Because I have to." The waves nearly drowned out her quiet words. He leaned closer to hear. "They believed in me. I have to prove they were right, that David and Justin didn't waste their time when they came to get me."

"Do you believe in you?"

She finally looked at him. Tears shimmered in her eyes. "I don't know. From everything I've remembered so far, I don't exactly have a great history of making the right decisions when I'm left on my own."

"You won't be alone. I'll be with you, talking you through the whole process. The whole team will be behind you."

"I'm sure they're thrilled with that, too, aren't they? They get pulled in cold, and the success or failure of the entire case, all their efforts, rests with someone they don't know and have no reason to trust."

"I trust you. That's reason enough for them."

"Why? Why do you trust me? You've known me for barely a week. Most of that time I didn't even know myself. So how can you be so sure I'm worth trusting?"

"Because I got to know the real you when you weren't loaded down with a lot of history." He rested his hands on her shoulders and turned her to face him. "That's a pretty rare opportunity. David and Justin knew the real you. They knew you were worth any amount of effort it took to bring you back."

"How can you know that?"

"Because it's what I'd do." He threaded his fingers through her hair, cupping her head, forcing her to meet his eyes. He needed her to understand what he was trying to say. If his words didn't do the job, he hoped she could see the truth in his eyes. "I'd storm the gates of hell if that's what it took to save you. To do anything less would be…" His voice broke. He couldn't complete the thought, much less say the words.

Tears spilled over her lashes, leaving silvery moonlit trails across her cheeks. "I'm not worth that. No one is."

"Some people are. For me, you are."

He kissed her eyes shut. The taste of her, the salt of her tears mingling with the salt of the ocean air, filled his senses. He pulled her into the shelter of his arms, molding her close enough he could feel each breath she took.

Her arms threaded around his waist, warm and strong,

sending shafts of want and hunger deep. The part of him he'd buried as a little boy stirred to life.

This was different. This woman…the mix of her strength and vulnerability called to his deepest need, answered some unasked question he'd never allowed himself to voice.

Hunger took over and for a brief moment he allowed the world to fade to nothing but the feel, the taste, the warmth of the woman in his arms.

She pulled away enough to look in his eyes. "If things go wrong tomorrow—"

"They won't." He willed her to believe him. He needed to believe it himself. Because, if things went wrong, someone was likely to end up dead.

"But, if they do, don't risk the team for me."

He tried to protest but she wouldn't let him interrupt her. "You have the book and the translation. If things go wrong, you'll also have Pela and the others on whatever charges you can bring if they…if anything happens to me."

Fear for her slid through his veins. "This isn't a suicide mission. You can't go in there believing—if you think that's how this is going down, you're not ready to take this on. I don't care what John said. I'm not putting you at risk."

"It's not your choice, Ryan. I have to do this. Breaking this ring was important to Justin and David and it cost both of them their lives."

"So you're going to sacrifice yourself for them."

"Whatever it takes. Their sense of justice drove them after Frank Sullivan. I won't let them die for nothing."

"I'll go in with you, then."

"You can't. Pela knows who you are."

"I don't want you to be alone."

"I won't be." She tapped her ear. "You'll be inside, talking me through the whole thing. Remember?"

He remembered all right. He pulled her back into his arms. "It's not enough. I want to be more than just a voice in your ear."

"You are." She wound her arms around his neck, hanging on as though the last thing she wanted was to ever let him go. "I know I won't be alone tomorrow. I know you'll be with me every step of the way. Tonight…"

He rubbed his cheek against the midnight silk of her hair, brushed a kiss to her temple. "What about tonight?" he whispered, daring to hope.

"I don't want to be alone tonight."

"I know, baby, I know." He dragged in a deep, shuddering breath. His arms tightened, drawing her closer. "I don't, either."

She turned her head, stretching up to get closer, fitting her soft curves to his aching hardness. Their lips met and he lost himself in the need.

His.

Hers.

It was all the same.

Whatever happened tomorrow, he needed her tonight. They needed each other. He scooped her into his arms and headed for the guest cottage.

For tonight, need would be enough.

RYAN SETTLED INTO the dim interior of the van and flipped a switch on the control panel in front of him. "Sit rep." The request for the team members to report in with their status went out over the mission frequency.

Everyone except Alex wore miniature wireless headsets with microphones, allowing constant communication. Since the signal wasn't scrambled or secure, they'd agreed to use code names for the duration of the mission.

"Tweety's in the clear. Nice day for bird-watching, but no action yet." Casey reported in first. She sat at a nearby coffee shop, looking like one of a dozen other patrons hooked to the virtual world via a laptop. Matt had rigged her headset to pass as a cell phone headset.

Her position put her across the street from Island Visions, a former warehouse converted into an art gallery. Kimo had filled in the details of the gallery staging Alex's upcoming show. While Ryan would have preferred a more controlled setting for the meet, the gallery provided their best option on short notice.

The gallery owner had happily provided a key and free access to the building when Alex called with a "wealthy patron" interested in a private showing. The possibility of a healthy commission during the downtime had proved irresistible.

From her sidewalk table at the coffee shop, Casey had a clear view of the street and partway into the gallery. Her position had her close enough to observe any people entering or leaving the gallery, but far enough away that she wouldn't attract undue attention for loitering.

Matt's position had him on the low rooftop across the alley from the gallery's back door. He'd be guarding their six with his handy sniper rifle. His soft voice came through the headset next. "Eagle has landed."

Casey groaned. "He just loves saying that. I think that's the whole reason he does what he does."

"Condor would be more appropriate, don't you think?" John asked.

Under normal circumstances Ryan would have joined in the banter. But this was far from normal. Worry about Alex dampened any desire to share the humor. "Cut the chatter. Tracker, where are you?"

"In position." John's response came over the headset. He watched the estate Casey had found listed to Frank

Sullivan. "There's some activity indoors, but our friend hasn't left yet. I'll report in when he moves."

"Copy." Ryan opened the switch to Alex's receiver. "Sugar, where are you?" He had done his best to ease Alex's nerves before he left that morning. But several hours had passed since then. There was no guarantee she'd maintained any level of calm.

"I'm just hitting the city." Alex's voice sounded even enough. Maybe she tended to settle down once business started. He didn't know, not for sure. Of all the variables they were dealing with, Alex and how she'd react held the biggest unknown. Having your key player also be your biggest question mark fell far below ideal.

Nothing about this mission approached ideal. They were shorthanded, underequipped and unrehearsed. *Too late to do anything about that now. Just get on with it, boyo, and get the job done.*

He stretched back in his chair in a vain effort to relax tensed muscles. He should be out there, closer to the action rather than stuck in an alley blocks away. The tight confines of their makeshift control center seemed tighter by the minute. The darkened van windows gave the illusion of twilight, a fitting atmosphere for the foreboding chill crawling up his spine.

Watch your back, Jamie had warned him more than once in the past week. His back didn't worry him. Alex was the one out there all alone. Casey's position put her closest to the action, but a lot could happen in the few seconds it would take any of them to respond if Alex raised the alarm.

The mission clock, red numbers glowing in the gloom, ticked off another minute. T minus forty minutes before the scheduled meet. An eternity before he could expect to see any action.

All he could do was sit there, rerunning all the scenarios in his mind. And wait.

ALEX KEPT CHECKING the rearview mirror, half expecting to see a dark sedan on her tail. If anyone followed her, they were more skillful than she. Which wouldn't take much. *They must be crazy to think I can do this.* "I must be crazy."

"No one's crazy, sugar." Ryan's voice came through her earpiece. Heat raced up her neck and over her cheeks. She hadn't meant to speak out loud. At least she was on a closed circuit with Ryan so the others hadn't heard her slip.

"Everything will be fine." Ryan's calm tone continued. "Just stick to the plan."

How could he sound so relaxed? If she wasn't already sitting, she'd have collapsed from nerves. "He scares me, Ryan. You don't know Sullivan."

"I know his type. Ruthless, controlling, manipulative."

"He's that and more. Justin and David aren't the only ones he's killed. Promise me he won't get away."

"I promise you, we'll stop Sullivan, no matter what it takes. Everyone's in place, ready to do their bit."

"Now if I can do mine…"

"You'll do fine, sugar. Don't worry none."

Sugar. Ryan had reverted to his original endearment for the mission. He tended to call any woman *sugar.* The impersonal term meant nothing to him. She was the only one he'd referred to as *baby*.

She'd barely been aware of his shift in endearment. It hadn't been until she caught a silent exchange passing between Casey and Matt that the significance registered.

Coming from any other man, she would have found the term belittling. Yet, she missed him calling her *baby*.

Maybe she was overreacting. It didn't necessarily mean anything. Maybe it just got confusing to call everyone *sugar*.

Still, there was that meaningful look.

"Sugar?" Ryan's voice jolted her into the present. "You still there?"

"I'm just a couple blocks away." She stopped any further musings. Now was not the time. Here was not the place.

Never and nowhere, that would be a more appropriate setting for her to ask him about his intentions.

Ryan didn't have intentions. He'd been quite clear without ever saying the words. He had no home and no room in his life for a relationship. *Especially not with a weak-willed coward like me.* He didn't need someone like her to screw up his life. She shouldn't mistake his affection for love.

The fact that she'd fallen in love with him meant nothing. She refused to let it mean anything, because the only men she'd ever loved, who had loved her in return, were both dead. She couldn't let that happen again.

Resolved to do whatever it would take to protect Ryan, she parked in front of the gallery. She could see Casey across the street, but neither acknowledged the other in any manner.

"Show time, sugar." Ryan's voice sounded comforting in her ear. "When you're ready, I'll start running a tape so we have a record of what happens in there."

Alex sat in the car, taking deep breaths. She wanted to still the churning of her stomach, but nothing helped. *Might as well get this over with.* She smoothed her hair over her ear. Satisfied no visible evidence revealed the earpiece, she stepped out of the car.

She pulled her camera-bag strap over her shoulder, hugging the reassuring weight close like a security blanket. The notebook was tucked in the front pocket, along with the gun.

Ryan had taken her to the beach that morning, reloaded the Glock, and showed her the basic steps of gun safety. The last thing she'd wanted to do was handle that ugly reminder of David's death. If he'd kept the gun, rather than giving it to her for protection, he might have survived the meeting.

The only good thing about learning to handle the firearm had been Ryan's arms around her as he taught her the proper grip and shooting posture.

His warmth had enveloped her, tickled over her skin, rekindling memories of the prior night. Their lovemaking had provided welcome distraction from what the future might be holding.

Now the future had arrived. Ryan had insisted she take the gun with her. She didn't want it, hated the sight of it, but took the heavy thing anyway. She knew that he, like David, found a comfort in her being armed. She shuddered at the thought.

The gallery's display windows gave a partially obstructed view of the interior. A large sign on an easel inside one window announced her upcoming show; a smaller sign hung on the door, declaring the business "available for private showings." The borrowed key opened the well-oiled lock with a quiet click.

With a last glance over her shoulder, she pushed through the glass door and stepped into the cool semidusk of the gallery's interior. She stopped, not moving any farther into the building, letting her eyes adjust to the low light levels.

Freestanding walls formed a random pattern in the large open floor plan of the gallery. She recognized her own pictures hanging on some of the walls, but found no desire to look at them. Instead, she forced her breathing to slow and concentrated on listening to the silence around her.

Nothing moved in the building. If it hadn't been for the

presence of the earpiece, she would have believed herself to be utterly alone.

She stepped farther into the room, away from the minimal security of knowing Casey could see her through the window. She moved through the main room of the gallery, looking behind each wall, verifying that she was, indeed, alone.

At the rear of the large refurbished space, an office had been built. The plan called for her settling in the small room before anyone else arrived.

The door swung open on silent hinges. A small pharmacy lamp sat on the otherwise empty desk. She turned it on with trembling fingers. The large high-backed leather executive chair faced the back wall of the office. She stepped around the desk with the intention of sitting in the imposing thing. That would put her in the power position, with her back to a wall, facing anything that might come toward her.

Before she took a second step, the chair moved on its own volition. Her breath caught in her throat. She hugged the bag closer.

"Hello, Lexa," a hatefully recognized voice said.

She'd wanted to be wrong, to believe she'd escaped this devil when the Angelinis had brought her home.

The chair stopped its slow revolution. In the dim light she came face-to-face with her past.

She tried to step back, wanted to flee, every instinct screamed "escape." Her heart pounded a furious rhythm but she didn't move. Ryan and the others were depending on her. She prayed her voice wouldn't reveal her fear. "You're early."

Ryan's soft oath joined the buzzing in her head. "Tape's rolling," whispered in her ear. "We're with you, baby."

Calm settled over her with the reassurance that Ryan and his team knew the sting was starting early.

"What, no joyous greeting, my dear?"

"Did you really expect one?" Her throat ached as she pushed the words past tight lips.

"I must admit I was rather surprised to receive your message. You seemed rather anxious to see me."

The team had run through dozens of scenarios. She thought they'd covered every eventuality. But none of the rehearsals had come anywhere close to preparing her for the reality.

She took a steadying breath. "I was curious about what enticed the mighty Frank Sullivan to leave L.A."

"Think about it a moment." Sullivan glanced at his Rolex watch. "I'm sure something will come to you. You were always the brightest, Lexa. You usually figured things out quite easily. When you weren't in a drugged stupor that is."

"I'm not her, not anymore. She died when I got out of L.A." She hated the nickname. Frank Sullivan was the only one who'd ever called her Lexa.

"Come now. Is that any way to behave? I thought I taught you better than that."

"You taught me nothing I need to remember."

"Oh, I think you're very wrong about that, Lexa. You learned well enough." One corner of his thin-lipped mouth tipped up in what might have been called a smile by someone less familiar with his character. "Otherwise you wouldn't have called my associate and insisted on meeting with me."

Her heart pounded in her throat.

"Keep him talking, sugar. You're doing great."

Great? She was dying. She could barely breathe. Her pulse had to be off the charts. The only reason she still stood was because fear kept her immobile.

"What are you doing here in Hawaii?"

"Like any good businessman, I always look for opportunity. Honolulu's potential caught my attention several years ago. I took advantage of a situation and expanded my operations to include this fair island."

"Why are *you* here? Don't you trust your associates to run the business?"

Sullivan chuckled. "As much as I trust anyone. Which is not at all." He glanced at his watch again. "We're almost out of time, Lexa. Why don't you ask me what you really want to know."

"David and Justin. Why did you kill them?"

"The Angelinis took something that belonged to me." Sullivan raised an eyebrow and tilted his head in a slight nod at her. "That was their first mistake."

"Me?" Her world dipped and swayed. She wished for a chair, a wall, something to lean against before her strength deserted her completely. "You killed them because they helped me?"

Sullivan shook his head. "Now, Lexa. You know me better than that."

She did know him. Better than she wanted to. Each of his answers had been carefully worded, falling short of admitting wrongdoing. Ryan would need something more concrete if they stood any hope of stopping Sullivan. She focused on his words as he continued.

"They set about trying to destroy a very lucrative branch of my business. No one does that and gets away with it. Those who wrong me must pay the price, to serve as a warning to others."

A muffled sound came through the earpiece. Ryan. Hope stiffened her knees. If she kept Sullivan talking, Ryan would be able to get all the evidence on tape. The Angelinis would finally be avenged.

Help me, Ryan. What do I do? No guiding words came

over the earpiece. He was leaving the direction up to her. She released her held breath on a near-silent sigh. "So you sat back in the shadows and directed your 'associates' to do the dirty work. That is how you normally operate, I believe."

"Very good. You would have been a worthy partner for me, if only you hadn't let the drugs take control."

"Just one of the things I have you to thank for." She hadn't wanted to remember that detail. Now Ryan knew, too.

"Judging by the call you placed to Mr. Pela, it would seem you did manage to learn a little about the blackmail business while you were with me."

"You always said you were the master of the perfect scheme."

"Unfortunately, you should never have attempted to follow in my path. You simply aren't up to it. Why don't you give me the book you claim to have and we can be done?"

"No. You don't get what you want until I get what I want."

"And what would that be, Lexa?"

"You're the master. Why don't you tell me?"

"Money?" That had always been the ruling tenet in Sullivan's business. Money equaled power.

"David and Justin were idealists." *Trust me, Ryan, please.* "I've learned to be more of a realist. Money is part of it." She didn't elaborate and let the silence lengthen. People tended to become uncomfortable with lengthy silences. The ploy might not work with Sullivan since she'd learned that particular stratagem from him. But she needed every chance she could find.

Sullivan heaved a condescending sigh. "Really, Lexa." She didn't respond to his chiding tone.

"Very well. One more lesson. You say you have information that is damaging to me. That is your primary tool. With that as leverage, you can make certain demands. We've established money is one. I imagine another is that you want me to stay out of your life.'' He stood, shot the cuffs of his handmade shirt and smoothed the creases from his Armani suit jacket before moving around the desk.

Nothing about him had changed since her escape. He still seemed to loom over her, even though she nearly matched him in height. From his impeccably groomed dark widow's peak to the tips of his Bruno Magli shoes, he oozed dominance.

Her instinct screamed to keep as much distance between them as possible. The urge to step back nearly got the better of her, but retreating would reveal weakness. She stood her ground.

Sullivan stopped next to her, too close, invading her personal space. The subtle scent of his expensive cologne threatened to choke her. She swallowed convulsively, but didn't move.

He smiled, leaned closer and whispered in her ear. ''Is it revenge you hope for, Lexa?''

Yes, she'd like revenge. Against him for trying to destroy her life, first in L.A. and now here. Against Pela for killing David. Against whoever had pulled the trigger on Justin.

He walked past her, forcing her to turn and follow him into the gallery. The shadows deepened as he led her farther away from the light streaming in the front windows. The only illumination came from security lights recessed in the high ceiling.

At last he stopped. Three partitions, her photographs covering the surfaces, surrounded them, forming an open U. He stood in front of a triptych of miniature prints.

''I must say, you do nice work, Lexa.''

She wished he'd stop using that name. Telling him to

quit would do no good. That would reveal too much and give him even more of an edge. She'd learned the hard way that standing up to Frank Sullivan got you hurt.

Or dead.

He turned to face her. "The proper response to a compliment is a gracious 'thank-you.' Surely you remember that lesson, Lexa."

A shudder of memory trickled down her back.

Lexa was weak, dependent, barely a shadow of a human. That wasn't her, not anymore, no matter how often he tried to remind her. She'd escaped that persona. David and Justin had freed her from that hell when they brought her back to the island.

Alex pulled her shoulders back and raised her chin. David and Justin had believed in her. So did Ryan. He must. He hadn't said a word to her in the last seven minutes. Surely that meant he trusted her to make the right decisions.

If nothing else, she could pretend to believe in herself. At least until this was over.

"You're stalling, Sullivan." That felt good. Lexa would never have dared use his last name so casually.

Frank stared at her a moment before he raised his arms in a gesture of innocence. "I can't imagine what you're implying."

"You're waiting for Pela to arrive. Then you can keep true to form and leave the dirty work to him."

"I must say, this new you is quite impressive." He gave her a slow once-over. "I believe you've actually grown a backbone. Perhaps we can come to an agreement."

He turned away and moved to the next partition to study that arrangement of photographs.

Panic simmered, eating away at her stomach. Everything was wrong. Pela should have arrived by now. Ryan should be giving her direction.

Why wasn't he talking? She needed his help. She needed him to tell her what to do.

The confident façade she'd pulled around herself began to crumble faster than she could rebuild.

Sullivan turned to glance at her. The smug expression on his face prodded her determination. *Trust your instincts,* Jamie had told her.

She could do this. She had to. She had to rely on herself, not Ryan. Facing down Sullivan would be the hardest test she'd ever have to endure.

"Before he gets here, why don't we work out an agreement?"

Sullivan faced her fully. "You've piqued my interest. Go on."

"You can't really expect to get away with this scheme much longer."

"Which scheme? The blackmail or the murders?" He waved a hand, dismissing his own question. "No matter. The answer is the same. Both will function exactly as long as I require."

"Not if the information I have gets out in the open." She shifted the camera bag from her left shoulder to her right.

"Continue."

"You're right. I want money and revenge. One will accomplish the other."

"Intriguing." Sullivan glanced at his damned watch again as he crossed his arms. "Perhaps you could explain that a little further?"

"You're a patron of the arts. I have no desire to be a starving artist. What I propose is that you provide sufficient funds so I can pursue my photography career. As long as the money arrives on a timely basis, the notebook never sees the light of day."

"And the revenge?"

"Actually, making you pay me…"

"Very good." Sullivan smiled. "Of course you don't have all the pieces for a successful transaction yet. You've yet to prove your little notebook exists or that it links me to anything."

"It exists. Even without it, you've just bragged about everything to me. Do you think I wouldn't testify against you?"

"Hearsay, nothing more. And what court would give credence to a former junkie bent on revenge. Especially when the victim of that misguided revenge is a respected businessman?"

"There is the link to Pela and Walker. When they go down, so will you."

"My, my. You seem very confident, considering you're here alone, unarmed. What makes you think you could ever succeed in exposing my operation?"

"What makes you think I'm alone? I may have a little angel who whispers in my ear, telling me what to do."

"Really? What is he telling you to do now?"

Her angel stayed frighteningly silent. She desperately wanted Ryan's reassuring whisper telling her she was going in the right direction. *Please, Ryan, tell me what to do.* The silence in her ear continued. Why didn't he say something?

"Perhaps your angel has fallen silent?" Sullivan lifted a hand and signaled. "Perhaps he's just fallen."

Shadows beyond the display walls shifted, separated from the encompassing blackness. Two men came forward, dragging a third form between them.

Pela and Walker. All the pieces of the puzzle together. Now. Too late to do any good.

They stopped halfway between her and Sullivan and dumped a man on the floor. Walker prodded the unmoving figure with one booted foot, rolling the unconscious man onto his back.

The dim light revealed the man's bloodied face.

Bile churned in her stomach. She would have collapsed if horror hadn't frozen her in place.

Dear God, it was Ryan.

Chapter Sixteen

Alex struggled to breathe. How had they found Ryan? What had they done to him? She watched for some indication that he was still alive.

"This wouldn't happen to be your angel, would it? You didn't waste much time finding a replacement for your last angel. Or should I say Angelini?"

Sullivan's words registered in one part of her brain, the part tallying every foul deed that could be pinned to him. Another part focused on Ryan, praying in silence, urging him to move. His eyelids flickered but remained closed.

Panic and relief rolled through her stomach in a sickening dance. He wasn't dead. She drew a slow breath and forced her attention away from him.

The other team members had to know something had gone wrong. If not when Ryan fell out of communication, then surely when Matt saw him being dragged in the back door. The team would be regrouping.

She had to continue the charade until they arrived and hope that, somewhere, a tape still ran. Her nails dug into her palm as she tightened her grip on the camera bag. She forced her features into a calm mask.

"I am sorry, Lexa, but it looks like I hold the more valuable item."

She looked up, a bitter smile twisting her lips. "He was

nothing more than a means to an end.'' Inside, she died a little. ''He's a fed.''

''Yes, so Pela mentioned.''

''Did Pela also mention that Special Agent Williams is from the OPR? Do you know what they specialize in?''

''Enlighten me.''

''The Office of Professional Responsibility investigates FBI agents suspected of, oh, let's call it straying from the straight and narrow. His assignment—'' she nudged Ryan with her toe and his eyelids flickered again ''—is to investigate David's disappearance. I figured I could use him to get to you.''

''It doesn't seem to have worked very well.''

''You're here. This guy disappearing is going to really muddy up your operation. One agent, you might be able to cover up. Two in as many weeks, even for you...''

''Will be a bit more difficult to explain.''

''Right. Not to mention the pictures I have of Pela and David's last meeting.'' She caught Pela's startled glance. ''Do you think the legion of agents descending on Honolulu to investigate would be interested in those?''

''You seem to have given this some thought.'' Sullivan turned his back on all of them.

A whole Polaroid minute.

Silence descended upon the surreal tableau. Sullivan appeared to study another set of photographs. Alex studied Walker and Pela, trying to gauge their states of mind.

Pela presented the easiest face to read. He had the most to lose in an FBI investigation. Which made him the easiest to pit against Sullivan.

Walker, for his part, wore the mask of a stoic, giving away nothing. Except the very absence of expression hinted that he hid something—most likely fear, provided he had any sense.

If the two men hadn't already learned, they were about

to discover that Sullivan considered everyone expendable, regardless of how far up the organizational food chain he may have climbed.

Alex forced herself to maintain a calm façade all the while her thoughts zoomed from fear of Sullivan to fear for Ryan.

Where was the rest of the team? How much time had elapsed since Ryan had been taken? They must have had enough time to regroup by now.

Ryan's eyelids flickered. She held her breath as he opened his eyes just enough to make eye contact with her. She lost herself in his gaze in the seconds before he closed his eyes and seemed to sink back into unconsciousness.

"Tell me, Lexa," Sullivan turned to face her. "What do you want to do with Mr. Williams?"

She composed her features into an expression of disinterest. What she wanted had little bearing on the situation. All she could do was play out the role assigned. "Reinforce the direction of his investigation."

"How do you figure on doing that?" Walker asked. "He's lying right in front of you."

She ignored the snide comment.

"He does have a point." Sullivan strolled to the next display wall.

"True, it might pose some challenges. If he saw either of these goons, then we're sunk." *We.* The subtle hint that she considered herself a part of this scheme nearly choked her.

Sullivan's gaze lingered on her face as he turned to Pela and Walker. "Did he?"

Pela shook his head.

Sullivan turned back to her. "Well, Lexa. Do go on."

Alex thumbed her triple-band ring, rolling it along her ring finger. *Trust your instincts. Please be right because if this doesn't work, Ryan will be dead.* "Then you get Williams out of here before he wakes up. Pela can 'find' him someplace. That gives him some credibility as being one of the good guys.''

''And you?''

''My materials remain out of sight, unless something happens to me. In which case the book and pictures find their way to the OPR.'' She held her breath, hoping Sullivan would agree.

''Interesting.'' Sullivan stared her down. ''In return, what do you get?''

''Just what we talked about. A nice income and you stay out of the rest of my life.''

He seemed to consider the plan. She shifted the camera bag, hitching it a little higher on her shoulder as she slipped her right hand into the front pocket. The handle of the Glock nestled into her palm.

''There is one condition.'' Sullivan held his hand out to Pela, palm up, fingers flicking in a ''give-me'' gesture.

Pela stuck his hand inside his suit jacket.

Her fingers convulsed around the gun. She forced herself to relax, stay calm, don't overreact.

Pela pulled out a tiny gun and handed it to her at Sullivan's prompting.

She looked at Sullivan. ''What's that for?''

''Let's call it my insurance policy. Take the gun, Lexa.''

She released her hold on the Glock, wiping her sweaty palm on the camera case as she withdrew her hand from the pocket. The gun had looked tiny in Pela's hand. In her hand, it still appeared small and had a decidedly feminine look to it.

''It's a derringer,'' Sullivan explained. ''A handy thing for a lady to tuck in her purse for protection.''

''What am I supposed to do with it?''

Sullivan pursed his lips in thought. ''Now that I have

your fingerprints on it, I suppose we could let it go at that. But I think a little more 'insurance' wouldn't hurt.''

A sickening knot of dread settled in her stomach. She looked from the gun to Sullivan.

''You're going to have to shoot him, my dear.''

The knot leapfrogged its way to the back of her throat. ''What if I refuse?''

''One of them will take the gun and shoot him for you. The end result will be the same—a bullet in his body that can be traced to a gun bearing your fingerprints.''

''You want to risk a second dead agent?''

''Oh, don't worry. The gun is loaded with special ammunition—effective, but not too powerful. It should be nonlethal, depending on the target area. I'll even leave that choice to you.''

Sullivan's goons dragged Ryan to his feet.

''You seem confident that I won't shoot you.'' She forced the words out, prayed she sounded calm. ''Or one of them.'' She raised the small gun toward Walker and Pela.

The two men pulled their guns. Walker aimed his at Ryan. Pela's gun trained on her.

She focused on Ryan, fighting nausea with every breath. Shoot Ryan. Stomach acid burned at the back of her throat. She couldn't do it.

''Whenever you're ready.'' Sullivan turned his back on her, for all the world appearing to not care when, or whom, she shot.

For two seconds, she considered pulling out the Glock and shooting him in the back. It was no better than he deserved. Then she looked back at the trio in front of her. Ryan's head lolled back, his eyes open.

Time stopped.

He was conscious and watching her.

She wanted to go to him, feel his arms around her, hear

his reassuring whisper that everything was going to be okay.

But if she did that, they'd both be killed.

The small gun weighed down her hand. She couldn't do it, she couldn't shoot Ryan. She loved him too much.

"Lexa." Sullivan's voice broke into the thoughts raging through her brain. "I consider myself a patient man, but I do have other business today. Please get on with it."

Ryan opened his mouth and her eyes widened. If Sullivan discovered Ryan was conscious, Sullivan would order him killed.

She had to stop him. Her eyes filled with tears. She blinked them back, furious. *Not now.*

Her hand swung up and she pointed the gun at Ryan's shoulder. She risked another glance at his face. His expression said everything. He believed she'd betrayed him.

Alex squinted through her tears and squeezed the trigger.

The gun barely jerked in her hand, nothing like the Glock had. Even so, a bloom of red darkened Ryan's shirt.

Sullivan appeared at her side. "Very good." He turned to Pela. "Get rid of him. Dump him someplace he won't be found."

She stared at Sullivan as Pela and Walker dragged Ryan away.

His impassive look mocked her. "You didn't really think I would allow you to direct me, did you?" He took the gun from her slack grip, slipped it into a small paper bag and tucked it into his suit jacket. "Do behave yourself, now. You never know when or where this—" he patted his pocket "—might turn up."

Her throat closed around a scream. This couldn't be happening. "You're forgetting something. I have the notebook."

He shrugged. "I doubt it exists."

Her stomach cramped into a tight knot.

Sullivan turned and walked away from her.

She sank to her knees. Her hands fumbled as she dug into her camera bag. She finally pulled out the notebook. "Let me ease your doubt, Sullivan. I have the notebook, right here."

He stopped and slowly pivoted to face her.

She held the notebook up in her left hand. In her right, she held the Glock. "And I have this." She got to her feet and leveled the gun at his chest.

"Lexa. You were barely able to pull the trigger on the derringer. Do you really expect me to worry that you might try to shoot me with that?"

"You're forgetting a very important factor."

He crossed his arms over his chest, impatience developing in his narrowed eyes. "I can't imagine what that might be."

"You killed my best friends. Now, because of you, I've destroyed the man I love." She dropped the notebook to the floor, gripped the gun with both hands as Ryan had taught her. "I have nothing to lose." Taking a deep breath, she slipped her finger onto the trigger and squeezed.

The Glock roared in her hand, filling the air with an acrid stench.

Sullivan stumbled back and collapsed.

Alex fell to her knees and bent over, heaving, one arm wrapped around her waist, the other braced against the floor. Her ears rang from the gunshot report. It almost sounded like footsteps bouncing off the gallery walls.

"Get the EMTs in here, fast," a vaguely familiar voice shouted.

She looked up and realized people were swarming into the gallery. Two figures huddled over Sullivan's body. Someone grabbed her and pulled her to her feet.

"I'm okay." She tried to pull away from the hands patting over her body. "Where's Ryan?"

Her right arm was pulled behind her back. "I've got the shooter." Cool metal pressed around her wrist. Her left arm was pulled back and the handcuffs ratcheted closed.

"What—" She twisted, trying to see who held her. Her hair fell in her face and she shook her head, blinking away tears, trying to make sense of the chaos surrounding her.

John Danse appeared in front of her.

Relief robbed her strength. The hands holding her arms from behind tightened as she sagged. "Is he going to be okay?"

"You're zero for two, *sugar*." John spat the word at her. "They're both going to live."

His icy glare stabbed at her before he looked over her shoulder at the person holding her. "Read her her rights." He turned his back to her and addressed the room at large. "I want everything done strictly by the book. No one's getting off on any technicalities, is that clear?"

Bitter understanding registered, along with the words being recited behind her.

"You have the right to remain silent...."

Chapter Seventeen

Ryan fought through the fog wrapped around his brain. His tongue felt thick as a cotton boll. Just as dry, too. He tried to raise his arm and a bolt of pain nearly sent him back to unconsciousness.

Cool hands wrapped around his hand and squeezed.

Tension eased. "What happened, baby?"

"Ryan, it's me, Casey."

He pried his eyes open, squinting in the glare of light bouncing off white walls. "Where's Alex?"

"Everything's under control." Casey squeezed his hand again.

Like hell. He needed Alex beside him and she wasn't there. He frowned, searching the room. "What happened? Where is she?"

"Ryan." Casey forced him to look at her. "Alex shot you. And she shot Sullivan. She's in jail."

"No." For an instant he had a taste of how Alex must have felt when the amnesia held her memories hostage. Nothing made sense.

Then memory flooded over him. A single image formed. Alex, standing in front of him, a tiny gun clutched in her hand, tears in her eyes.

Pain sent him sinking back to dark oblivion.

RYAN PUSHED HIS WAY into the police station. The combined FBI and HPD task force had set up there. His team had been going at it almost nonstop for two days and that's where he belonged. Not lying in the hospital, driving himself and the nursing staff crazy.

A uniformed officer led him to the conference room that served as the hub for the task force.

John looked him over as he sank into the nearest chair. "You look like hell."

"Thanks. Tell me something I don't know, like where are we on the investigation."

Casey entered the room with three tall paper cups in a carrier. She set one cup on the table in front of Ryan. "I thought I saw you crashing through the doors. The coffee here is pretty bad, you'll want to drink this."

A sling immobilized his right arm so he pried the lid off the cup with his left hand and inhaled the rich aroma. The caffeine would do him a world of good. He took a cautious sip and grimaced. "Sugar?"

Casey froze, glanced at John then looked at him. *She thinks I mean…* He rushed to clarify, "For my coffee."

Casey tossed a few packets to him. "I'm surprised the doctors let you out of the hospital already."

"There wasn't much 'let' about it." His right shoulder hurt like the devil and he had to do everything left-handed but he managed to empty four sugars into the cup before he tried another sip. "I wasn't doing anybody any good lying around there. Now, why don't y'all fill me in on the sit rep here."

"I've gotta check on a…thing." Casey made a beeline for the door.

Ryan turned to John. "A 'thing,' huh? What am I going to hear that she didn't want to be around when I heard it?"

"We're having a difference of opinion. She's not happy with the direction the investigation is taking."

"Which is?"

"A downward spiral, according to her." He ticked the pieces off on his fingers. "We've got a missing and presumed dead agent, a notebook written in code, three suspects who aren't talking, two gunshot victims and two guns with a single set of fingerprints. Everything traces back to one person."

"What about the tape backup?"

John shook his head. "Whoever clocked you over the head also took a couple whacks at the equipment. Matt's salvaging as much of the tape as possible." He walked over to a bulletin board that filled one wall of the room. Index cards with names had been arranged across the top. Running down from those a few more cards had been pinned. Most of the cards fell under Alex's name.

Ryan started to shrug and thought better of it. "We've worked with less to go on. Sooner or later someone's going to roll and the case will break."

John unpinned a few cards from the board. "Until then, we work the evidence." He pushed the cards across the table to Ryan. "These are what's been transcribed so far."

He turned the cards facedown without looking at them. Time enough for that later. "What else do you have?"

"Nothing."

"Walker and Pela?"

"They lawyered up fast and aren't giving us much."

"Sullivan?"

"In critical condition. He won't be talking anytime soon, either. The Glock did a lot more damage to him than that peashooter she used on you."

Ryan pushed at the cards, but didn't turn them over. "Did Casey get anything from L.A.?"

"She's still working that angle. Mostly she's just got confirmation of what we already knew."

Ryan took another sip of coffee. The wall clock ticked off the lengthening silence. His mouth was still cotton dry. From the painkillers the doctors had given him, no doubt. It didn't have anything to do with the one person neither of them had named.

He was tired of dancing around the topic. He needed to know. "What about Alex?"

"She's not talking, either." John crossed his arms and scowled.

"What does her lawyer say?"

"She refused getting one. All she does is huddle in a corner of her cell."

Ryan's throat tightened at the image of her caged. "I never should have involved her. She shouldn't be sitting in jail." Nothing had gone down as they'd planned.

She was supposed to be safe at home with that cat of hers. Or out wandering around the island, taking pictures. He should have protected her.

"Her involvement began long before you found her." John broke into his thoughts. "She's right where she deserves to be."

Ryan shook his head. Gut instinct disagreed and it had never let him down.

Of course, he'd never been in love before. That thought derailed him every time. The image of her aiming the gun at his chest mocked him.

He flipped over the first card, then the next and the next. Every phrase twisted around his heart, contradicting what he wanted to believe, damning her with each neatly typed word.

...I get what I want
...work out an agreement?
You pay me.
He was nothing...

He turned the cards back over, shuffled them together in a pile and pushed the pile across the table to John. "What about the videotape?"

"What video?"

"From the gallery security system." He stared at John, stunned. "You mean to tell me that no one has checked that?"

"We know what we saw when we got in there. I made salvaging the audio Matt's priority." John tried to stare him down.

"Appearances can be deceiving. We need to know what's on that tape."

Reluctance etched into every line of his face, John lifted a phone and dialed an internal number. "Matt, do you have the security camera tape from the gallery? Right, put Casey on it." He hung up. "Do you really think it'll show us anything?"

"We owe it to Alex to check it out, don't you think?" He pushed himself up from the chair. "Where is she?"

"They're bringing her up to interrogation." John stood. "Let's take a walk."

They walked in silence as John led the way through the halls. The door to the interrogation room was swinging shut as they rounded the corner. They slipped into the cool dimness of the adjacent observation room.

Through the large one-way mirror they could see Alex standing with her back to them, just inside the door of the next room. A female uniformed officer stood beside her.

"Someone'll be in before too long." The officer's voice came over a wall-mounted speaker.

Ryan stepped closer to the window. This was the first time he'd seen her since the shooting.

He rubbed his arm, but the ache he wanted to ease was located more in his chest, in the vicinity of his heart.

"D'you want anything?" The officer spoke again.

Alex shook her head. Ryan squinted through the smudged glass, studying her, wishing she'd turn around. He couldn't summon up much emotion looking at her back.

"You sure?" the officer asked. "You're gonna be in here for a while."

When she didn't respond, the officer shrugged and left. Alex turned then and looked straight at him through the mirror.

Dark crescents beneath her eyes revealed how little sleep she'd had since the arrest. Her shoulders sagged and her hair…he swallowed around the rock in his throat. Her hair hung dull and lifeless, like her eyes.

His heart fell to the pit of his stomach. He didn't want to hurt, dammit, not like this, like he was six years old again and losing the only woman who loved him.

She looked away and he could finally breathe. His pulse pounded in his chest. He turned his back to the one-way mirror, sagging against the cool glass for support.

Her image still burned in his mind's eye. He knew what the evidence said. Her own words condemned her.

None of that mattered, because he knew something else. He pushed away from the window.

John stood, arms crossed over his chest, watching him with narrowed eyes. "What are you going to do?"

"Talk to her."

John stepped in front of him, blocking the way. "She's a criminal, Williams, charged with blackmail and two counts of attempted murder. That's so far. It will be a lot worse before we're done."

"You're telling me this because…"

"Don't fancy yourself in love with her, because if you do, you won't like the road it takes you down."

"Tell me something, John. When you realized you were in love with your wife, could anyone have said anything that would have changed your mind?"

John scrubbed one hand over his face and shook his head. "It's too late, isn't it?"

"Yes." Ryan pushed past John. "Whatever hell she's headed for, I'm not letting her go alone."

When he entered the interrogation room, Alex stood in a corner of the windowless room. Her eyes were closed, her head leaned back. She looked as if she was trying to push herself into the wall and disappear.

He turned to close the door and came face-to-face with Casey, holding a videocassette. She stepped closer and he shut the door on her. What he needed to say to Alex would be said without an audience in the room.

No audience at all would be better, but he knew there was little hope the other team members would allow them any privacy. They would have to work mighty hard to hear anything, though.

Ryan crossed the room to stand in front of Alex, blocking her from the observers behind the one-way mirror.

It didn't seem possible, but she hunched tighter into the corner. He wanted to touch her, but he needed to talk to her more.

"I doubt any cracks in the wall will be big enough to hide in." He kept his voice soft, tried to put a smile in the tone, but it hurt too much.

She flinched but didn't open her eyes.

"I will admit to wishing we could slip away somewhere." His voice cracked. He stopped, wet his lips, then continued. "Together, just the two of us."

Her eyes fluttered open and she finally looked at him. When she saw his arm in its sling the last bit of color left her cheeks. "I'm so sorry," she whispered.

His throat ached. Evidence be damned. He saw the truth in her eyes. She'd been fighting for her life. And his.

She touched his arm with trembling fingers. "I tried to remember what you taught me about shooting but it happened too fast. Will you be okay?"

He nodded, not trusting his voice for a moment. "I lead a charmed life, remember?"

"Is Sullivan…" She bit her lip. "Did I kill him?"

"No, you didn't hit anything vital. You're not a very good shot."

Some of the tension left her body.

"Not that he doesn't deserve it."

She shook her head and looked away. "No one deserves that."

He touched her chin, drawing her gaze back to him. "Baby, what did he do to you?"

"He came here because of me. He had Justin and David killed because of me. He was going to kill you. Because of me."

"You'll testify against him?"

She nodded.

"You'll be given full immunity." He brushed her hair over her shoulder. "I'll get you a lawyer and work out—"

A hammering knock on the door interrupted him. They turned to see John standing in the open door.

"Williams, we need to talk."

"Come on in, John."

"What the hell are you doing?" John slammed the door shut.

"Alex is going to provide her complete testimony in exchange for immunity on any charges."

"You can't do that."

"I just did." John could scowl all he wanted, it wouldn't change Ryan's course.

"Blackmail, attempted murder, that's just in Hawaii. Add in the California charges and she's going away for a long time."

"No. She is a member of our team. She did what she had to do, the best she could do, same as any of us would have in that situation."

"Pela and Walker are pinning her." John braced his fists on the table and leaned toward them.

"Yeah. They're a reliable pair."

"The tape—"

"Is incomplete and misleading."

"You don't know that."

"I was there." He turned and looked at Alex. "I know."

A glass-rattling door slam witnessed John's departure.

"That boy's going to break a window if he's not careful."

Alex sighed, relief clear in the relaxing of her shoulders. "I was so scared. I thought it would be just my word against the others." Tears shimmered in her eyes. "You were conscious and heard—"

"Nothing." Ryan shook his head. "I was out the whole time, right up 'til the end."

"You didn't hear any of it?"

"No."

"You lied."

"Did I?"

She shook her head. "But you don't know that."

"I know what's here." He rested his hand over her heart. "You're ready to sacrifice yourself because you think that will make up for someone killing your friends. The better choice would be to make sure the people who are really guilty are put away. You need to be free to honor Justin's and David's memory by living the life they brought you here for."

She turned away.

"Don't forget your cat. Someone's got to be around to take care of Ansel. I like him and all. I'll even admit to having grown kind of attached to him, but when I'm gone on assignment, he's going to need you."

She looked at him with a puzzled frown.

"There's something else." He threaded his fingers through her hair, cupping her neck and drawing her close. "When I come home, I'll need you."

That got her attention. "Home?"

"I'm not quite sure how it's going to work." Hope began to grow. Maybe he could make this happen. "I'm gone for months at a time. But there's an opening in the Honolulu office, and I was thinking of posting for that. It would make maintaining our relationship a lot easier."

"Relationship?"

"Yeah. It seems, if we love each other, that's pretty much the start of a relationship." His heart beat with an unsteady rhythm.

"Love?"

"I'm not claiming to have much experience, but I'm pretty sure I do." His throat closed around the words. "Love you, that is."

He pulled her close, wrapping his good arm around her. The silence nearly killed him. Had he misread her? "The hoped-for response is…"

"I love you." Her words were a mere whisper.

"Yeah." He nodded, took a deep breath.

She nodded. Her arms wound around his waist.

They stood in the interrogation room, holding each other, words no longer necessary.

Epilogue

Ryan ran along the water's edge, reveling in the sensations of sand, sea and wind surrounding him. The sun hovered above the horizon as though reluctant to leave the comfort of the night.

Jamie's house came into view as he rounded the bend. As usual, Jamie stood on the patio, waiting with a towel and a glass of fresh-squeezed lemonade.

Ryan hesitated for a moment, torn between returning to the guest cottage and hearing the latest news from Jamie. News won out. He trotted to the patio, accepting glass and towel. "Good morning."

Jamie nodded. "It would seem that all is right with the world today. Indictments came in late last night."

Ryan lowered the glass. "That was fast."

"The gallery security tape provided rather compelling evidence when combined with other testimony. Mr. Sullivan and his cohorts will be out of circulation for some time to come."

Ryan blew out a sigh of relief.

"How is Alex?"

"Sound asleep when I left this morning."

"I must admit being surprised to see you up this early."

Ryan smiled. "It's easy enough when you never went to sleep in the first place."

Jamie raised an eyebrow.

"Alex was so wound up after the opening last night she kept me awake sketching out plans for her next show."

"The show went well then?"

Ryan smiled with unashamed pride. "More than just well. She sold a number of pieces. I have a feeling several more will go before the week is out."

"And you?"

Ryan looked out across the ocean. "I finally understand why you stay here when so much of your work is on the mainland. This is as close to home as I've ever come."

A movement at the edge of the palm grove caught Ryan's eye. Alex was walking toward them, a cell phone to her ear. When she reached the patio, she handed the phone to Ryan and slipped her arms around his waist, snuggling in close. He wound his free arm around her, the action automatic, the need to hold her unfailing.

"Williams?" Jacquelyn's voice demanded attention.

"Yes, Miss Jackie?"

"Your posting for the Honolulu office has been approved. Is there anything you need before you can begin?"

"No, ma'am. I reckon I've already got pretty much everything I could possibly want. Thanks." He ended the call.

"She was very insistent that I bring the phone to you. What did she want?"

"She was giving me my new assignment."

Alex went stone still in his arms. He hugged her closer, before she could even try to pull away. Over her head he met Jamie's questioning look. "Looks like you'll finally have your guest cottage back. I'll be needing a more permanent place to call home."

He loosened his hold on AJ, just enough that he could look into her warm gray eyes. "I'm kinda hoping you and Ansel might be willing to share yours."

"Really?" A smile lit her eyes.

He nodded. "I've got a permanent assignment here. The woman I love is here. Seems logical to have a home here."

"How would you feel about finding a new place, together? Something that's ours and not a friend's hand-me-down?"

"Yeah. I like the sound of that." He lost himself in her smile.

The where didn't really matter. For him, home would always be Alex.

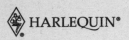

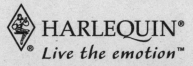

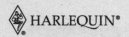

HARLEQUIN®

INTRIGUE®

**presents a new force of rugged lawmen
who abide by their own rules...**

COWBOY COPS

They live—they love—by the code of the West.

A riveting new promotion featuring
men branded by the badge!

BEHIND THE SHIELD by Sheryl Lynn
March 2004

RESTLESS SPIRIT by Cassie Miles
April 2004

OFFICIAL DUTY by Doreen Roberts
May 2004

DENIM DETECTIVE by Adrienne Lee
June 2004

Available at your favorite retail outlet.

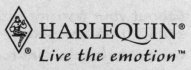

HARLEQUIN®
Live the emotion™

Visit us at www.eHarlequin.com

HICC2

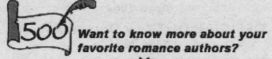

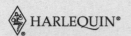

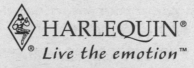

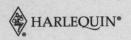

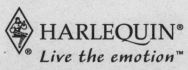